PRISONERS

OF WAR

SARAH GRACIA

Rivershore Books
8982 Van Buren St. NE • Minneapolis, MN 55434
763-670-8677 • info@rivershorebooks.com

CHAPTER 1: MATT

Location: Boston, USA

I woke up with a feeling of fear. I didn't recognize my surroundings—ghost white walls, a green chair with an ugly polka dot print, and dull lights blinking above me. There was a woman, a stranger, in the room on a computer.

"Where am I?" Then it dawned on me that I didn't know anything about myself. "Who am I?"

She peered at me. "You have amnesia?" Amnesia. The definition of the word flashed in my head: loss of memory. She questioned, "Where are you?"

She obviously wasn't convinced I had no clue. "I asked *you* that."

The nurse wrote that down. "What did you have for breakfast?" A sneaking suspicion told me I didn't have breakfast.

"I don't know."

Can she cure me? Probably not. I'll most likely have to see a professional.

She thrust my wrist out before me, where there was a bracelet with a name on it. "Your name is right here: Matthew Garrings."

Matt sounded right, but "Garrings" had a foreign sound to it, like even before I was in that room I had never heard it before.

She abruptly stopped typing. "I'll call your parents. Sit tight."

A man entered, clutching a book with the word "Bible" on it. Hope surged in my chest. "Are you my father?"

He cracked a smile. "I am a spiritual father, not a biological one. I visit patients in the hospital. Do you need my help with anything?"

"I don't know anything about myself besides my name."

He pressed, "What is it?"

"Matt Garrings."

He shook my hand. "I'm Father Derek Wallace. Pleased to meet you."

The door swung open once again, allowing two adults with watery eyes to tumble haphazardly into the room, and a teenage girl who seemed distressed quietly followed them in.

I was unsettled at the sight of so many strangers. "Who are you people?"

The dark-haired and dark-eyed adults rushed over and hugged me while their tears splashed on my cheeks. "We're your parents!"

The girl walked over to me. "I'm your younger twin sister, Tara."

I asked, "What happened to me?"

Tara frowned. "I didn't know you existed until we were on our way here."

That perplexed me. "I have amnesia, so I don't remember anything, but you never knew about me, even with all your memory?"

She confirmed, "Yep."

I noticed a Saint Dymphna medal around her neck.

Saint Dymphna?

There was something about Saint Dymphna that nagged me . . . "I'm Matt."

She beamed. "Awesome! I finally have a sibling! Why is there a random priest in here?"

I filled in, "He was visiting me."

She nodded. "Aw, that's nice."

I had an intense desire to bond with her, like she was the most important person in the world to me.

I desperately attempted conversation while getting an answer to one of my questions. "Where am I?"

She replied, "A hospital. You're in intensive care for a deadly head wound. You have a nasty scar on your forehead, with a small mark on your neck. They took something out of your neck."

I instinctively touched my head and felt waves of pain. "What happened to me?"

Another anxious look appeared on her face. "I don't know."

I sighed. At least I knew I was Matt Garrings, and I was in a hospital.

I quizzed, "Do I have any friends?"

Then I remembered Tara's words. *"I didn't know you existed until we were on our way here."*

"Did you live with our parents all your life?"

She blushed. "Yeah. I actually never spent a night away from them. None of the girls at school wanted me to sleep over at their house."

That meant I never met Tara, even before amnesia hit. And if Tara lived with our parents all our lives, I never met my parents before, either.

I have a head wound from a mysterious incident and I've been separated from my family my whole life?

This isn't sounding good . . .

I inquired, "Why didn't I live with you? What happened?"

Mom brushed her tears away and bit her already bloodied fingernail. "We should tell you later. You must be in shock. I don't want to make it worse."

I decided to find out more about the "where am I" question. "What country are we in?"

3

Tara responded, "America."

Politicians have ulterior motives! All they care about is money!

Where did that thought come from?

I changed the subject. "Are people nice in America?"

She snorted. "I was bullied at recess, lunch, and in the classroom in elementary school. In eighth grade, kids I didn't even know called me big. One said I was chubby. But I wasn't overweight. That made me go into the early stages of anorexia. I think. I recovered since. And there are certain policies . . ."

I scowled. "I'll have to beat those punks up."

Mom intervened, "Don't get into fights, Matt."

I protested, "Some kids almost gave her anorexia, and I can't even punch them in the face?"

After Mom didn't budge, I decided to talk about something else. "How many grades are there in school? Which one are we in?"

"Twelve in total, and we're in ninth grade."

I beamed. "Then we're almost done! Wait, how old are we?"

Tara giggled. "We're fourteen. I think you have to get a tutor to catch up to the state's standards."

I made a face and said a sentence in Belarusian.

Dad's eyes nervously darted around the room. "Whoa, there. What does that mean?"

I translated, "It sounds awful!'"

Tara prodded, "What language is that?"

I grinned. "Belarusian, the native language of Belarus."

Her eyes widened. "You lived in Belarus?"

"I don't know. I know German, too."

She sat in a chair. "I'm impressed."

I tried to make her feel better about those kids.

"My favorite thing to say in German is 'people are the real monsters in life.'"

She raised an eyebrow. "Matt, I'm okay. Society says I'm not a human because I have a mental disorder. Since I'm not tough, everyone says how I hurt feminism.

"More people hate me for mental health. After all, why do they . . . never mind. Let's just say there are some laws that prove their scathing hatred. I'm used to it. I'm always the freak that gets picked on."

I was heartbroken at her words. "You're not a freak, Tara! Those 'feminists' are actually sexist by saying all women have to be tough. People shouldn't fit women in a narrow box of what they think girls should be like."

She looked away. "Those annoying chicks don't bother me. The mental illness stuff is worse."

I questioned, "What do they do to you?"

Tara fiddled with her medal. "I was born with . . . OCD. I have to fight it every day. OCD is torture, but everyone says it's just liking things neat. In reality, I'm dying on the inside."

I didn't comprehend why, but I recognized it. OCD, obsessive-compulsive disorder.

Saint Dymphna is the patron saint of anxiety and mental illness! That was what I was trying to recall! When did I learn that?

I inched forward on my bed. "I'm your twin brother. You can tell me anything."

Her features lit up. "You want to hear it all?"

I announced, "Hit me."

She began, "I was born with it, but the symptoms didn't really show. On the day before the last day of second grade—"

I asked, "You mean the second to last day of second grade?"

She corrected, "No. The last day was a Monday, so this was a Sunday. I ... ... get ready, okay? I ... became ... afraid ... to ... to ... eat."

I froze. "That sounds agonizing."

Tara seemed very satisfied. "You're not laughing at me? I'm not pathetic deadweight to you?"

I assured, "You're the most important person in my life. Continue if you wish."

"Okay. I became afraid to eat because when I swallowed a cheese sandwich, it felt weird. I swallowed again, and it felt weird. It happened twice in a row. That really freaked me out. I didn't need the Heimlich Maneuver, but it still triggered OCD, and that's when it got really bad."

I analyzed, "Are you afraid of choking as well as eating?"

She didn't answer.

I figured she confessed a lot for one day. "Do you want to stop talking about it?"

She nodded.

Mom kissed my cheek and put her arms around me for ten minutes. "We'll come back tomorrow. You must have had an exciting day." All three of them left.

Father Derek remarked, "That's strange how she trusted you with so much so quickly."

"We must have a special connection. We're twins."

He watched me. "I heard. Still, it's unusual for such a bond to develop so fast. It's like you're a Delaisan."

I paused. "What's a Delaisan?"

He clarified, "The demonym for the country Delais."

I was intrigued. "I never heard of it. Can you tell me about it?"

He stated, "Delais is a small island in the Indian Ocean. It's the top country for medicine and intellect, and they are very trusting to certain people. Anyway, the eighth graders there are as smart as college graduates here."

I gushed, "They're the smartest country in the world? That's so cool! What type of government do they have?"

He scratched his head. "I think a democracy. I'm not sure after . . ."

A nurse came in. "Excuse me, Father Wallace, but," she checked my identification bracelet, "Matt can't see more visitors today. He needs a lot of rest."

He rose. "Right. Hope you recover your memory."

The nurse fluffed my pillow. "Try to get some sleep. I'll see what you can eat. Food might make you vomit. If that's the case, you can only drink liquids." She left.

I laid down while my eyelids grew heavy.

Accident . . . I wonder if another will happen again . . .

A voice woke me up. "He's sleeping now. Come back later."

I saw Tara, Mom, and Dad in the doorway with a nurse.

Did I sleep for a whole day? I must be tired.

I tried to sound more awake than I actually was. "Nope, I'm up. Hi, guys!"

The nurse jumped in surprise. "Well, now you can come in to see him."

Dad checked, "Hey Matt, how's your head?"

Throbbing. Terrible.

I didn't want them to worry, so I waved the pain away. "Fine."

Mom cleared her throat. "Now that it's a new day, I'll tell you why you didn't live with us. On the night you were born, you went missing."

That was fishy. "One of the hospital staff misplaced me?"

Dad's eyebrows furrowed together. "No. Someone kidnapped you."

A chill struck my spine with as much force as a sword. "Why? Who wanted me? Do we have any political enemies?"

Tara laughed. "Sorry, but 'political enemies' makes it sound like we're royalty. Clearly, we're not. But that was good comic relief, Matt."

I turned red. "Thanks, but I wasn't kidding."

She bit her lip. "I wasn't trying to make fun of you."

I stretched. "You weren't. But why would someone want a baby? Are we rich? Did they want a ransom?"

Mom crossed her arms. "If we were rich, I'd have the sunroom I always wanted, and Tara wouldn't go to the public school."

I was starting to get frustrated. "No ransom? Then what could someone gain by capturing me?"

Someone started humming. Startled, I turned to see who it was.

Oh. Just a nurse. I'm getting jumpy by all this kidnapping talk.

Tara turned to him. "When's Matt coming home?"

His smile faded. "He can only drink water right now. It'll take a long time for him to be ready to leave."

That's discouraging. I should make Tara feel better.

I winked. "You can come see me every day. Tell anyone who gives you a hard time that once your brother enrolls in school, he'll destroy bullies who get in your way."

Mom scolded, "Matthew Joseph Garrings, no

fighting!"

That baffled me. "Hold on a minute, 'Joseph'?"

Tara informed me, "That's your middle name. Most people have a first, a middle, and a last name."

I tried it out. "Matt Joseph Garrings."

Tara held up the palm of her hand. "High-five!"

What is she doing?

After a few moments, Tara explained, "You take your hand and hit mine like this." She slapped my hand.

Mom walked to the door. "I'm getting lunch."

Tara looked at her feet. "I wanted you to know how much yesterday meant to me. Because I found my brother, but also . . . because I found a brother who really listens. The world thinks I'm a freak, but I don't think you do. And," she finally looked up, "There's a lot more to say, but I don't really want to talk about it right now. But do you know? Do you . . . understand?"

I folded my hands. "Yes, some people are against you, and there's still more OCD things we haven't discussed. But you're not a freak. Whenever you feel comfortable confiding in me, I'm here. Except when I'm unconscious, but I think you get that."

I leaned closer as she pulled me into a bear hug.

She glowed. "I'm glad I have you now, Matt. You're special."

I grinned. "You are, too."

Mom handed Tara a grilled cheese sandwich. Tara was tackling her OCD and eating it, but I could tell it was hard for her. Dad encouraged, "Good ERP work!"

I questioned, "What's 'ERP'?"

In between bites, Tara defined, "Exposure Response Prevention. Basically, it means I'm exposing myself to my fear and preventing my normal response to OCD, giving in to it."

I poked her after she finished eating. "Do you like school better now?"

She made a so-so gesture. "The kids are all right because I'm in the higher levels this year, and I love the academics. I'm in Latin."

I said, "*Tam pulchra regia filia capit suam linguam.*"

Her countenance shone. "Oh! *Lingua* means 'language', *tam* means 'so', and *regia filia* means 'princess.' That's all I know."

I translated, "'So the beautiful princess seizes her language.'"

She rolled her eyes. "Of course! I can't believe I missed that *capit* is a form of *capiō*! Ms. Greenwood would be so annoyed with me!"

"It's fine, everyone messes up once in a while. It's good that you know Latin. *Latina est mater de multae linguae.*"

Tara clapped her hands. "Latin is the mother of many languages! I got it that time!"

Dad's eyes gleamed. "Speaking of Latin, I can tell you all about the Roman emperors!"

Tara made a face. "Nero and Diocletian *disgust* me."

I never expected an aggressive response from a girl who never spoke up for herself. "How come? What did they do?"

Dad supplied, "They martyred Christians in various gory ways. I won't tell you so you won't throw up. That would be a setback for bringing you home."

The nurse beckoned them to the door. "Visiting hours have ended."

I waved. "Bye, Mom and Dad . . . I love you.

Tara, I love you. Enjoy school! Don't let horrible people bring you down!"

After they headed out, I focused on theories as to why I would be a target for kidnapping. I had no explanation, but I intended to find out.

After a glass of water, I dozed off.

A five-year-old version of me beamed. "It's my first mission with a partner today, Giovanni!"

The man, Giovanni, ruffled my hair. "You're growing up. Your partner is Adrian. It's pronounced like the name 'Hadrian', except the 'h' sound is gone. The first syllable is the word 'age.' Don't worry; he's nice."

My heart sank. "Truman Shaw wouldn't have stolen me if I wasn't useful."

"You're very special, Matt. Adrian is very special, too. Try to teach him about God, okay?"

I scowled. "Are you sure? A lot of people don't like Catholicism."

Giovanni wouldn't make eye contact. "Adrian was taken from his parents, too; the only difference was that he was baptized before it happened. His parents would want you to."

I sat up straighter. "When can I be baptized?"

He leaned back in his chair. "I don't know, buddy. I don't know."

Another scene vividly unfolded.

I approached a boy with sapphire blue eyes, blond hair, and a light complexion. "Are you Adrian?"

He shied away from me. "You can call me Age. I love writing poetry."

I relaxed. "I'm Matt. You know that I'm your partner, right?"

He took a giant breath. "I do. Ready to do this?"

I almost screamed when I woke up. I mentally counted the things I found out from my slumber:

1. A man named Truman Shaw was

the one who abducted me.

2. A man named Giovanni taught me Catholicism, and, even though he was likely a kidnapper, we were fond of each other.

3. I was on a mission to be baptized.

4. I had a partner named Age who liked poetry.

Was Giovanni really a captor?
Was I baptized?
Then there was Age.
Were we friends? Did something happen that made us hate each other?

CHAPTER 2: AGE

Location: Lithuania

I heard Truman Shaw's steely voice thunder, "Is the kid still in the trunk?"

A door slammed, and someone opened the trunk where I was tied up. A goon gave me a disgusted expression. "Cheer up. You should be honored we took you out of the old facility and are taking you somewhere else. We're doing this because you're our new favorite."

I shot him a loathsome glance. "I'm insulted! You took me away from my poetry notebooks! This is not okay!"

The perpetrator slammed the trunk shut. "He's still there, and he's still irritating."

The truck started again. I laid down, wondering who that guy was. There were so many captors from all over the world; there was no way I could memorize all their names.

I only knew Truman Shaw since he was high up in the ranks, and liked to kill people.

Then my mind drifted to something that signaled a red flag.

"New favorite"? What happened to Matt?

Matt was one of my best friends, and Truman Shaw had a particular hatred for him. He was sometimes mockingly referred to as "precious" or "favorite."

He definitely helped the hostage life improve. He laughed at all of my jokes and taught me religion. It made being locked in a closet (recently replaced by the trunk) when I wasn't forced to do a mission bearable.

God, please let Matt be in Heaven. He taught me everything about You! It's not like he wanted to be forced into doing illegal things!

My plea ended when a voice became audible. "How did they possibly find out where the Belarusian base was?

"The signal in the tracking device isn't working, so Matt could be anywhere, and we can't kidnap him again! We need to relocate Adrian before they find out about him, too."

YES! Matt is alive!

The tracking device didn't work? That's bizarre. How is that possible?

Apparently the authorities freed Matt, so maybe they did something to it?

I couldn't bolt on a mission; I was being spied on whenever I was allowed out of the closet, and I had a tracking device implanted in me. It was the same story for Matt and the other hostages.

Maybe I can make a run for it and pray that the spies aren't paying attention and the authorities get rid of the device before the kidnappers arrive.

It won't work. The spies always pay attention. You check every time to see if they let their guard down, and they don't.

Truman's voice boomed, "Let's stop for the night. We can torture Adrian for entertainment. I'm itching to break a few bones."

The trunk opened again. A burly guy threw me on the ground and spoke, "Do you like trees?"

"What?"

"Do you like trees?"

One of my abductors is interrogating me about my opinion of trees. This is odd. Never mind all the torture. This is just odd.

I blinked. "Um . . . sure?"

He rubbed his hands together. "Excellent. You're going to spend the night being tied to one."

That makes more sense.

I retorted, "I hope environmentalists frown upon trees being used like this."

He leaned in closer as if to stab me in the throat with a blade, but only uttered, "What's an 'environmentalist'?"

Through gritted teeth, I managed to mutter, "A person who tries to protect the environment."

Truman cast a furious glimpse my way. "Don't smarten up my henchmen! I hire the brawny and dumb! They know how to hit, use a gun, use a knife, and kidnap people. Now, it's time for you to meet your new tree friend. Tie him."

Someone tentatively wondered, "Should we feed the kid now?"

Truman examined me from head to toe. "I suppose so, since he's our new favorite."

The title made me nauseous. "Stop calling me that! I am not your pet!"

Truman held his chin up. "Yes, yes you are. The definition of the word pet I am referring to is 'favorite person or thing.' That's right. I have a high school diploma. I actually have a very excellent education."

I scowled. "I thought you'd be expelled from every school you set foot in."

He admitted, "You're right; I was. My sister was heartbroken. I wonder where she is now . . ."

Truman's not going to make me relive this backstory, is he?

He smirked. "I'll stop there. After all, I don't want to bore Your Highness."

I had enough of his manipulation games. "For the last time, I am *not* royalty!"

He sat on a tree stump. "How many times do I have to tell you that you really are? Your name is Adrian, Hereditary Prince of Liechtenstein, Count Rietberg."

"Just because you keep telling me that doesn't make it true. Go away. I don't want to talk to you."

He tapped his foot. "Maybe I told you the truth because your first instinct was to label it as a lie. It could be a lie, though. I am known for my endless cruelty. I am technically a mass murderer."

I decided to make him scram. "Does anyone want to teach Truman the definition of an environmentalist?!"

A thug leapt up and proceeded to educate the dim-witted criminals about the denotation. All of them got up to listen.

Sensing my window of opportunity, I motioned to the one closest to me. "Where are you taking me?"

She guffawed. "You don't have the appropriate level of clearance for that."

I decided to use her lack of wisdom against her. "My full name is Adrian, Hereditary Prince of Liechtenstein, Count Rietberg. I assure you I have proper clearance."

The others were so engrossed in finding out what an environmentalist was that they weren't paying attention to the conversation.

She displayed a doubtful countenance. "Truman said you don't have clearance."

I feigned offense. "How dare you! Do you want to go to war with my people? We never lost a battle."

I had no clue about Liechtenstein's military history, but I was being intimidating.

She hesitantly peeked around to see if anyone was eavesdropping on us. "We're escorting you from Lithuania to Estonia. But we have to travel across Latvia first."

I'd have to memorize those countries. "Thank you. Please enjoy learning now."

I was in Lithuania for ten years. I'm going to Estonia. But, to get there, we have to go through Latvia.

Right. That's why I speak Lithuanian and Latvian.

Truman punched a tree in anger, and pieces of bark flew everywhere. "I was taught about environmentalists already! Don't you idiots know by now that I own you? Do as I say!"

One man puffed out his chest. "Hey, Shaw, I'm sick of you running your mouth! You're not going to boss us around anymore."

His comrades chuckled, but Truman's veins were pumping a lot of adrenaline. "You're fired! And when you get fired . . ." Truman took out a knife and struck the man down.

The man's face became ghostly white, and blood poured out of his wounds. "Curse you . . ." He started to wheeze, leaned his head back, and died.

Truman eyed his inferiors as if they were cockroaches and he was the exterminator. "You think his joke was funny? You'll be next."

I have to sleep with a bloody corpse gawking at me. It reminds me of the good old days when I was six.

They weren't good, actually.

I should have been disturbed that a man died in front of me, but I had seen murder so many times that it lost its original scarring effect on me. The same thing applied to the men since they all went to rest without any display of emotion.

Two portly men appeared at my side, making sure I would remain there throughout the night.

The first taunted, "You'll never get away. This is the only life you'll ever know. Your God abandoned you."

The second got in my face so we were micrometers apart. "Around here, you worship us."

I had witnessed scarier villains than those clowns. "Give me a break. Who would bow down to a bunch of men who smell like meatloaf, blood, and body odor?"

The first took a whiff of me. "You're not so fresh-smelling yourself. At least we have access to showers and deodorant."

The second snarled, "You're worthless. Why do you think no one rescued you by now? Nobody wants you back."

I exhaled. "Really? Then why do you hide me all the time? If you'll excuse me, I need to sleep."

The first put his arms around my throat. "Not so fast. Truman's going to give us a hard time tomorrow. If we're going down, we're taking you down with us. Your punishment will start with no rest tonight."

Their logic was self-refuting. "By making sure I stay up, don't you have to stay up and be exhausted, too?"

The second punched me in the jaw so hard I saw the ground spin and fell as much as the ropes would allow me. My skull cracked against a huge boulder, and I was out cold.

When I came to, I noticed that the first pair of guards had been replaced by another set. A set that was snoozing on the job.

It's happening! I might be able to make a run for it!
That is, if you don't pass out again.
Brain, now's not the time to be negative.

I struggled to undo the knots that fastened me to the tree.

These are loose! Some are giving way!

In a matter of minutes, I was no longer stuck

to the tree, but the original knots that bound my hands, knees, and feet together were impossibly tight.

What do I do? What do I do?

Think calmly, like you're in complete control.

I observed my surroundings to see if anything was useful. My eyes fell on rocks scattered on the ground.

Aw, thanks, rocks! That makes us even for the boulder nearly shattering my skull.

I found a very pointy one and cut the rope. I quickly undid my feet and knees.

I did it! I'm finally free!

Except for the tracking device, but I need to get help first.

I took a few fearful steps away from the watchmen, and an ear-splitting crack of a branch punctured the air.

Bracing myself for the eventuality of someone waking up, I was immobilized with terror while my heart dropped. A cold sweat broke out on my forehead and gripped me with a sudden chill. No one aroused. My breathing slowed, and I jogged away into civilization.

Hey . . . am I still in Lithuania, or did we cross into Latvia?

I kept running, unnerved by the lack of civilians on the sidewalk. I kept scanning shadows in case one was a stealthy human silhouette.

Argh, why are all these streets empty?

Is there a curfew as to how late everyone can be out?

Was there a fascist takeover while I was a hostage?

I kept searching for someone, racing down countless blocks. It felt like a lifetime before I spotted someone.

As I got closer, the features came into focus. My new ally was an intellectual-looking man, with dark skin and hair, reading a fat book on a bench.

I was as charming as I could be. "Excuse me, sir, do you know where we are?"

He didn't look up from his novel. "Dūkštas."

That's in Lithuania, right?

You're speaking Lithuanian, Age. Duh.

I rocked on my toes, trying to be more adorable than a mugger with my messed-up appearance. "What country?"

He closed his volume. "Lithuania. Are you lost?"

I bobbed my head up and down. "Yes! Very. Can you help me?" I spun around in a circle to make sure Truman wasn't creeping up behind me with a baseball bat.

The man offered, "Would you like me to call the police so they can bring you to your relatives?" He took out a cell phone and dialed a number. "Hello? I am here with a boy who needs to find his family."

About twenty minutes later, a police car arrived. An officer came out and kindly smiled at me. "Are you the lost boy? What happened?"

I gulped. "I'm a fugitive from a bunch of kidnappers."

The officer took me into the car. "Do you know any of the captors' names?"

I revealed, "Truman Shaw. That's it, sadly."

He reported the story into a walkie-talkie. "What's your name?"

I disclosed, "Adrian. I'm not sure of my last name."

He made a left turn with ease. "I'll have the hospital do a DNA test. Don't be scared; you're safe now."

Unless you're a criminal, too.

We drove on without a sound until we approached a hospital. The officer parked the car, and we started to walk toward it.

Out of nowhere, three familiar convict forms materialized, sprayed something in the air, and the world turned black.

CHAPTER 3: TARA

Location: Massachusetts, USA

Mom called, "Tara, time to get up for school."

I saw the black sky through my window and went downstairs for breakfast. As always, Dad was already at work. Mom handed me breakfast and packed my lunch.

I scooped up the contents in my pudding cup and gulped down my juice that contained a surplus of vitamins like I did every morning.

After I was done, I went back upstairs. I went to the bathroom and washed my hands. I brushed my teeth, washed my hands, washed my face, took off my sleepwear, washed my hands, changed into jeans, washed my hands, put on deodorant, washed my hands, and put on my shirt.

Mom volunteered, "I'll brush your hair for you, dear."

Since my brush had germs on it, I let her comb through my horrible frizzy hair until it behaved itself, and I clasped on my Saint Dymphna medal.

After I made sure Mom put the brush away and washed her hands, I put on a few bracelets and went downstairs.

I jammed on my shoes without touching them, since they touched the floor, and the floor had a bunch of germs.

Contagious deadly diseases. You'll cough up blood and have a raging fever. . . then you'll die with a burning sensation and pass it on to Mom and Dad . . . then they'll cough up blood, having a fever, and die . . .

Mom reminded, "Put on a long-sleeve jacket, Tara! Nobody can see your birthmark!"

Once I was dropped off at school, I went into first period early. Ms. Greenwood was already writing the day's Latin lesson on the board with examples.

What? Ablative of agent? Like a secret agent?

No, Tara, that makes no sense.

Well, what the heck is it?

I copied it down in my notebook, deciding to just fake it through the test and hopefully get a good grade.

At lunchtime, I sat with people I barely knew, and started consuming my crushed-up peanut butter sandwich. I crossed my legs, and my knee scraped underneath the table.

Ahh! What if it touched gum?! I could get Ebola or the Bubonic Plague!

More unwanted images bombarded my brain.

I was at the doctor's office, with a bunch of sick patients hacking up an infection and covering me with a slimy coating of saliva with thousands of viruses and bacteria.

Bacteria and viruses swam inside my body and started touching body cells, effectively destroying them.

I was on my deathbed, throwing my back with the intense effort it took to try to get all of the mucus, blood, and air out of my decaying lungs.

I was lying down in a coffin, dead. Worms started climbing on my arms and through my eye sockets, absorbing the nutrients from my body until I was a skeleton.

My heart was running a marathon, and my hands started shaking. I swiftly checked to see if the girls noticed, but they were gossiping. I took out a notebook and started doodling to ease the pain.

When I finished, it was a portrait of Matt and me, without my birthmark. Bianca winked at me. "Ooh, is he your boyfriend, Tara? He's cute."

I didn't want to share the happy news with them that I had a brother, especially since I really didn't know them well. "No."

I really didn't have any friends, except for Piper Bison. I was a loner, even at family parties. I just didn't feel right during them.

Hey, you have Matt now! He's your twin, so you can't drift apart like what happens with every other human being in existence!

Thanks, self! Or OCD? I can't tell the difference anymore . . .

Huh.

Does Matt have a birthmark, too? It never occurred to me to look for one.

Another girl at the table wore a smug expression. "Something wrong, Tara? Your lips are moving, but no words are coming out."

I blushed. "I do that when I'm thinking, which is all the time. It's nothing."

They exchanged a there-is-something-wrong-with-her look, but I was used to people doing that.

A teacher yelled, "Get back to class!" That signaled the end of lunch.

I heard Bianca whisper, "She's really too socially awkward to be associating with us. Tara Garrings is an embarrassment."

Another chided, "How have the doctors not recommended euthanasia yet? It's time to kill the animals around us."

The very kind euthanasia laws. I'm used to people suggesting that I should be taken to a slaughterhouse.

I trudged into third period, History. Mr. Burnem started writing about the American Revolutionary War on the board.

Is this really necessary? I learned about that war in third grade, fifth grade, and now again in ninth?

Out of all the planet Earths humanity lived on, why is the school curriculum so focused on the first Earth? There's a lot more they could talk about!

Mr. Burnem snapped his fingers. "I forgot to give out progress reports. Some of you are in danger of failing the semester and staying back a grade."

I'm fine; I never failed an assignment.

Mr. Burnem handed me my grade: a ninety-four.

What? How do I have a ninety-four? I do every single homework assignment, and never got less than 100 on a quiz or test. This is absurd.

Once the bell rang, I hastily picked up my stuff, and my bad mood became worse once I realized I was traveling to the fourth period, Algebra.

After eighty minutes of being hopelessly confused about elimination and substitution, the last bell of the day rang.

Yes! Freedom!

I ran into the school library, signed in, and started doing homework. I did the Latin translation, read the short story for English, filled out the history worksheets, and wrote down random answers for the algebra page when Mom texted me that she'd arrived.

Your Latin translation is all wrong. You don't get Latin, and you are the worst at algebra. Look them over again! Can you get any subject right?

Are you kidding? I'm not going through that again!

I went inside the car. "I'm all done with homework, but you have to sign a progress report." I fished it out of my backpack, and she took out a pen and did a quick signature. I put it back in its folder, and Mom sped off.

At home, I tossed my bag on the floor and darted into the bathroom after holding it in for six and a half hours.

The school bathrooms are so gross. If the kids can't even wipe their urine off the toilet seat, imagine what germs would be on it. I'd catch a terminal disease in those restrooms.

After I washed my hands after wiping, washed my hands after pulling up my pants, washed my hands after I pulled down my shirt, and a final wash after I touched the doorknob, Mom and I made our daily trek to Boston.

After an hour, I excitedly bounded into Matt's room. "Hi, Matt . . ." I noticed that the priest was there.

Shoot. I don't remember his name. This is going to be awkward.

I'm the Princess of Awkward. There's nothing I can't handle!

I cleared my throat. "What's your name again?"

He extended his hand. "Father Derek at your service."

I shook his hand. "I'm Tara."

His eyes lit up with amusement. "Yes, I caught your name when you introduced yourself to Matt."

My eyes flitted to Matt's arms. They were pale bony limbs with no color whatsoever.

So, the giant red birthmark is a Tara trait.

Ooh, I'm original. Awesome!

Like original in having OCD? You're not that special.

I swallowed the lump in my throat with great difficulty. "How was your day, Matt?"

He bit his thumb. "Father Derek, can you give us some privacy?"

After Father Derek departed, Matt held my hand. "This is really frightening. I have a memory. I've learned some things . . ." He retold us the whole story.

I was in shock. "Oh my gosh! That's insane! We have to call the police. It'll be a crime if we keep it from them. Are you going to be arrested because you did illegal things?"

He shook his head. "In the memory, I was forced to do that stuff against my will, so, no."

Mom fetched a nurse and requested a 911 call.

To break the tension, I lauded, "You really love me with all this OCD stuff, even if I have a germ thing and food issues? Nobody has ever cared that much about me. It's like I finally have a friend. It feels safe. I haven't felt safe in a long time."

Matt could fill in the blanks. "Because you have an anxiety disorder and are forced to watch the obsessions in your brain, which usually comes in a form related to death? But you never mentioned germs."

Here comes another vulnerable part of me.

Matt's different. He won't hurt me like Bianca and those other girls.

I croaked, "I'm afraid of getting germs from something and dying."

Matt nodded. "You're afraid of catching a deadly disease? You shouldn't unless there's an epidemic, but OCD repeats the fear in your head like a broken record, and you can't get the song out."

My jaw hung open. "How do you know so much about this?"

He inclined forward. "I don't know."

I decided I was in a safe place and could vent my frustrations. "OCD is more complicated than everyone thinks. They're like, 'I organize my stuff in alphabetical order, so I have OCD.' If you just like to do it, that's not OCD. Even when you have to do it, if you don't spend hours and hours and hours agonizing over it, it's not OCD."

He high-fived me. "Don't let them bother you."

I made a face. "They don't. I'm the one with Dymphna here." I fingered my medal.

"What's her story?"

I readied myself to get into my dramatic storytelling zone. "She was an Irish princess who fled with a court jester, his wife, and Father Gerebran to Gheel, Belgium, because her father wanted to marry her. He found out where she was hiding, and beheaded her, as well as Father Gerebran."

Matt was clearly impressed. "A warrior princess is the patron saint of anxiety disorders? Wow."

I blurted out, "Are you in danger? Does this Truman Shaw want to kill you? You can't die! You're my only friend!"

"No. He would've terminated me already if that was his intent. He wants something else."

I started pacing, something I did frequently, even when I was happy. I could pace and daydream to music all day.

I sputtered, "Will the authorities be able to catch him? He has this Age guy! What do you think he's doing to him now that you're not there?"

He paled. "Tara, don't stress out about this. That's not your job."

I argued, "I don't have a job, so it might as well be stressing out about you!"

"Please don't. I've lived this long. I'll be fine."

I glared at him. "I don't want you to leave me a second time."

Mom came in with the authorities, who were holding notepads. Matt detailed everything to them while I came up with a curious question.

Who is the patron saint of kidnapping victims?

I was still absorbed in trying to solve this enigma when they left and it was time to go.

I kissed Matt's cheek. "Bye! Don't get kidnapped! Love you! See you tomorrow!"

We scurried outside, and Mom drove home.

I groaned. "I don't want Matt to die."

She giggled. "He's not going to die. The hospital staff will protect him."

I'm not so sure the hospital staff can take down a crime lord, but whatever floats your boat, Mom.

If you don't shower and get all the germs off, you'll be gravely ill and die a horrendous, horrible death.

You'll have to wash your whole body, then your hair, but, while you're doing that, don't let it touch your body. That would re-contaminate everything.

I strategized my shower routine until we got back home.

Dad greeted, "How was your day?"

Mom popped in and closed the door. "Matt got a memory."

Dad's eyes widened. "What happened in it?"

Wanting to get away from it all, I proclaimed that I was going to shower and then head straight to bed.

But, before I did, I looked up the saint of captives on the computer.

Mom will have to clean it tomorrow. And the chair. And the desk that my elbows are touching.

I read the screen once it loaded the answer.

Saint Leonard is the patron saint of political prisoners, prisoners of war, and captives.

Prisoners of war? That sounds intense . . .

CHAPTER 4: AGE

Location: Nereta, Latvia

I gingerly sat up, and I saw the captors consorting with a teenager with black hair and brown eyes—similar to Matt's facial features—but aggressive and hostile.

He growled, "You almost lost the Liechtensteiner? I can see him watching us now like a scared puppy. Good thing I don't get attached to things, or else I would have pitied him."

Truman hardened. "Thank you for coming. We can handle the situation from here."

The boy narrowed his eyes. "My visit here was precisely because you *couldn't* handle him. If you lose him again, it's not my problem; my head won't be on a stick. I'll take my leave now that he's awake." The boy stalked off.

Truman turned on me, his eyes like those of a wild animal. "You'll pay for your little charade!"

The sound of the British pronunciation of "charade" perked me up a smidgen. It was those little things in captivity that made my day.

I suddenly remembered the officer. "You didn't kill anyone, did you? If so, I'll have to . . . tell your mother!"

Really, Age, really?
It's the only thing I can think of!

Truman said, "I released knock-out gas, so that man is fine. You, on the other hand, *escaped*! You'll pay for your scheme!"

I snapped, "What do you want, my soul?"

He responded, "Your soul would be nice, but that's impossible."

A woman brute cracked her knuckles. "Let me give him a couple blows on the head. He'll see so many stars he won't try that again."

Truman held up a hand. "Not on the head. His brain would suffer. We don't want that. Another area would be preferable, such as his face."

I piped up, "How about I don't get a punishment?"

Truman scorned, "Not going to happen. I hope you'll enjoy Latvia. We crossed the border while you were unconscious."

I grimaced. "You're always so thoughtful."

Questions about the whole being-kidnapped-at-five thing popped up in my mind.

What was the point in kidnapping us? What was the overall goal?

I guessed, "You kidnapped kids to have us do illegal things so your hands won't get dirty? Why don't you just do it yourself?"

He shot back, "That's not why we seized you. The time has not yet come when the true purpose will be revealed, so I have you do things to fill in the time. That's all you need to know."

I exclaimed, "You have a bigger master plan? What did they teach you at that high school?"

He stiffened. "Lots of things."

Six seconds later, Truman sat on the ground, staring at me, while I made a new tree friend (which was a bubbly fairy-tale way of saying I was tied to a different one).

I spat out, "Today I have spent more quality time with you than I would like in a lifetime."

He put a hand over his heart. "Thank you! I'm so glad the feeling is mutual."

I asked, "Are you going to search for Matt, or

did you give up?"

He threw a rock at me, which smacked my nose. I could feel blood and saw it stain my already grungy clothing.

Truman seethed, "You've been too nosy lately. The next time you want to stick your nose in my business, think about this. You're suffering from a nose bleed."

I sarcastically commented, "It's a mystery how that happened. Anyway, who was that boy? I never saw him before."

His face contorted. "You weren't supposed to see him earlier today; you should've still been out. You make my life harder than it has to be."

"You took me away from my parents. I really don't care if trying to get back to them is a nuisance."

Truman lashed out, "Matt was never as obnoxious as you, and yet I hated him more."

That wasn't logical to me. "He left you alone, and you still hated him? Why?"

Truman pinched my nose, which made more blood ooze out. "Maybe I'm lying to you."

I wasn't buying it. "You claim I'm the Hereditary Prince of Liechtenstein, an unlikely target for a random attack. You deliberately got us if I really am a prince."

He countered, "Are you really royalty, or was that a lie, too? You don't have the slightest idea of who you are. Maybe I don't know who you are."

I had had enough. "You always called me Adrian! My parents named me Adrian; you know that. You took me when I was five, so I still remember them! That can't be a coincidence."

Truman shrugged carelessly. "You got me there; your first name is Adrian. But are you really a royal Liechtensteiner, or a regular American boy? Do you remember that you were in America when I snatched you?"

I bristled at the mention of that traumatic day. "I am fully aware that I was at a museum when it happened and of the sacrifice I made."

He faltered. "Oh, that's right; you almost got away, but then you decided to save a little girl you had recently befriended. Stupid move. Do you know how this world is? She's probably dead."

That hit a chord. "Shut up, Shaw!"

Truman mocked, "Innocent high school girls have been slain before. She might not even be righteous anymore. Amusing, wouldn't it be? You saved a little girl, went through torture for her, but your precious princess is evil."

That can't be. I love her.

I yelled, "You don't know that! Maybe she's already fighting poverty."

Truman trailed on, "So, the princess saves the world alone, waiting for her prince to come. Sadly, he's still tied to a tree."

He dozed off eventually, and I immediately tried to untie my knots again. But they were tighter, and my hands wore out easily.

Everyone you care about is back in the real world. Mom, Dad, and the girl, but I don't know where Matt is . . .

I'll just take a quick nap. I'll be more refreshed in an hour or so . . .

"Looks like those held you. That crash course on tying knots was helpful."

I jolted awake and saw Truman right in front of me. "They have classes for that?"

He gave me a "duh" expression. "Of course. Another agent gave them out."

I predicted, "The boy my age who looks like Matt?"

"Did you see him teaching me how to tie knots?"

I demanded, "That's not an answer."

He snapped his fingers. "I'm answering your question with a question. That's how all those great thinkers operate."

Funny how you didn't include yourself as one of "those great thinkers."

Truman cracked his neck. "So, Prince Charming, are you ready to be thrown in a secret compartment and start the day? I upgraded the truck while you were unconscious."

As I was placed in my spot, I turned things over in my mind.

With every mile they take me, the farther I am from everyone. How do I escape? It seems like I can never get away from them for long . . .

CHAPTER 5: MATT

Location: Massachusetts, USA

After some time in the hospital, I made significant progress recovering from my mysterious accident.

A nurse tapped my arm. "The Lithuanian police reported that there was a man named Truman Shaw who kidnapped a boy named Adrian. Were these people in your memory?"

"Adrian was, but Truman's name was only mentioned. Was Adrian described having blond hair and blue eyes? Did they figure out the mystery of Giovanni?"

She searched the note from which she was reading. "Your description of Adrian matches with Lithuania's! But no, we still don't know who Giovanni is."

"Thanks for keeping me informed."

Tara raced over, followed by Mom and Dad. "Matt! Hi!"

I waved, while the nurse relayed the same information to them.

Tara cheered, "Adrian's still alive! That's awesome!"

I fidgeted. "Time has passed; he might be dead now. All we know is that he was in Lithuania."

Dad nodded. "So, Truman Shaw is definitely a 'Most Wanted' fugitive?"

The nurse scanned for confirmation in the note. "Yes. He's wanted in Lithuania for harboring Adrian there. Interpol is after him, so he's a fugitive.

"You're also free to go with your family. It was certainly an adventure taking care of you. Be extra careful now that you don't have maximal protection."

I gulped. "Aren't there government agents that will keep an eye on us?"

Tara informed, "Those were the old days. Now you're on your own."

We exited the building and went into a car. I inquired, "We live in Taunton? It's Saturday, so Tara won't go to school. What are we doing today?"

Dad advised, "Let's wait until we get home to decide."

After conversing with Tara for fifty minutes, we made it to our city.

Tara pointed out the car window at trees and other signs of forestry. "We live in East Taunton. Sometimes people treat the area like it's its own town because it's so quiet while the other parts are noisy all the time."

We live in the quiet part. Good. After all the excitement, I could use some peaceful afternoons.

I tried to understand Tara's social situation better. "Even though you said you don't have any friends, do you have people you talk to that have no clue about OCD?"

She responded, "There's Piper Bison; she lives in East Taunton like us. We met in middle school. And I talk to Peter Reynder at school."

I immediately got into protective-older-brother mode. "Whoa, a guy named Peter? He's not your boyfriend, is he? Will I have to beat him up?"

Tara crossed her arms. "I don't have a boyfriend. I'm not allowed to date until I'm sixteen. You're like Dad now."

Dad added, "You bet I'll beat up a guy who

wants to date you!"

Mom pulled into a driveway. "We're here!"

We walked up the driveway and entered the house. Dad turned off the alarm, and Tara sank into a chair.

Mom went into the refrigerator. "It's lunchtime. Want to eat?"

Tara reminded me, "You have to wash your hands before you eat, to kill germs that want to murder you."

I cleaned my hands. "I remember hygiene, but thanks for the tip. You don't have to be concerned about me."

She washed her hands in the kitchen sink and put suds on the handles. "You're right. The only contagious deadly disease right now is in Africa, not America. And Dad said that you die seven seconds after you get infected with it!"

I turned to Dad, who put a finger to his lips.

I see what's going on here.

Mom took a spatula out. "Matt, I'll find you a tutor so you can attend school once you catch up."

I grinned. "Sounds good. What's he or she going to teach me specifically?"

Dad stuck his tongue out at me. "Everything you need to be able to attend school! Do you not listen?"

He's hopeless with his humor. Hopeless.

I rolled my eyes. "That's nice, Dad. What are we doing today?"

Tara beamed. "Why don't we visit Bisavó? Matt, Bisavó is our great-grandmother. She never saw you. She's getting old; she should meet you as soon as possible."

Mom frowned. "I think it would be too much too fast. Matt needs to adjust to home life first."

Tara poked me. "Tomorrow you'll go to St.

Jane of Valois' for the first time!"

I remembered my wish to be baptized in the memory. "I don't know if I've been baptized or not. We need to find a priest as soon as we can."

She suggested, "Ask Father Leon after Mass tomorrow."

I noticed a bowl with small things inside. "What's that?"

Tara picked one up. "A candy. You take off the wrapper and eat it."

I put it in my mouth. "This is delicious."

She fetched her backpack. "While you have fun with your first chocolate snack, I'm doing homework. I have to write a story about Roman roads using three Latin words. Apparently, the roads smelled. The hotels smelled, too."

I was amused by that. "Because the roads were so bad?"

Tara considered that. "Makes sense. Want to help me write it? What was English homework . . . I think it was to read part of the novel."

I brainstormed what the Latin story could be about while she was tackling English.

An hour later, she slammed the book shut. "Done! Did you come up with anything for Latin?"

I launched into my creative burst of inspiration. "Our heroine is Veronica, a girl who is being chased by her family's enemies, only to have them attack her chariot, and meets up with a friend who protects her."

She took the main topic and lengthened it to a page. "Mission accomplished."

We didn't do anything else until Mom observed, "Bedtime. Matt, you're in the room next to Tara's."

I opened the door to my new room. It had white walls and brown carpeting. There was a floor lamp and a bed that faced the wall.

A voice squealed, "Cool! Our beds are only separated by a wall!"

I jumped at Tara's presence. "Why does that matter?"

She grinned mischievously. "That means we can send each other secret messages at night. If we can't fall asleep, we can play a game with each other. All we have to do is make up a code!"

I mocked, "My, my. So rebellious, Tara."

"I *did* get kicked out of the library once. I'm the worst girl in school!"

I wasn't convinced. "What did you do?"

She jumped up and down. "I stayed five minutes past closing time."

I rolled my eyes. "Oh yeah. You're going to get expelled."

Mom pretended to be angry. "Go to bed, you troublesome kids!" We parted ways, and I settled into bed.

God, thanks for helping me escape those people, and having Giovanni teach me Catholic stuff.

Saint Dymphna, help Tara fight OCD.

I woke up to Mom singing, "Good morning! Tara, you have CCD tonight!"

I got out of my room and nudged Tara. "What's CCD?"

She summed up, "CCD stands for the Confraternity of Christian Doctrine. It's religious education."

We went downstairs for breakfast. Mom put a plate of pastries on the coffee table. "We have donuts."

I saw a brownish black one with some white coating and dove for it.

Tara took one with an intense scowl. She was taking small bites and was extremely fidgety.

She must be fighting her choking obsession.

I caught Mom's eye. "When's the tutor coming?"

Mom replied, "Tuesday. I met up with him to make sure he's credible."

Tara grabbed my shoulder. "When you go to school, don't sag your pants! Don't let anyone see your underwear! Sometimes when guys walk past my desk, they bump into my folder and their underwear touches my stuff."

I concurred, "I will never do that."

She went back to her donut. "Good."

Mom put a basket of laundry down. "When I drop Tara off at school, I don't want to see boys' underwear in the morning. I've been thinking of starting a charity called *Belts for Boys*, so they can pull up their pants."

Tara exploded, "I'll get infected with their butt germs! They're going to start a disease that practically eliminates mankind with their sagging butt germs!"

I wasn't sure how to handle her anger. "Um, I'm sorry that bothers you, Tara."

She seemed to calm slightly. "Thank you. At least *someone* cares."

Mom looked at the clock. "Tara, we have to go teach."

I wondered, "Who are you teaching?"

Tara was still in her aggressive mode, but managed to elaborate, "We teach second grade CCD. I hate it. The kids are rude and germy. But I have to do it for community service hours to make my Confirmation."

I guessed, "Confirmation is a sacrament, right?"

She high-fived me. "Right. Teaching is really hard, too. I have to teach them transubstantiation."

Mom intertwined their arms. "Come on, Tara,

we need to leave, or we'll be late."

I watched as they left, then went on the computer to visit a website under the Favorites tab. But the History tab came up instead, and I found a description of a saint Tara must have looked up.

Saint Leonard is the patron saint of political prisoners, women in labor, prisoners of war, and captives.

Prisoners of war?

I feel like I'm in a war against my former captors. And I'm the prisoner.

CHAPTER 6:
TARA

Location: Massachusetts, USA

I checked off the kids that were there on the attendance roster. After glancing briefly at the agenda, I gave Mom the signal to start the lesson.

She began, "You're all about to make your First Communion. That's when you receive Jesus in the Eucharist."

All the kids stared at her with dropped jaws.

Oh. She's making them believe that Catholics are cannibals.

I jumped in. "That's hard to get used to. The bread doesn't become human skin. Jesus loves us so much that He didn't want to abandon us, so His Presence is in the Eucharist."

A boy shouted out, "So it's *not* like the priest dug up Jesus' grave and cut his skin off or anything? I don't want to eat people."

Huh. They're actually being nice today.

At the end of class, Mom opened the door. "How many of you have to go potty?"

Hands shot up. Mom and I waited outside of the bathrooms. Unfortunately, I could hear the boys hollering at each other.

"Lloyd, you have to wash your hands!"

One of the boys didn't wash his hands after going to the bathroom! The bacteria! The viruses!

OCD painted a picture of my inevitable future.

I walked down the block in a white dress; the side of my hair and face were covered in blood. I started hacking up the red liquid onto the street, where the droplets formed together to make puddles.

Cars splashed through them, drenching people in contaminated blood.

The doomsday virus was just beginning.

After the kids left with their families, I doused my hands with hand sanitizer.

We trudged to the car, where I opened the car door.

A woman wearing a huge hat decorated with blue ribbon and lilies walked over to me. "Are you under the weather, dear? You look as though you're about to pass out."

I played it off. "Thanks for the concern. My OCD about germs is just getting in the way."

She sniffed, "A mentally incompetent mutant. You shouldn't become a mother. Children are a blessing. People with OCD aren't able to properly care for a child. You'll only abuse your baby. You won't be able to change diapers. You'll leave the newborn in soiled undergarments!"

My cheeks flushed in embarrassment. "Don't worry. No one wants to marry me. My genes won't infect a new generation."

She raised a fist. "They better not! We need healthy humans, not a bunch of drama queens cutting themselves. Maybe you should cut yourself until you die so I won't have to worry! God wants what's best for the human race, and that thing does not qualify."

After she left, we drove in silence until Mom pulled into the driveway. I saw Piper ride her bike toward us. Once she made it over, she threw her helmet on the ground. "Tara, want to hang out today?"

I looked at Mom. "Can she come over? Please?"
Mom smiled. "Sure."

I turned to Piper. "But Matt has to be with us. I

don't want to leave him alone."

She gave me a funny look. "Who's Matt?"

I forgot Piper had no idea about him. She still thought I was an only child. "Matt's my brother. He just came back from . . . Portugal. He's a genius, so he attended a prestigious academy there. He's back."

She narrowed her eyes. "You never had a brother. You always told me that you were an only child."

I bragged, "Maybe he was being taken care of by relatives in Portugal from his birth because he was born with poor health and then he was a prodigy so he went to the academy. You know I'm Portuguese."

She accepted the cover-up. "I can't wait to meet him. Tara, my youth group meets on Wednesday; want to come? It's a few towns away from Taunton, so you should be able to go."

Mom fished her keys out of her purse. "Is your church Catholic? I thought you were Protestant."

Piper persisted, "But Catholics are welcome at our church!"

I pleaded, "It's just one time. How harmful can it be?"

Mom opened the door. "Ask your father. Matt, we're home. This is Piper."

He waved. "I'm Matt. Pleasure to meet you."

Piper examined him. "So, you're Tara's brother? She never mentioned you."

Matt handed her a piece of candy. "Tara didn't want to discuss the immense heartache of our separation. Don't blame her."

I informed, "Piper invited us to go to her youth group on Wednesday!"

He brightened. "At St. Jane of Valois'?"

Piper's eyes flickered behind him. "No, this is

somewhere else."

We chatted about random stuff for two hours until she had to go home. Once Piper picked up her helmet, dusted grass off of it, and sped off, Matt quoted, "'Somewhere else'?"

Mom filled in, "A Protestant church."

The phone rang.

Mom rushed over and glanced at the caller ID. "That's Dad now! I want his opinion before I allow it or not."

She picked it up. "Piper invited Matt and Tara to go to her church. You think they'd tell them that Catholics won't go to Heaven? Wait, some people from Piper's church said that to you? All right. I'll tell them."

Matt hugged me. "Sorry Tara. At least Piper thinks we'll go to Heaven." Before I knew it, Mom gestured it was time to leave. "Time to go to church! Tara has choir practice and then CCD right after."

I kept telling Matt about how awesome St. Jane of Valois' was until we arrived. I rushed into the church basement. Miss Ellen, the choir director, was setting up. I took out my community service sheet. "Can you sign this?"

She took out a pen and wrote her name with a flourish. Miss Ellen kept her pen in her hand. "Is that due tonight?"

I nodded. "I have CCD, so Emma should be here. She's in my grade, so she has to turn the slip in today."

After everyone else, including Emma, showed up, Miss Ellen patted her piano. "Let's do it."

After choir practice and Mass, I went in the parish center and made no eye contact with the other kids. I was the outsider no one wanted to talk to.

Why would they want to talk with me? I'm from another city, and I have OCD.

The speaker came forward. "Never let your boyfriend or girlfriend pressure you into anything, especially sex before marriage. Even medically, it's not good to sleep with someone and move on to the next person . . ."

Once the talk on chastity ended, I strolled into the parish office where Matt and Mom were waiting for me.

Father Leon was very animated. "Matt's going to enroll in the RCIA! He'll make his Baptism, First Communion, and Confirmation at the Easter Vigil Mass!"

He could die before then.

He will die before then. He's going to be taken away by the hands of Death itself . . .

I faked a smile. "Awesome! What if he dies before then? Will he still go to Heaven?"

Father Leon answered, "Since he's aiming to get the sacraments, he'll go to Heaven. That is, if he doesn't commit any mortal sins, but he seems well-behaved."

Mom changed the subject. "We'll take Matt to Aunt Brooke and Uncle Jimmy's tomorrow while I'm at work and you're at school."

We waved good-bye to Father Leon and left. Matt stopped at the end of the sidewalk. "How was the talk?"

Boring. She didn't teach me anything new. I already know to stay a virgin.

I managed to keep my tone in check. "A lady taught us about chastity. I have a vow, though."

He examined my hands. "I've never seen you wear a chastity ring."

I explained, "They're too expensive, but I still have the vow. How do you know about chastity rings?"

He shrugged. "I really don't know. Yet I remember that you usually wear a ring."

Once we got home, Dad yawned. "Guys, it's bedtime."

I showered, washing every particle of my being very carefully, and snuggled under the covers.

I woke up the next day and discovered Matt downstairs, ready to go to Aunt Brooke and Uncle Jimmy's. He elaborated, "I woke up at 3 AM like it was routine."

"You were kidnapped by a bunch of early bird people?"

He winked. "More or less."

CHAPTER 7: AGE

Location: Jēkabpils, Latvia

The best time to escape is now, while they think I'm securely bound.
Okay, did they leave me anything to untie myself?
Not really.
Hang on! There's a screwdriver from when the bulletproof window needed repair! I just need to get it over here.

I tried to scoot over to the tool without bumping my head on the ceiling.

I grasped it, and then plunged the screwdriver through the rope. I untied the rest of the knots on my body, took off my shoe, shoved the screwdriver inside it so they couldn't find out how I escaped, and focused on how to open the compartment.

I crawled over to the edge and tried to lift the doors open. An electronic voice buzzed, "Password."

What would Truman's password be?

I recalled something he bragged about, "*I have a high school diploma.*"

It was a long shot, but, "Diploma?"

"Incorrect. Access denied."

I kept brainstorming. "Environmentalist?" Denied. "Museum?" Denied. "Don't smarten up my henchmen!" Denied.

What could it be? Who's the one person Truman loves? Think, Age. Any conversation you overheard. Anything.

I remembered Truman lovingly say a name once, when I was six. I gave it a go. "Dolores?"

It paused. "Correct. Access granted."

I burst into the normal trunk, which was now very spacious. I could stand upright in it.

That must be the upgrade. More room I have to walk through. More time for them to catch me.

A crony sitting on the floor in the corner viciously smiled. "Going somewhere?"

"Um . . . yeah! Truman sent me to get snacks. Can you let me out? That would be helpful."

He advanced on me. "No can do. Truman and the black-haired boy ordered me to never listen to you."

Well . . . Truman certainly smartened up his henchmen.

"The black-haired boy? The one who taught you how to tie knots? Who is he?"

He floundered, "I-I-I . . . don't know. After you escaped, Truman called headquarters and contacted one of the best agents. The boy came. He was bloodcurdling. We're kidnappers, so we're intimidating. But this kid was a whole level above us."

"How?"

He shuddered. "The kid was so much smarter than us. He knew so many things. It was like he was trained his whole life for this business . . ."

I interrupted, "Abducting people isn't a business; it's a crime. Continue."

He jabbered, "He was so young and so high up! And there was something off about him."

Not that smart. Still revealing classified info to me.

He spat out, "Matt has a fraternal twin sister."

I didn't see that one coming. That was really random, too. A little odd, but I'll keep pumping him for information.

I didn't bother to sneakily get anything from him; he seemed dumb enough to just give me what I wanted. "He has a sister? What's her name?"

He crossed his arms bitterly. "Tara. If I ever see her, I'm going to nab her and never let her see daylight. You have no idea how much trouble everyone got in when we failed to capture her on the night she was born."

Another target. Poor thing. Look at the people she'd have to deal with.

I demanded, "You also want Matt's sister? Why?"

He glanced at the wall. "They were part of the plan, blah, blah, blah."

I prodded, "Do you know where Matt and Tara are now?"

He shook his head. "If I knew, I'd drag them back here. Plus, I don't even know if they're in the same place."

"Oh. Thanks. So, about those snacks, can I go get them?"

"I cannot let you out."

I scratched my chin. "What if I'm the good guy and Truman's the bad guy? Can I leave then?"

He seethed, "They gave strict orders that you can never leave until the day you die."

I feigned a cough. "The end is near . . . I'm going to die today . . ."

He smirked. "Cute. It's time you went back in that compartment where you belong." He whipped out a foamy, fizzy concoction with a napkin covering the noxious fume.

He lunged, and I blocked him. I shrieked, "Stay away from me!"

He removed the napkin and attempted to shove it under my nose. I pushed it in front of me. It went too close to the henchman and he collapsed.

I checked his pulse to make sure he was alive. "At least I'm not the one on the floor. They'll find him before he dies, so I'll make my leave."

I opened the trunk. I leaned forward, climbed on top of the truck, and spied a small woods. I jumped in that direction, feeling the wind blow through my bones as I hurtled toward the ground.

I tumbled into a creek and picked myself up off the ground. "I have to warn Matt . . . and Tara."

Matt's been on my mind ever since he escaped.

What about Sophie and Louis? I haven't thought about them in forever! I'll try to get them out of this mess, too.

A long-forgotten memory suddenly smacked me.

Sophie sat up. "Once we get out of here, I'm going to be a doctor."

Louis added, "And specialize in brain surgery. You'd be perfect!"

I thought out loud, "Sophie's held in Sardinia, and Louis . . . I'm not sure."

Sardinia was quite a distance I'd have to cover, and with the tracking device still intact . . .

I just have to make it to a hospital to prove my identity and contact my parents.

I'll miss my fellow hostages. Sophie was hilarious, and Louis was the kindest person. He had this aura about him that always calmed me down when I was freaking out.

I forged on until I saw a woman holding a newborn. I said in Latvian, "Excuse me, where is the nearest hospital? Where am I?"

She mumbled, "Jēkabpils."

Since she understood me, we really must be in Latvia.

"Are there any hospitals nearby? I have to go to

one very urgently."

She directed me to the nearest one. I took off in that direction, forgetting to thank her.

I kept running until I stumbled upon it. I skimmed the area for Truman or the countless others, and entered.

I jumped when I saw Truman questioning a nurse.

So, he knew I would come here.

Luckily, his back was toward me. I moved away from him and flagged down a doctor. "Excuse me, how can I prove my identity?"

He answered, "A DNA test."

Hope rose in my chest. "Can you give me one? I've been captured by this guy named Truman Shaw who is interrogating a nurse about me right now out there. He attacked a police officer in Lithuania, so I suggest knocking him unconscious while we wait for the authorities, if you are calling them."

He peeked out and saw Truman, who was screaming, "If I find out you're lying, I'll come back for you! Your head will be on a silver platter and I will gorge on your neurons!"

The doctor's face turned a snowy white. "I'll have security apprehend him."

I warned, "He has stuff that will make you faint!"

He dialed a number on a phone in the hallway. "Security? This is Dr. Jansons. There's a kidnapper in the front of the building. Be sure to wear masks while getting him. Yes, I'm calling the police, as well."

Dr. Jansons contacted the police, and the situation was immediately reported to officers on duty.

He thumped my back. "Let's have you take

that DNA test. That man might look around this corner and discover us."

We zoomed down corridors until we approached a room that resembled a laboratory. He opened the cabinet and took out a vial of ink. "I'll take your thumbprint. Put this ink on your thumb." I obeyed, and he pressed my thumb onto a machine. "Maybe you're not in our database, but there's a chance you are."

"I mustn't be; I'm not from around here."

He was still waiting for the machine to identify me. "That guy kidnapped you. If there's a missing person, their fingerprints automatically go into this database. Advanced medical technology is one thing that survived the Tech Crisis years back."

A picture of me when I was little showed up on the screen and a name popped up: Adrian Edward Maria, Hereditary Prince of Liechtenstein, Count Rietberg.

He whistled. "You're the long-lost Prince of Liechtenstein? Yeah, you'd be in the database."

"Can you call my parents?"

His jaw was open. "This man . . . did he capture Princess Sophie of Hohenberg, the descendant of Archduke Franz Ferdinand and his wife, Countess Sophie Chotek von Chothowa und Wognin?"

"A Sophie is captive in Sardinia, but maybe not her."

But now that I know I'm the Hereditary Prince of Liechtenstein, the girl he described must be Sophie.

He took a deep breath. "Wow. Today is one for the history books. When the police come here, you'll go with them."

I pleaded, "Please don't tell them I'm here! I don't know who I can trust! One of them could be a kidnapper!"

Dr. Jansons shut down the machine. "We might have to travel to an embassy. There aren't any from Liechtenstein, but there's an Austrian one. They'll take you to your family."

I restrained the urge to hug him. "Can we can drive there?"

He frowned. "The embassy is in Rīga. It'll be a two-hour drive. Truman might still be detained in the building, so we'll have to go out the back exit. But I have to help patients, so you'll have to wait until my shift is up."

"No problem, but what if Truman escapes and comes after me? Is there a room where he can't find me that I can stay in until our departure?"

He started thinking. "There is one empty hospital room. But, if it's needed, you'll have to go somewhere else."

"Okay. Where is it?"

He led me to a room secluded from the others. "Right here. The door doesn't lock, so Truman could waltz on in . . . but you can lie down on your bed, so, if he walks by, he most likely won't see you."

I hopped into the bed and covered myself with the blankets. Before he closed the door, Dr. Jansons assured, "I'll get you when I'm done."

My eyes lingered out the window, and flashing lights danced on the glass. Police stepped out of a car, armed with guns and masks, and burst inside.

They must be here to arrest Truman, and he can't knock them out now that they have the proper equipment!

Someone knocked on the door. "Truman got arrested! He's being detained for questioning. You're safe now."

Phew! It's only Dr. Jansons.

I sighed. "Not really. He had so many accomplices. One could break in, but I could probably outsmart them. They aren't the brightest."

He snorted. "Keep hanging in there. A few more hours, and you'll be free." Dr. Jansons returned to his patients.

A flat voice droned, "Excuse me, is a boy by the name of Adrian here?"

That's the boy with black hair's voice!

I quivered on the bed, determined not to move.

A lady's voice sounded angry. "That's strange; another man was looking for him. He was arrested."

"Truman Shaw was arrested? What an idiot!"

I heard shoes step backward. "He was taken in for kidnapping. You're searching for Adrian, as well? Are you with him?"

A forced laugh chilled my bones. "Of course not! I'm Adrian's brother. That Truman Shaw is an idiot; he made the mistake to take *my* brother."

"I see. Well, your brother isn't here. He must have run away somewhere else."

He persisted, "My mother installed a tracking chip inside him. It points to this building."

I perceived the agitation in the air. "Honey, he could've removed it. Now please, I have patients who need meals. Go back to your mama and let the police handle it."

Thank you, nurse lady.

"I must have been mistaken. Where do you suppose my brother has gone?"

I risked looking at her expression, which was extremely vexed. "I told you to let the police handle it. You're too young for this."

He crossed his arms impatiently. "Ma'am, to inform the police of his possible whereabouts, I must know."

She turned on her heel and left. "How would I know?"

He stayed put. "Adrian, you have proven to be very clever. Unfortunately, I will find you, and, this time, I will drug you until we reach the base. I know you can hear me! Your tracking device points here. I'll tear this place apart until I find you."

I closed my eyes. He walked in the room. "Resting, are you? That makes my job easier."

He approached me, but I didn't move. I had the element of surprise on my side.

When he was directly over me, I punched him in the face. "You can't hide everything from me! I already found out I'm the Hereditary Prince of Liechtenstein!"

"Who told you that?"

"A DNA test."

He glowered. "Congratulations; you know your name."

I raised an eyebrow. "You're talking to the person who outplayed Truman Shaw."

He shot me a dirty look. "The organization is displeased with him."

I yelled, "Dr. Jansons, another kidnapper broke in!"

The boy slapped me. "Shut up! Your doctor friend won't save you now." He tackled me to the ground and started hitting me in the face.

A lady shrilled, "What is going on here?"

I answered, "This boy broke into the hospital and attacked me!"

The black-haired boy denied it. "He's lying! I was visiting my brother, and this savage beast just came after me."

I pointed out, "If I came after you, we'd be in the hallway since I would have had to leave my room to get you if you were really visiting some-one. But we're in my room, so you came after me!"

She seemed very confused. "I'll call security." Then she ran away.

The boy heaved me over his shoulder. "Don't worry; you'll be gone by then."

I realized I had the perfect angle of the side of his head and struck it repeatedly. He flinched, and I kept doing it until he dropped me on the floor.

I bolted out the room. "Dr. Jansons! Can you *please* send someone to take me to the embassy? Doctor! Where are you?"

I bumped into another doctor in a lab coat. She smiled. "We can't have someone screaming in the hospital! What can I do for you?"

"I need to find Dr. Jansons! There's another person trying to take me!"

She examined me. "You're the Adrian that man was after? Okay, Dr. Jansons is in this room."

She led me to him. "Dr. Jansons, this boy is here to see you."

He scowled. "I told you to wait until my shift is up."

I felt very discouraged at his admonishing. "I know, but then this person came after me."

"What's his name?"

I only had disappointing news. "I don't know. He has black hair and brown eyes."

He sighed. "Dr. Ozols, can you cover me? I have an international incident to take care of."

She took his clipboard away from him. "Sure thing."

A voice bounced off the walls. "There you are! You will face my wrath!"

I squeaked, "That's him! *Run!*" We sped out as fast as our legs would allow, and he guided me to his car.

Dr. Jansons started the engine and drove onto the road.

I glanced behind me, and pinpointed the boy gliding into a vehicle and turning it on. "He's onto us!"

Dr. Jansons kept going as fast as the speed limit would allow. "We just need to get to the embassy!"

The black-haired boy's car rammed into our backseat.

I moaned, "Why are there so many people trying to kidnap me?"

The boy marched to my side of the car, and I could hear him even inside. "It's the end of the line, Adrian. You can't stop me now."

CHAPTER 8: MATT

Location: Taunton, USA

I couldn't contain my excitement after we got home from Aunt Brooke and Uncle Jimmy's the next day. "Tomorrow's my first day of tutoring!"

Tara high-fived me. "Congratulations! That must be exciting. You know English, so you'll excel at that."

I wasn't sure if I was really as smart as Tara claimed I was. "What about history? I only know about World War I."

Tara snapped her fingers. "Archduke Franz Ferdinand got assassinated."

I included, "His wife Countess Sophie Chotek von Chotkowa und Wognin died, too."

Talking about it made me feel despondent and hurt.

Even though that was a tragedy, why I am acting like it's personal?

While Tara was busy doing schoolwork, my thoughts of the mystery returned.

How can I help Age and Giovanni escape?

Was Age forced to do criminal activities against his will?

Are Age and Giovanni even good guys? They could have been friendly to gain my trust in order to use me . . .

I turned to Mom. "Can I call Interpol about the case, or would that get in their way?"

She took a break from her show. "I'd let Interpol do the investigation without probing them."

I lingered. "I just thought of a possibility that

might help them. With murderers out to get me, they should know."

Mom digested that. "I'll call them." She dialed a number on the phone and handed it to me.

I spoke, "Hi. I'm Matthew Garrings, the boy captured by Truman Shaw. I'm proposing the idea that Adrian and Giovanni, believed to be innocent civilians, might actually be criminals trying to pose as victims as part of an act."

The agent replied, "We'll take care of that if it turns out to be true. Mr. Garrings, we have an update on your case."

My stomach twisted in knots. "You do? Can I hear it?"

He informed, "Truman Shaw was arrested in Latvia and is being interrogated. Adrian was alive in Latvia, but now he's missing. Giovanni is still elusive; we have no records of him. Thanks for calling! Please contact us if you have a new memory that might give us a lead."

I breathed a sigh of relief. "Will do. Thank you for updating me."

I hung up. Tara's ears perked up. "Update? What's new?"

I briefed, "Truman Shaw was caught and taken in for questioning. Adrian was alive in Latvia, but now he's off the grid."

Tara started jumping up and down. "Yes! That heartless man is having justice served to him on a plate with ketchup on the side!"

"Why ketchup?"

Her eyes became misty. "When I was afraid to eat, ketchup became my friend. If there was a food I didn't like the taste of, I could conquer OCD and eat it if I squirted ketchup on it. Ketchup helped me eat a lot of stuff. Before we knew it was OCD, I thought eating a cheese sandwich was going to make the disorder go away, since that was the food that went down funny. So, Mom put ketchup on it, and that was the first cheese and ketchup sandwich I had. In middle school, kids gave me a hard time for eating them, but they weren't there when I thought I was going to die every day and spent every second of my life in painful agony, so I didn't give them the time of day."

Anger flashed in my chest. I was seriously getting fed up of those kids who bothered Tara. They called her 'fat', 'chubby', and wouldn't leave her alone when she ate certain foods. Sure, not a lot of people ate cheese and ketchup sandwiches, but that didn't give those brats a right to pick on her.

I kept my voice calm. "They stopped?"

If this keeps up when I enroll in school, they're going to pay.

She scratched her head, and, when she pulled her hand away, particles of dandruff clung to her fingernails from compulsive washing. "Yeah, but now I eat peanut butter sandwiches."

I went returned to pre-ketchup conversation. "Isn't it great that Truman can't bother anyone anymore? But Adrian . . ."

Age shook my shoulder. "Hey, how do we get them to leave us alone?"

I glumly stated, "There's no way they'll get off our backs."

He sank against the wall. "We're never going home. We'll be trapped here forever. I'll be tortured by some agent, and you'll be tortured by Clementine."

A clammy revulsion washed over me that overpowered the memory.

Who's Clementine?

I certainly don't like her; the way Age said her name disturbed me. She must be one of Truman's people.

Tara sat back in her chair. "Spill it. You just had

a new memory; you zoned out."

I summarized it for her.

She clutched her books against her chest anxiously. "Should you tell Interpol? They should find out about this girl."

I hesitated. "But I already called them once today. Would I be harassing them?"

Tara gave me a knowing look. "Would you rather irritate them or have this Clementine chick stalk you?"

That was easy. "Irritate them! I don't want her to get me! Or be near me, for that matter."

Tara concurred, "Feel free to call them. Don't let the criminals win."

I called Interpol and informed them of the new threat. "There. I did it. Back to those kids picking on you, do you really feel pain all the time?"

"Every moment. If I get married and have children, there's an increased risk that my kids will have OCD. It feels like I'd be passing on poison to another generation. I don't want my future children hating me because of this awful disorder. I'll adopt children so they won't resent me."

Mental pain was one of the most dangerous kinds because no one could tell how much you were bleeding from internal scars.

I held her hand. "Tara, your future children will not hate you. They'll get that you thought about the pain they might suffer, but that they would be your miracle children.

"Your children will understand that they were evidence of victory because their birth meant that, despite the trials of OCD, you found a husband who wouldn't abandon you! Even though OCD made you afraid to eat, you won."

She started crying. "I don't want my descendants to kill themselves! Some OCD sufferers commit suicide! I couldn't handle knowing that the disorder I transmitted to them through these detestable genes made them do that.

"In this time and place, there aren't any therapists I could bring them to who would tell them that God doesn't want them to do that because He loves them and doesn't want them to hurt themselves. I have to wake up every day and acknowledge that no prince will save me."

Grimness coated the air. "It's going to be okay. There is at least one man out there who will love you despite OCD."

Tara burst, "It's too late! You don't know what happened! No Catholic boy will ever like me after he finds out what I did!"

I knew there was more OCD stuff we didn't talk about, but it made me alarmed at how perplexed she was. "What did you do?"

She turned away from me. "I can't tell you. Mom and Dad say that people will take me away if I tell."

Something that gives people the right to take her away? I'm not going to lose my sister.

"What did you do, Tara?"

She ran to the staircase and flew up them. I crept up behind her. "Tara, I'll love you no matter what it was."

She wasn't budging. "I'll tell you eventually, but not now."

Tara didn't tell me all night, and I went to bed wondering about her.

Mom sang the next morning, "Time for school! Matt, your tutor will be here at ten. Tara, get ready."

I bounced up. "Do you want me to go back to sleep or wait for him?"

Mom chose, "Wait for him. We can't have him

knock on the door while you're asleep."

At ten, I apprehensively waited for my tutor until someone pounded on the door. I brushed the curtains aside to inspect the visitor. He seemed safe, but that wasn't a guarantee. I opened the door a crack. "Who are you?"

He took a step closer. "I'm Mr. Chives, Matthew Garrings' tutor."

I opened the door. "That's me! It's nice to meet you, Mr. Chives. What shall we start with?"

He took out a suitcase. "Let's test your English." He had me say common phrases and complete piles of worksheets on English grammar. "Oh my! Your English is already at the high school level; you did the whole pile! Let's work on math."

I finished all the problems he gave me. He double-checked them, amazed. "Again, you're at the high school level. Science is next. We live on a planet called Earth, and we rotate around a star called the sun. In return, the moon rotates around us."

I raised my hand. "Mr. Chives, I know astronomy. Our current solar system is based on the original system humans first lived in. The planets are Mercury, Venus, Earth, Mars, Jupiter, Saturn, Uranus, and Neptune."

"Impressive, but there's more material, such as black holes . . ."

I blurted, "Black holes are regions of space with a gravitational field so intense that not even light can escape. If a person gets trapped in a black hole, spaghettification occurs. Spaghettification is painful and deadly."

We did more science until Mr. Chives concluded I was at the high school level. He stretched. "On to history. The Greco-Persian wars were fought between the Persian Empire and the Greek islands . . ."

He taught me about the battles until Mom and Tara came in. Mr. Chives seemed troubled. "Your son is at the high school level in everything but history. You might have to register him in Golden Lake High soon."

Mr. Chives and Mom then proceeded to discuss his rate of pay. Mom pawed through her wallet. "I have insurance. Does this cover it?"

Tara tapped my shoulder timidly. "Thanks for your support yesterday. That means a lot to me."

I returned, "You mean a lot to me."

Mr. Chives picked up his belongings. "Goodbye, Matt. I'll see you tomorrow." I waved as he left.

I turned to Tara. "How was school?"

She threw her backpack down on the same spot it always sat. "More confusing Latin, more English assignments, more easy history, and impossible algebra, but that's the average day for a freshman."

I offered, "How's Latin? Can I help you out with that?"

She unzipped her backpack and took out her Latin folder. "Yes. On the practice test, I got a D. Can you please help?"

We went over all of the vocabulary and grammar rules. Tara pointed at the mythology section. "I got that down."

After Tara was all set and taking her hour-long shower, I had spare time on my hands, which resulted in my mind drifting off to the mystery looming over my head.

Who are Clementine and Giovanni?
Where is Age?

I attempted to figure it all out. "There are no records on Giovanni, so he's a mystery. Same thing with Clementine. They have records on Age, but he's off the grid. He must be in Europe, since he was spotted twice there."

I returned to Tara after she showered. "I have an idea."

She put her hands on her hips. "Did you have another flashback?"

I let her in on my plan. "The easiest bit to figure out is Adrian's location. Where was he found so far?"

Tara answered, "Lithuania and Latvia. Is there anything they have in common?"

I grimaced. "Not that I know of. This is a job for the Internet."

She turned on the computer and found an online map. "Latvia is north of Lithuania! They must be taking him north! Estonia is north of Latvia. If Adrian was captured again, he must be in Estonia!"

I wasn't satisfied. "Why are they taking him north? What's up there?"

Tara brainstormed, "You were held in a base, right? So was Adrian. Witnesses reported that he was trapped in a truck. Maybe they're taking him to a new base up north. If they continue north, they'll arrive at Svalbard, more specifically the island of Nordaustlandet. The island currently has no inhabitants. Good place to hide someone."

"But all we know is this north pattern. We don't know if the destination is Nordaustlandet or not. Another thing to call Interpol for?"

Her mouth straightened into a thin line. "Not sure. They probably figured it out. Then again, it's a big organization, so maybe they can take our call. Would you rather e-mail them? Here's where you would send it to."

I typed up an e-mail and sent it.
Why north? What's up there?

CHAPTER 9: TARA

Location: Massachusetts, USA

I went up to my room, took out my notebook, and started writing while thoughts kicked open the door leading to my mind.

Matt still cares about me even though I have OCD, but he's my brother. How can a guy seriously like me romantically?

Let's face it; I'm going to die with OCD. There's not going to be a cure while I'm alive, so I'm going to have to deal with it.

I really don't want to have kids. Matt said they'd still love me even if it was my fault they got OCD, but I don't want them to kill themselves like others have.

I feel so sick.

Just go back to writing.

I took a few deep breaths and submerged myself in the story as my alter ego Lara Ralace.

I filled up a page when Mom shouted, "Dinner!"

I shuddered as I smelled the wafting scent of food. Sometimes smelling food triggered OCD, which really bugged me. If the smell turned me inside out, how would I cook for myself once I moved out?

When I was nervous while eating, I chewed with my mouth open to take deep breaths as a soothing skill (no one can ever deal with the comments I face from family members at holiday parties. Extended families are *evil*). I felt like a mutant misfit.

I trailed down with my stomach doing somersaults. I swallowed the lump in my throat, ate my vitamins while sweat started soaking my skin, drank a sip of water, and noticed my hands shake when I picked up a piece of chicken.

You won't eat it. You'll be so afraid of choking that you'll ever eat again. You'll starve to death. You won't eat. Even if you eat one chicken tender less than usual, you'll enjoy eating less and slowly cut down until you eat nothing. You'll starve.

After I was done eating, I put my head on Matt's shoulder. "I'm so exhausted. Do you want to sleep?"

He paused. "I'm beat, too."

I cowered under the covers, goosebumps prickling my body after the ordeal. Being that petrified took a lot of energy, so I fell asleep quickly.

Mom shook me awake violently and hysterically screamed at Matt to rouse himself. "Tara! Matt! Wake up! We're going to the hospital!"

I murmured groggily, "What's going on?"

Mom shrilled, "Dad has severe stomach pain! We have to go now!"

I descended the stairs, thrust on a pair of shoes (without touching them, of course), and we barely remembered to turn on the alarm before heading out.

We got into the car, and Mom was definitely ignoring the speed limit.

I grabbed Matt's hand. "Is everything going to be okay?"

Matt bleakly stated, "Not sure, but we'll find out soon."

When does this nightmare of fear end?

I resolved, "Let's recite all of the presidents America ever had to take our minds off this. George Washington, John Adams, Thomas Jefferson, James Madison, James Monroe, and John Quincy Adams . . ."

While we were waiting for the results of Dad's entry exam, I was still going. ". . . Grover Cleveland, Benjamin Harrison, and Grover Cleveland again, William McKinley . . ."

The doctor entered. "The results point to a stomach bug . . . a very painful one, though. You'll recover shortly."

The worst place to get sick is in a hospital. Superbugs. Germs that can't be beaten with modern medicine.

You're going to catch something deadly just by sitting in this chair. Then you'll get a fever, then hack up blood. The blood will drench everything, and the stench of death will suck the life out of every room.

You can't escape your fate. You're going to die soon.

I announced, "I'm taking a shower when we get home. I'm getting germs off me."

Matt boosted my confidence. "You did great just by coming here."

After my extra extensive shower, I numbly walked into the living room to devour breakfast, feeling like a robot with my limited sleep.

Dad high-fived me. "I'm taking a sick day today."

I stammered, "I'm just happy it's nothing serious."

Wait. Dad high-fived me. He didn't shower! He still has the superbug germs! And now he contaminated me with them! I'll have to have another extra extensive shower!

I was doing homework after a noneventful day at school when the phone blared. Dad picked it up. "Hello? You want me to go back right now? You found something? Okay. I won't eat anything, Doctor. See you when I get there." He hung up. "That was the hospital. I have to go back." He hurried out without even turning on the alarm.

I grabbed Matt's shoulders and squeezed them. "Is Dad going to make it out of this?"

He apologized, "Tara, I don't know. I'm sorry."

I did algebra homework to pass the time. A lot of time. I wailed, "I don't know how to graph a line! I'm hopeless!"

Matt encouraged, "Keep going! Give it a shot; that way the teacher can't give you a failing homework grade."

I held my head in my hands. "You do realize that some teachers grade homework on accuracy, right? Lucky for me, Mrs. Macintosh only cares if I try. On test day, I'm going to fail."

He pouted. "There's probably someone who will get a worse grade than you. Come on, laugh. You have a marvelous laugh."

I was flustered at the compliment. "Yeah right, like you've heard my laugh before."

Matt persisted, "I heard it a couple times. It's a pretty sound, like a maiden from a medieval movie."

That comforted me. "Aw! That's one of my dreams."

Mom came in after doing errands. "Where's Dad?"

I wavered. "The hospital. They called and ordered him to go back. We don't know what's happening."

She held up her car keys. "Let's go find out."

Once we got there, Mom paraded to the receptionist. "What is going on with my husband? His name is James Garrings."

The receptionist checked the computer. "He's in here overnight. He has diverticulitis."

I let OCD wreak havoc. "What is that? Is it deadly? Is Dad going to be okay?"

He gave me a gesture which meant to shut up. "No, diverticulitis is not deadly or contagious; he is going to be okay, and diverticulitis is inflammation of diverticula. That was the pain he felt the other day."

OCD was not done with its rampage. "If diverticulitis isn't life-threatening, why was Dad rushed here?"

He made a disgusted noise. "If you must know, even though it's not life-threatening, the sooner it's treated, the better. Diverticulitis can be activated by some parts of a diet, so we were making sure he wasn't going to accidentally make it worse."

Matt nodded. "Thanks! And, next time, if you're nice to my sister, we might give you a tip."

Mom and Matt turned their backs to him while we navigated the hospital for Dad's room.

More superbugs. They're on the walls. They're on the floors. They're on the ceiling. They're falling off the ceiling and into my mouth! There's no escape!

When we made it to his room, I reported, "Dad! You're going to be all right! I interrogated the guy at the front desk."

Dad's shoulders drooped. "That's good to hear. I'm on a liquid-only diet."

I spouted off, "You should only drink things for now. I found out that some foods make it act up."

Dad approved, "You could be a detective."

We chattered about random things until Mom fidgeted. "We should go home and have dinner. I trust that you two completed homework? Even though you're being tutored, Matt, you still have homework."

We asserted, "I finished."

We waved at Dad, left, and scooted inside the car. Mom peeked back at me. "Since you went to the hospital, even with OCD, I should reward you. You can go to Piper's Youth Group. Just be careful if they start trashing Catholicism."

When we got home, I rushed to the phone and called Piper. "I can go! I can't wait to see you there!" She informed me that the youth group meeting had been pushed ahead to that night.

I flagged down Mom. "Youth group is tonight now. One of the preachers is visiting his sick grandmother, so they picked today to do it instead."

After dinner, Mom drove us there. "I'll be here at eight. Have fun."

We entered the church, signed up for the day's activities, and I saw a girl I knew. "Hi, Alicia! This is my first time coming."

Her eyes sparkled. "I'm glad you're here, Tara. Who's that with you?"

I introduced, "This is my brother Matt. Matt, meet Alicia." They shook hands. I craned my neck to see another familiar face. "Is Piper here yet?"

Alicia pointed to a room. "Everyone else is in there." I opened the door and jumped back in culture shock.

This was so different. Where's the altar; is it that big stage? And why are kids sitting *on it? Isn't that blasphemy?*

Piper grabbed my hand. "Tara! Matt! You made it!"

I froze when I saw Simon, a kid who bullied me in elementary school and in fifth grade. As a matter of fact, he was the first person who told me I was fat, even though my weight was normal for my age and I was skinny.

In seventh grade, he randomly hit on me. He was absolutely disgusting.

A bunch of girls batted their eyelashes at him.

Piper illustrated, "They all have crushes on him."

I bitterly fixed my gaze in the opposite direction. "They can have him. I don't date barn animals."

Piper dropped my hand. "We'll play dodgeball in a minute. I hate sports."

I shuddered at memories of eighth grade gym class. "I'm good! I don't need kids deciding to hit me in the face and chest. That really hurt."

I seriously got chest pain spells after that. The person whipped it so hard and so fast it caused damage.

Matt motioned for me to go with him in private. "Why did that guy trigger you?"

I told Matt what Simon did to me. Matt seethed, "Now I have to knock him out of the dodgeball game for your honor."

I was in disbelief. "'My honor'? This isn't the 1500s. That was millions of years ago."

He cracked his knuckles viciously. "Chivalry is not dead, Catholic princess."

The pastor grabbed a microphone. "Who's ready for dodgeball?!"

I'm in the Coliseum! I'm in the Coliseum!

Matt rushed up to the dividing line, waiting for the signal. I dove to the back with Piper and her friends. The four unknown entities all put on mocking smiles when they saw me. I inched toward Piper. "Who are your friends?"

She acquainted, "This is Ginny, Marcia, Georgia, and Molly. This is Tara." Their taunting smiles widened, and they said nothing.

Do these girls ever say anything, or do they just fantasize about eating people for lunch? That's the expression they've been giving me for like three minutes now.

Simon was getting everyone out, while Matt deftly avoided balls.

Soon it was down to Simon and Matt. Simon looked like the athletic hero, while Matt looked like a bug avoiding getting squashed.

The people-eaters cheered, "Go Simon! Get him out!"

They're acting like stereotypical girls fawning over a jerk from the movies. Who are secretly cannibals.

I felt bad no one was on Matt's side. I was always that kid in Gym class who was never cheered for. I clapped my hands. "Yeah, Matt! Carve him like a pumpkin!"

Matt winked at me.

I could hear the people-eaters whisper, "She's so weird. Why are you friends with her, Piper? She should be dead."

Of course they say that. Of course.

Simon hurled a ball, but Matt agilely moved out of the way and threw the ball he was holding right at Simon's face, exactly the way the kids in eighth grade did to me.

Simon staggered back, stunned at losing. The people-eaters licked their lips, as if picturing him drenched in ketchup to be eaten as punishment for losing.

The pastor raised Matt's arm in the air. "What's your name?"

"Matt Garrings."

"Matt Garrings is the King of Dodgeball!"

Matt turned to me. "My first order is to make my sister, Tara, the Princess of Dodgeball. Anyone who tries to mess with her messes with me. Let me tell you; you'll pay." He made eye contact with Simon.

After the event, the leader preached about God (and *didn't* claim Catholics went to Hell), and then it was time to leave.

I took Matt's arm. "We aren't coming back

here." My face was hot with embarrassment after the encounter with the people-eaters.

Some kids there were super sweet, like Alicia, but I didn't want to get bullied every time I attended.

Mom backed out of the parking lot. "How was it? Did they do any anti-Catholic stuff?"

Matt launched, "They weren't anti-Catholic today, but a few kids were awful to Tara. Mother, I shall not participate in any activity they host again."

She was befuddled by his official tone.

I explained, "He won the dodgeball game, and was crowned the King of Dodgeball."

Mom's eyebrow arched. "That's nice . . . Wait, if a few kids were rude, why didn't Piper stick up for you?"

My face grew warm again. "It doesn't matter; I'm not going back."

We got back to the house, and I patted the top of Matt's head. "Thanks for taking out Simon for me."

He kissed my hand, imitating a knight. "My pleasure, princess. It gave me pride to avenge you. That nasty beast won't sink his fangs into you again."

I yawned. "That's rad. I'm going to shower and go to bed."

After my hour-long shower cleansing, I flopped onto my mattress and pulled the covers over my head.

The next morning, I got ready for school, jamming my shoes on without touching them with my hands (as always). My hands were cracked, red, and as dry as the Algerian Desert from washing.

Someone knocked on the door. Mom mused, "Who's that? Nobody comes this early." She opened the curtains, which unveiled Piper.

I had a nagging sense of exposure. I intuitively checked to make sure my birthmark was still hidden.

Piper rocked back and forth on her heels. "Can you take me to school? The bus left without me, and my mom grounded me from using my bike. I had to walk here. I had to jump out of the cars' way."

Mom softened. "Of course! You poor thing!"

Piper carefully worded, "How was the group yesterday, Tara?"

I contained the urge to scoff. "Not what I imagined."

Piper asked, "Will I see you there next week?"

I wasn't going to be trapped into attending another meeting. "No."

Mom called, "Come on, girls; time to go. Matt, have fun learning with Mr. Chives!"

I stepped out the door, very incensed. I stomped over to the car, yanked open the passenger's side, buckled the seat belt, and slammed the door closed with a passion.

Mom teased, "You sure moved swiftly! Have a date before school or something?"

I snarled, "Maybe I do. I got kicked out of the library once; I'm a rebel. You don't know if I have a secret boyfriend or not."

I was bluffing; I never had a boyfriend, except for one guy in preschool.

Piper was caught off guard. "You had to leave the library? What did you do?"

Mom rehashed with relish, "Stayed five minutes past closing time!"

They both hooted. Mom criticized, "Really Tara, that was pathetic."

I contended, "I was hanging out there with the basketball team. There was a really nice tall girl named Cara O'Sullivan."

Piper checked, "You got kicked out of the library for staying past closing time with the basketball team for a school project?"

I snapped, "No one mentioned it was for school!"

In reality, Cara needed help finding a book for a project, but I wasn't going to admit that.

Piper haughtily assumed, "But I'm the only person you hang out with outside of school; you told me so."

"That was before I met Cara."

Cara and I never went to each other's houses,

but, whenever we saw each other waiting for a parent to pick us up, we talked very excitedly. I pretended to care about sports, and she pretended to care about writing.

Mom surveyed me. "You never hung out with Cara after school."

"We'd talk about things on the benches outside school. She's fascinating. She and her friends raise money for their basketball team by doing tricks on the street."

When we arrived at school, I got out as fast as possible, sprinting to get inside. I opened the front doors, climbed the stairs up to the library, and logged on a computer. I loaded an online map again and tried to figure out what could be up north.

There's still the possibility of the frozen, uninhabited land of Nordaustlandet.

Matt e-mailed Interpol; there's nothing else I can do. I should just relax and wait for them to get back to us.

I'm on a computer. These are ancient. Isn't it funny how the computer was used in the 1900s and 2000s, and then technology got even better?

But then the Tech Crisis happened, so now we're back to telephones, computers, and cell phones, like ancient times . . .

Since I had some time to kill, I researched Saint Leonard again, and the same summary of him popped up:

Saint Leonard is the patron saint of political prisoners, women in labor, prisoners of war, and captives.

A philosophical or spiritual analysis flooded my mind.

Prisoners of war, people who have been captured by the enemy.

I wonder if Adrian's a prisoner of war since he was captured by those people. It's not a war between countries, but trying to escape seems like his own personal war.

Am I a prisoner of war, too? I'm going to die with OCD with no hope of freedom.

Could that be a war? A lot of people describe OCD as a hostage situation. I'm the prisoner; OCD the captor.

Maybe. Maybe we're all prisoners of war of some kind . . .

CHAPTER 10: AGE

Location: European Continent

The atmosphere felt as cold as ice itself. I held on to Dr. Jansons' arm. "How close are we to Rīga?"

He calculated, "Halfway there."

The boy marched over glancing at me murderously.

I took a few deep breaths. "Are there any police stations nearby I could go to?"

Dr. Jansons shook his head. "I think he's going to take you again."

I would not go with him. "I made it half-way to Rīga! I'm not going to Estonia!"

"Estonia? Why are you going there?"

I hatched a plan. "A guy told me I was going to Estonia. They have a base there! If I get captured, please tell the Austrian embassy I'm in Estonia."

In case I get taken, he'll know where I'll be.

But how do I confront this criminal without losing?

When he approached the passenger's side, I opened the door, which slammed into him. I dashed to the opposite side of the car.

He warned, "You escaped twice. You better not do it again. The top man found out about your habit of disappearing, and he's starting to want to discipline you himself."

"Why don't you just kill me? Why do you want me alive?"

He wrinkled his nose. "Do you know anything, Adrian? The solution isn't crystal clear? You're as stupid as one of Truman Shaw's goons."

Okay, that was just insulting.

I started running.

The boy yelled, "You can't hide from me!"

I kept going, but my legs gave way, exhausted. Desperate, I crawled with my hands.

The boy stood over me. "What are you doing?" I kept trying to push myself forward. He pulled me back. "You won't flee with that effort."

"I can't go back with you! I can't go back to being forced to do things!"

He struck me in the face. "What is wrong with you? We never had you destroy anyone! Stop being so dramatic!" He took out a cloth and sprayed something on it.

Dread overcame me.

Why do all of my escapes end like this?

I couldn't move my legs, so I swatted the cloth out of his hand. "I will fight you for as long as I live!" I proceeded to clutch handfuls of dirt and slowly move along.

He crouched over me again and pinched my ear. "When was the last time you drank water?"

"I don't keep track!"

He took out a water bottle. "About three days without water, death won't be far."

I remarked, "Good to know."

"When was the last time you've eaten? I can see your ribs. Have the agents been neglecting to feed you?"

"Why do you care?"

He slapped me. "I'll hit you every time you ask a dumb question. I have to keep you alive for a reason. I can't have you die of dehydration or starvation. We have too much at stake."

"Who is 'we'?"

With a flourish, he tore out more mixtures from his pocket. The liquids trembled in their container. He ridiculed, "Your Majesty, it is time I imprisoned you in a more secure location. You're used to that, aren't you, Prince Over the Water?"

A sound pulled me into semi-consciousness. "Is that Age? It's been so long since we've seen him."

"Let me do tests." A stab jarred me into full awareness.

I jolted upright and saw who was there. Astonishment pounded in my chest. "Sophie? Louis? Is it really you?"

Louis beamed. "Age! It's us! Where's Matt?"

I replied, "He got rescued. He has a twin sister named Tara; the convicts want their hands on her. Is she okay?"

Louis bobbed his shoulders up and down. "I haven't heard anything about Matt having a twin."

Sophie poked me. "Age, lay down on that cot. I'm going to perform tests. Some creepy Matt-look-a-like barged in here with you."

I obeyed her command. "Where are we?"

She took out test tubes. "Welcome to Sardinia." She put alcohol on a cloth and rubbed my finger. She stabbed it with a needle, and blood trickled out.

That wasn't good enough for me. "Where in Sardinia?"

She put the sample in a machine. It buzzed and glittered red. "Age! Don't lift a finger! You're in the danger zone! Is there any water in here? Or food? The nutrients level in your body is really low."

Louis chattered, "We're in Oristano, Sardinia, located in Italy, in an abandoned building. It's big with agents posted everywhere, including outside this door."

Sophie opened a can of ravioli. "Got a meal!

Now we just need some water. Thanks for the help, Louis."

I shoveled the food down, starved. "You're the best! That was delicious; the best meal I ever ate."

Sophie opened a crate. "Here's a water bottle!"

I gulped the water down. "Why would they just leave food and water in here?"

She sighed. "They don't interact with us much. They give us the basic essentials for living. Food, water, medical stuff, that sort of thing."

I went on a hunch. "But no priests, huh?"

Louis' tone became dreamy. "I wish!"

While he fantasized about meeting a priest, Sophie had me lay down again. "Matt escaped? Do you think he's coming back for me? I mean, us! Is he coming back for us?"

I covered my eyes with my hands, forming the combination of words that would work. Sophie was very sensitive when it came to Matt. "I only know he made it out. But he wouldn't just leave us to rot and die here."

Shame surged inside me as I recalled my fatal error. "No! I botched it! A henchman told me I was being taken to Estonia! I contacted a doctor and told him if I went missing, I'd be in Estonia! Everyone would look in Estonia! It's all my fault!"

Sophie forced me back down. "You couldn't have possibly known that you'd be taken to Sardinia. They'll figure out we're here eventually."

Louis punched the wall in a fit of anger. "That's wrong! I got relocated here from Minnesota a while ago with the help of a sleazy American senator! I'm still not over it! I'm very upset with that man and Minnesota, even though the state itself had nothing to do with it!"

I had an idea. "Are there any windows we can access?"

Sophie moved to the edge of the room. "Here, but they're bolted shut and boarded up, and we're not on the first floor. None of us are strong enough to rip metal and wood apart with our bare hands, and we can't jump out and live. There aren't any tools in here we could use, either."

I banged on the wood. "There goes my plan to throw a letter out of it! Any vents we can climb out of?"

She shook her head. "The only exits are the door being guarded and the windows covered with metal and wood. Anyway, get back to doing nothing! You're going to get to Heaven a lot faster than you want if you keep exhausting yourself. You barely have the nutrients to survive. Sit down, or I will beat you up." I complied, but only because I wanted to. "You know martial arts?"

She confessed, "No, but I am an expert at assaulting people when I need to."

I warmed inside. "It's so great to have you guys back. I missed you."

Louis went back to business. "We missed you too, but if we do make it out, in order to get help, you'll need to speak Italian."

I colored. "You mean learn a whole new language? I can't do that! Why can't you do all the talking?"

Sophie glared at me. "We might get separated! Think, Age, think! Anyway, what are all the languages you speak?"

I simply returned, "Lithuanian, Latvian, French, German, and English."

She cheered, "Italian is easier to learn than English or German. Believe in yourself, Age!"

I abruptly remembered Dr. Jansons talking about Archduke Franz Ferdinand. I clung onto Sophie's arm. "This is crazy, but are you a descendant of Archduke Franz Ferdinand?"

She gritted her teeth. "Let go of me before I beat you up. You need to rest, you dork!"

I released her. "Sorry if my grip was cutting off your circulation."

Sophie made me lie down again. "Why would I be? Are you becoming delirious? Louis, get me more needles; I might have to do more blood-work."

I responded, "Dr. Jansons told me that a descendant of Archduke Franz Ferdinand named Sophie is gone.

A thought suddenly materialized in my mind. "Wait! I told him there was a Sophie in Sardinia! Maybe after they figure out we're not in Estonia, they'll go here. Oh, Dr. Jansons, please tell them about Sardinia . . ."

Louis sat on the grimy floor. "You did that? Smooth move, Age. You might have saved us. I'm sure it was God."

I noted that I was on the only bed. "Where do you guys sleep?"

Sophie pointed to the floor. "I sleep on the left side; Louis sleeps on the right. You get to rest on the flimsy bed."

Responsibility was poking at my conscience. "Are you sure you don't want it, with chivalry and all?"

She patted the top of the machine, which was still red. "You're close to death. You can have the bed. If you keep moving around and draining your energy, I will tie you to that thing."

I couldn't hide my smirk. "Ouch. Your science improved a lot since we last met."

She was definitely flattered. "It did! I can perform brain surgery now."

I was incredulous. "You cannot! No way!"

She simpered. "I saved three lives doing it. The captors were so impressed with me rescuing three of them that they gave me warm soup one time."

Louis certified, "That happened. Once we're free from this stuffy room, Sophie's going to be the best doctor the universe has ever known."

Pride blossomed in my chest. "I bet she will. Do you want to start with the Italian lessons? What's the first thing I should know?"

She instructed, "The first thing you should know is 'help me!'. Say it after me," she said a word, and I repeated it, "you now know one word in Italian. How does it feel?"

I bantered, "I feel like a culturati."

Sophie teased, "Oh yeah, you're such a cultured young man after being locked up for a decade."

"Why, I admire your articulately-phrased adulation, Miss Sophie, future doctor destined to change the world. I admire it very much."

Louis interrupted, "Quit fooling around; we have work to do before we reach freedom. Then you two can play English Aristocrat as much as you want!"

I asked, "Do you have a plan?"

He moved closer to us to form a huddle. "Not by any means, but we need to form one without the guards overhearing."

I griped, "I came up with a ruined plan already; why should I keep going . . . Sophie, when do new shipments of food come in?"

She shrugged. "Beats me. They just whirl on in."

I put my trust in her. "You really can fight someone and win when you have to, right? Because when they come in, you clonk them and we run out the door."

She held up two fingers. "Crummy plan number two. There are more individuals securing the place than just the people bringing in packages and the ones outside the door."

We can make it work!

I said, "We'll get them, too!"

Louis recommended, "Sophie, do you want to teach us how to fight?"

She rubbed her hands together. "This is going to be the best day of my life! I'll teach you the pressure points . . ."

She showed us various techniques, and I was again amazed. "Do you have any other fortes? Can you pick a lock with your fingernail or cook?"

Sophie laughed. "My only talents are the arts of battle and science."

Louis reminded, "I can handle technology."

I wondered, "What's my talent?"

Louis provided, "You come up with crafty ways to get out of sticky situations, despite them all failing."

I was getting bored. "I'll take it. What do we do in the meantime?"

Sophie put her hands on her hips. "I'll tell you what! Lay down before you die, you oaf! It's not safe for you to be walking around! How many times have I told you?"

I voluntarily listened to her. The key word was 'voluntarily'.

Louis was equipped with a can. "Should we give him more water and ravioli?"

She twisted the ring she wore on her finger. "Water, yes, but are there any other foods, like chicken? He needs protein." She plunged her hand into a crate and pulled out a package. "Oh, fish! This is acceptable."

I dug into the feast. "I'm so stuffed. This is the

most food I ever ate at once. Am I dying from lack of nutrients now?"

She pricked my finger and put the blood in the machine. "Better, but you still need rest. You are still banned from moving."

I stretched out on the bed. "See you guys tomorrow; I have an appointment with sleep not induced against my will."

For the first time in a long while, I didn't resist when my eyes closed.

Thanks for bringing Sophie and Louis back in my life, God.

Please have Dr. Jansons tell the authorities about Sardinia.

Also, You should watch over Matt and Tara. I doubt the organization will accept that they're gone.

CHAPTER 11: MATT

Location: Taunton, USA

Tara told me what those girls said about her. They're Piper's friends, and Piper invited us to go. I don't trust her at all.

I was starting to get furious, so, to calm myself, I checked our e-mail to see if Interpol got back to me. Sure enough, there was a new message.

Dear Mr. Matthew Garrings,

A medical doctor recently came forward with evidence that the captive boy Adrian from your recollections is the long-lost Prince of Liechtenstein. The doctor also tipped us off that he is being taken to Estonia.

Also, Adrian is reported to have revealed that a girl named Sophie is hidden in Sardinia.

Someone pounded on the door. I called, "Coming, Mr. Chives!" I shut off the computer and opened the curtains to be sure it was him, and, once I saw his face, I allowed him to enter.

He shook my hand. "Hello. Since you're already done with everything but history, we're going to do lessons on that. Back to the Greco-Persian wars . . ."

After covering a few battles, he was pleased with our work. "We finished that. Let's do Ancient Rome."

I flipped to a new page in my notebook, and he began, "A man named Julius Caesar was popular with the people of Rome. The Senate was afraid of his power and assassinated him, with Caesar's best friend Brutus delivering the final blow."

I bristled. "Ouch."

Mr. Chives snickered. "Yes. It was a very famous event in human history." He flipped through pages in his teacher's handbook. "Which emperors should we go over? Caligula seems like a good place. At first, he was kind and welcomed back citizens unjustly exiled. He became ill but survived. His behavior after that altered considerably. He pretended to be a god and forced people to kiss his feet. One time, he was about to kill an animal as a Roman sacrifice, but, at the last second, he struck a Roman priest and killed him."

I jotted that down. "What did Caligula catch that made him so violent?"

He struggled for the right words. "Caligula's health is a whole different lesson on its own. There are so many theories.

"After Caligula died, Claudius ruled. He was the one always made fun of at family gatherings, the victim of pranks. He improved Roman life tremendously. His second wife, Agrippina, had his doctor poison him so her son, Nero, would inherit the throne-"

Tara would like Claudius.

I interrupted, "Tara doesn't like Nero. He persecuted Christians."

Mr. Chives softened. "Yes, he did. At first, he helped people. Then he started wandering streets murdering innocent people for fun and eventually killed his mother. The Great Fire of Rome was aflame, and everyone found out he did nothing to assist the victims. He used the Christians as a scapegoat to take blame off himself, and tortured and martyred them brutally. Later on-"

I finished, "He got killed, too?"

He frowned. "No. This is a more troubling way to die, suicide." I shivered at the thought of it.

Mom and Tara came in the room. Tara threw her backpack in its usual spot and got out cookies. We started munching on them while Mr. Chives was going over stuff with Mom.

I said, "We did the Roman empire today. We went over Julius Caesar's assassination, Caligula, and Nero."

Tara mumbled, "What? You skipped over Augustus? Whatever. At least you did the Ides of March."

I frowned. "What's 'the Ides of March'?"

She answered, "March 15. It's associated with Caesar's death."

Mr. Chives picked up his teacher's handbook. "Time for me to leave. Have a nice day."

After his departure, Mom walked to the door. "Let's visit Dad in the hospital."

After we got home from our visit with Dad, I led Tara to the computer. "I got an e-mail." I opened it up.

Her face looked like mine when I ate chocolate for the first time. "Whoa, Adrian is a prince? And there's another hostage named Sophie? Backtrack, Age is a prince? A Catholic prince?"

"Yep. It's funny; I don't recall a Sophie. I hope I remember her. Poor Sophie. I remember Age, but not her."

Tara was still glowing. She must have still been thinking about Age's newly-discovered royal status.

I deduced, "It would be better if they went to Sardinia. They might even rescue Sophie!"

Tara touched the screen. "That would be good, but some of them are going to Estonia, right? Adrian should be searched for, too."

I clicked off the e-mail. "I'm sure they won't give up on him. He's a tough kid, anyway."

She sank in a chair. "No! He's mean like Simon? He's supposed to be a knight in shining armor!"

I assured her, "He's not mean. I meant tough in the sense of 'resilient'."

She made a face. "Now what? There's nothing more we can do about the mystery."

"Help each other with school? I'll help you with math; you'll help me with history."

Tara complained, "Right after I find out Age is a prince, I have to pass algebra."

CHAPTER 12: AGE

Location: Oristano, Italy

"But you're used to that, aren't you, Prince Over the Water..."

"The descendant of Archduke Franz Ferdinand?"

"You're the long-lost prince of Liechtenstein?"

I groggily rubbed my eyes. "Do you guys know what 'Prince Over the Water' means? The Matt-look-a-like-creep called me that."

Sophie took out another needle and antibacterial wipe. "Never heard it. Let's see how healthy you are today."

She dabbed my arm, punctured it, and put my blood sample in the machine. "Improving, but you're still teetering towards death. Here's some breakfast."

I wouldn't drop the question. "It just caught me off guard. I'd love to know what it means."

Louis twiddled with the opening to a crate, moving it back and forth. "If I had access to the Internet, I could find out for you."

Sophie went into her doctor mode. "You need rest. Finding out your princely lineage or whatever can wait. Eat your bread!"

I bit a good portion off and started chewing. Only because I wanted to.

She praised, "Good. Drink your water, too! You'll die of dehydration before starvation."

I finished the bread and water. She pricked me again. The machine had a reddish-orange-ish hue. She gasped. "It's even better! Keep eating and drinking."

I smiled. "Sounds good to me."

Sophie fiddled with her ring. "Let's move on to Italian."

Louis was enamored with the sparkly aspect of the ring. "Before we do, that's pretty. You've always had that, haven't you?"

She glanced at it. "It's my chastity ring. My parents got it for me on the day I was baptized. On to Italian. Let's learn 'call the police!'" She pronounced a phrase, and I followed suit.

Sophie got excited. "Now you have to learn 'I was taken away from my parents.'" She said something, and I felt like a seal being trained while repeating it.

Louis jumped in, "Put it all together, 'help me; call the police; I was taken away from my parents!'"

I did so.

Sophie finished, "So, now you can tell a civilian to save you. But you'll probably have to describe the situation. Say, 'a guy brought me here against my will.'"

More? That's a lot of words.

I pleaded, "How about you just write it down for me on a piece of paper? This is getting complicated."

She disapproved, "You have the attention span of a goldfish. But I'll just write down common phrases on this grocery receipt. 'Where is the bathroom?' will be a lifesaver."

I was relieved. "You're one of the best, Soph."

She threw her pencil at me. "Stop groveling and take the sheet already!"

I crumpled it up and shoved it in my shoe. I touched cool metal.

The screwdriver from when I untied myself in the

truck!

I dropped my voice so that it was barely audible. "I forgot I have this screwdriver. This could unbolt the windows!"

Sophie examined it. "There's still the wood. A screwdriver can't get through that."

A crafty plan formulated in my head.

I challenged her, "You're right. None of us can break wood. I guess you're not strong enough. We'll just have to go with Plan B, then."

Her eyes turned to slits. "Let's see *you* try to tear that wood!"

I smirked. "I never promised I could fight. You did."

She was vehement. "I did not! I just said I could attack someone when I needed to!"

I let my cocky attitude get even more annoying. "Yeah, you see, we need this wood taken down. Unless a piece of wood conquers you . . ."

Sophie's fists curled. "How dare you!"

I turned to Louis. "Can you write in Italian?"

He saluted me. "You bet. Why?"

I went closer to him. "Can you write a letter saying that we're being held here? Are there any other receipts around?"

He fished one out of a box filled with medicine and started writing. I crept to the windows and unscrewed the bolts.

I buried the metal under cans strewn around. "Sophie, it's time to prove yourself worthy."

She readied herself and shattered the wood with a deafening crackle.

I recoiled. "They might have heard that!"

Sophie threw the wood shards on the ground, and Louis flung the letter out the window. I peered outside. "Are there any pipes we can climb down?"

"What is going on in here?!" The door burst

open with our wardens standing there pointing guns at us.

I screamed, "Sophie, get them!"

"The windows are open! Take them down!" They aimed at us.

I dove behind a crate.

Another plan by Age ends in disaster.

But Louis still got the letter out the window! There's hope!

Sophie started kicking a captor repeatedly, then threw him against the wall, where he slumped to the ground, unconscious.

They advanced on her, so I grabbed the piece of metal hidden under the cans. I snuck behind one buffoon and bashed her on the head with it. She swooned.

Sophie complimented me, "Not too shabby, Age!"

I caught Louis running out the door. I jerked my head toward it. Sophie winked, and we both took off after him.

I warned, "Louis, there are more people on the way!"

We made it to a big room. There was a computer on a desk. The desk was decorated with a snow globe with something small on it.

Louis lunged at the computer, typed maniacally, and punched a button. Paper shot out of a machine. He hissed, "Get the paper out of the printer!"

I snatched it and shoved it in my shoe. Louis turned the computer off. "That has all the information you wanted, including what that phrase meant, and who we really are."

I tugged his arm. "We need to keep going!"

Dozens of agents broke in the room and blocked all the exits. "Secure the place!"

Sophie started fighting a guy, and the other criminals moved toward us.

One slammed me against the wall and took hold of my hair. He squeezed it, making me flinch. "None of this happened before you came along. This is your fault, isn't it?"

He grabbed the snow globe and smashed it on my head. I closed my eyes to shield them from the glass. I could feel cuts open on my skin. Water splashed the floor, mixing with blood droplets. The room was spinning slightly.

Louis struggled against his captors, and when all eyes were on me, he crammed the small thing in his pocket. "Age, are you okay?"

I retorted, "Still alive!"

The guy who trapped me started beating me. "Not for long!" He dragged me away, making the disorientated feeling worse, and brought me to an elevator without taking his hand off of me. He pressed a button.

Once the elevator came up, he pushed me inside and ducked in. The doors closed, and we went down.

He's bringing me to a secret torture chamber to destroy me! I'm going to die!

God, if it's not too much, watch over my friends.

Salvation is my only hope now . . .

We finally reached our destination. He lugged me over to a dimly lit room with shelves full of vials.

He strapped me down on a thing that looked like it came out of a horror movie.

I coughed. "Is Sophie a descendant of Archduke Franz Ferdinand?"

He grabbed a blindfold and tied it around my eyes. "I don't want you to see what's about to happen to you."

Searing pain shot through me. "Is she?"

"If it'll comfort you, yes, she is. You're the Hereditary Prince of Liechtenstein, and Louis is the Prince of Belgium."

"What does 'Prince Over the Water' mean?" More affliction made me tense my aching muscles.

"I'll let you ponder that until your last breath. You bleed a very appealing shade of red. I might get a vial and fill it with your blood to keep as a sample to use *forever*."

I bit my tongue in anguish as my brain registered more torture. It grew more and more agonizing. I finally stopped holding back the screams.

"It takes that much to bother you? That takes a lot of effort; I'm going in really deep. No more flesh wounds. You're a challenge; I like that."

My slow death has started!

CHAPTER 13: TARA

Location: Taunton, USA

I mournfully covered myself with blankets in my bed.

No more mystery to take my mind off OCD.

New sibling, Dad in the hospital, school stress . . . I'm going to wade through OCD spikes.

OCD's going to be so bad with food I won't be able to fight it, and I'll starve to death!

I never told anyone about scrupulosity except my parents, like three years ago, before they started to get agitated at me for telling them about it.

I'm going to starve to death and go to Hell.

Ugh! You know what; I don't want to think about my doom.

I clicked a pen and flipped open the notebook with Lara's adventures to the page where I left off and let my imagination cope with all my scars.

You're going to Hell. You're going to Hell. You'll never be happy again. You're going to Hell after a slow starvation after the whole family will tell you how much they couldn't wait for you to die.

Especially after seventh grade.

I put more attention into writing to block out the thoughts, but it was in vain.

Over and over, the thoughts hissed, sinking fangs into me.

You're going to Hell. You're going to Hell. You will not have salvation. You lost the hope of going to Heaven.

I covered my ears, but I knew that wasn't going to stop the thoughts.

You're going to Hell. You're going to Hell. You don't deserve to be Matt's sister.

Tears stained the page, and I buried my head in the sheets and wept.

Mom caught me in the act. "Tara, why are you crying?"

I went with the usual response. "Nothing."

"There has to be a reason you're crying. What is it?"

I clammed up. "Nothing."

She pursed her lips. "Don't tell me then." She went down the steps.

That's the exact reason I never tell you anymore! You don't really care!

I hid in my room for the rest of the day.

Mom knocked on my door in the morning. "Time for school!"

I crept downstairs to get breakfast. Matt put his arm around me. "Mom said you were crying last night."

I swiped my glass, jostling the juice inside. "I bet she did."

He sensed the strain in my voice, the acerbity. "Do you want to talk about it? That might make you feel better."

Matt's not going to love you if you tell him about scrupulosity. Matt will never talk to you again.

I ate a spoonful of pudding. "Let's just say it's OCD."

Tiny beads of sweat adorned his forehead, right where his scar was. "We can always talk about it."

"Is the vow that you'll love me no matter what still on?"

Matt jabbed me. "Definitely."

I gripped my pudding cup tightly. "I have . . . scrupulosity, so I dealt with OCD telling me I was going to Hell. I started crying."

He soothed, "You can talk to me whenever you have an OCD thought."

I exploded with disbelief. "What if it's during the night? You want me to wake you up?"

His head pricked up. "Why wouldn't I? Tara, you can talk to me whenever, except at school. Worst case scenario, you can go to your guidance counselor, right?"

Just discussing OCD made me tired. "This isn't the 2000s millennia! Of course I can't go to a guidance counselor at school! Can we talk about something positive?"

"Sure. I'm almost at school with you! We might be in some of the same classes! Wouldn't that be great?"

We went over the possibilities of that happening until I finished my little meal and got ready (with, of course, many washings).

A knock on the door propelled me to check if my birthmark was hidden. Mom opened the curtains to see who it was. "It's Piper again." She let her inside.

Piper asked nonchalantly, "I can walk to school from now on. I just wanted to know if you're free on Monday at three o'clock."

Mom watched the clock while talking. "No. Why?"

Piper stated, "I need a ride. I have Drama Club rehearsal."

That was dubious. First of all, she never mentioned she was in Drama Club. Secondly, there was no upcoming performance.

I slammed the door shut and made the trek to the car. Piper caught up to me. "So, Wednesday nights are busy for you?"

"I can't go to your youth group anymore."

She wasn't offended. "That's fine. Wednesday's in the middle of the week; a lot of people can't make it. There's a group at my house on Fridays. Since the group is at my house, there'll be different kids."

My heart beat faster. Even though there were new kids, I was scared to go after meeting the people-eaters and Simon.

She kept going, "These are really sweet kids. They won't bother you."

"I'll think about it."

At school, my thoughts roamed to the seemingly ending mystery.

It turns out Adrian's a prince, and there's a girl named Sophie.

Maybe we'd get along. She dealt with kidnappers; I bet she can handle high school kids. If the people-eaters came along, she could stick up for me.

But who would really like me? My only friends are Matt and Piper, even though she and I aren't on the best terms.

There's Peter, but he's only an acquaintance at school.

I have Cara, but . . . I don't know. If I had a panic attack, I'm not sure how she'd respond.

After school, I opened the door to the house. Mr. Chives hurried over to Mom. "Hildegarde, Matt is almost done with the entire tutoring curriculum."

Skepticism crossed her face. "So soon?"

He showed her his teaching book. "Most students take time to go over English, mathematics, and science. Matt and I only go over history, so we can fly through it. And, at school, the freshman curriculum starts with the exploration of America, beginning with Christopher Columbus. We're already finishing Ancient Rome. Next, we'll do feudalism . . ."

I couldn't contain my excitement. "That's the time of chivalry and Catholic monarchs!"

Mr. Chives chuckled. "That is accurate, Tara. Matt and I will do feudalism and the Renaissance. That's all he has to know to be caught up to district standards. He'll be eligible to be registered in school this year, and, since Tara seems to have a passion for that time period, it'll be done quickly."

He wasn't wrong; I adored feudalism and the Renaissance. Last year we had to memorize the order of knights' obedience in the feudalism days: God, their landlord, and then their wife.

Then there was the Renaissance, with Michelangelo painting the Sistine Chapel and the Medici family, a powerful unit in Italy who supported scientists.

Mom shook his hand. "Thanks for letting me know, Mr. Chives." He exited.

I couldn't stop my bubbliness. "I can't wait to go over that with you!"

Matt got out cookies and milk for our snack. I felt a twinge of acknowledgement at myself for not having a full-blown OCD spike at the sight of them.

Good for you, Tara. You stand up for yourself.

Matt brushed my offer aside. "I can handle the material."

I complained, "But going over them with you will be like reliving them. I won't be able to study them again until college! If I'm lucky."

He gave in. "If you want."

After studying vocabulary terms for feudalism, we visited Dad (We just updated him about school, nothing serious).

Once we got home, I showered until my skin was sore and red, and started writing Lara's journey, with OCD torturing me.

Matt breaks his back doing everything for you, and you're deadweight. You never do anything for him.

You do nothing to benefit humanity. You are deadweight destined for Hell, especially after the seventh grade! You sold your soul!

I fought back those thoughts with vigor.

I don't want to sell my soul! I'd just get anxious about something, like a test, and a thought would pop in my head like, 'If I got an A, I would sell my soul'.

But I never wanted to! But something weird happened one time . . .

I tapped my chin with the base of the pen. "Does anyone else have problems like taking the Eucharist without going to Confession and worry about if they sold their soul?"

You're all alone. Nobody else commits sacrilege and sells their soul like you do! Stop acting like you have hope! You'll never have anyone who will understand you, you freak!

I sighed. Eventually, I'd have to confront it, but a deep feeling inside told me that no one would help or care.

I have Matt.

Shut up, mutant; he won't love you after this.

No, you shut up, OCD! Or myself! Or whatever you are!

I took a nap, wiped out from the constant war I was dragged into.

CHAPTER 14: MATT

Location: Taunton, USA

The fact that I was almost going to Golden Lake High kept my good mood going. I handed Tara a cup of pudding and a glass of juice for breakfast. "What things should I know about high school?"

Tara listed, "You need to pass your courses. You need to take three semesters of the same foreign language, and you need to take P.E."

I was puzzled. "What's P.E.?"

Tara winced. "Physical Education. That's when you play athletic games all semester."

I can deal with that.

She obviously hated P.E. I tried to make her feel better about it. "At least we won't have homework if all we do is play tag and stuff."

A captivating grin spread across her face. "I didn't think of that! There is a bright side to a world of competition and bullying for the not-athletically-gifted kids after all!"

I turned on the computer. "Enough about school; let's check e-mail. Maybe Interpol found Age or Sophie."

Tara chirped, "Wouldn't it be so cool if Sophie and I got along? I'd fit in with your friends."

I didn't want her hope to be dashed. "Hold your horses. I don't have any memories of Sophie; she might be a mean person." I signed in and clicked on the new message.

We browsed its contents. Tara's shoulders

sagged. "This is atrocious! They searched every-where in Estonia, and no Adrian!"

I read the next paragraph. "They found a lead in Sardinia! On a street, there was a letter that said Sophie, Age, and someone named Louis were in Italy! According to the letter, they didn't take Age to Estonia; they took him to Sardinia."

"That means the north pattern was off."

I wasn't done assessing. "Maybe the criminals figured that, after the sightings in Lithuania and Latvia, it was getting too noticeable they were go-ing north."

Tara speculated, "I bet every building in Italy is being investigated now, especially on the street where the letter was found."

I wasn't won over with that hypothesis. "Not necessarily. Maybe the wind blew the letter from the initial location to that road, or the letter was planted there on purpose."

"You have a flair for this secret stuff."

I was flattered. "Thanks."

Tara said, "I still think the antagonistic people are coming back to take you again."

"Why would they? I've met my real family, so the authorities know more about me now. If I were kidnapped, it would be easier to rescue me now. Plus, whatever they wanted from me, they can get from Age."

She argued, "They took you *and* Adrian. You must put something on the table that he doesn't. Otherwise, why would they have captured you in the first place if all they needed was Adrian?"

"Tara, I don't know their motives. They could be prowling the American countryside looking for me for all I know."

Tara pulled up an online map of Sardinia. "Do you think they're in the crowded places like Cagliari, Olbia, or Sassari? It makes more sense to escort them to a more secluded area, but you never know."

Mom appeared in the doorway. "Tara, you have to study. Saving the world can wait two hours."

CHAPTER 15: AGE

Location: Oristano, Italy

A girl's frantic voice broke through the waves of aching. "What are you doing? You can't kill him yet! We need to find out his special thing for the plan to work. If he's a hassle conscious, just knock him out."

Clementine.

I did not want Clementine anywhere near my deathbed. "What are you doing here? Aren't you trying to figure out where Matt is so you can try to convince him to marry you?"

She snarled, "If you must know, he is madly in love with me; he just doesn't realize it yet."

I was repulsed. "He will never like you. He has made it clear that he has no romantic feelings for you whatsoever."

I heard a shoe slap the floor. "He doesn't yet! But he will. My persistence will win him over. That's how it is in the movies."

This girl is hopeless.

I kept my annoyance out of my voice. "Clementine, being one of his captors is a deal breaker."

She roared, "Former captor! He got rescued by the meddling authorities."

The man butted in, "Enough! Even though I hate every fiber of Adrian's being, he's right about Matt not liking you. You're going to have to blackmail him to marry you; he's not going to of his own free will."

Clementine hissed, "That will change one day!

How many times do I have to go over it?!"

Even with the blindfold, I could tell Clementine was as red as a tomato. "Knock him unconscious already; I didn't come here to be insulted. I only came to chastise you about almost wrecking the plan." Her footsteps faded.

The man pinched my shoulder. "If that's what the big man wants, I'll do it. Get ready to sleep for a hundred years, Liechtensteiner, because that's your destiny."

CHAPTER 16: SOPHIE

Location: Oristano, Italy

After Age was taken away, Louis and I were overpowered and brought back to the room.

They put even stronger wood to board the window up and applied ten sheets of metal.

They went back out, with extra guards outside of the door. Louis whimpered, "They're going to kill him. They're going to kill him."

"At least Age's going to Heaven."

He gasped and held up a small device. "Hey, when no one was watching, I stole this. It was on the desk with the computer. I don't see how it's useful now, but it might be later, like Age with the screwdriver."

I held up a carton of gelato, changing the somber atmosphere to strategic like a certain deceased Liechtensteiner friend would have. "Have a little treat tonight. The gelato comes with a spoon." I tossed it to him.

Louis opened the carton. "Age was right. He is, or was, the Hereditary Prince of Liechtenstein. You are a descendant of Archduke Franz Ferdinand. I'm the Prince of Belgium."

"That's stellar! Is Matt a prince?"

He joshed, "Why? Do you plan on marrying him and becoming his queen?"

I let out a girlish giggle that was very unlike me. "I didn't say that."

"That's a nice daydream, but I couldn't find any information on Matt. My hunch is that he's a normal kid with a super brain. His sister is even harder to track."

I wanted to stay optimistic. "But, if he's a prince with a huge brain, that'd be the best!"

"If I were you, I'd be more concerned about living than getting married."

His words made me stop. "You're right, but I have to do something to escape depression from being a hostage for ten years!"

He scooped a spoonful of gelato and put it in his mouth. "Why would they kidnap the Hereditary Prince of Liechtenstein, the descendant of Archduke Franz Ferdinand, the Prince of Belgium, and two geniuses? A ransom is the blatant answer, but they're killing Age. Why would they kill him?"

"In all likelihood, they want a ransom, but Age was difficult to keep under control, so they don't want to put up with it anymore. But Age was such an angel! He had all those poetry notebooks he wrote about the girl we saved at the museum."

Louis sighed. "Poor Age. All those notebooks must still be in Lithuania."

I choked on the words. "They wouldn't leave evidence there. They must have burned them."

I started crying for my slain friend. Even the toughest warriors cried sometimes.

Louis put on a cheesy grin. "Do you want some gelato? It might make you feel better."

I sourly took a carton and ate the contents. "What was that girl's name? The one we saved at the museum."

Louis leaned against the wall, squeezing every drop of memory his brain possessed. "The name Tara rings a bell."

I stood. "Isn't Matt's twin named Tara? What was the girl's last name?"

"Garrings. Her name was Tara Garrings."

I put the carton down. "You can remember that?"

He put his hand up to stop me. "I could be wrong. Her name might be something else."

I started eating again. "Is Garrings a common surname, or is it super rare?"

"I'm not sure. We'd have to sneak out again in order for me to find out, and I don't want to die."

I wasn't giving up. "A DNA test would tell us if they were really twins, but we'd need DNA from them both."

Louis rolled his eyes. "Perfect. And how would we get their DNA?"

I rummaged through the crates. "We have to have something from Matt that contains his DNA! Like a fingerprint or a hair particle!"

My search only came up with some spare euros. I put them in my pockets. I now had a secret stash that was a fair amount in the event of an emergency.

Louis joined me. "These are from Italy; Matt was held in Belarus. Nothing here can help us. Let's take a break for tonight. Maybe, if we sleep on it, we'll be better prepared. You can sleep on the rickety bed if you want."

I took him up on his offer and dozed off.

CHAPTER 17: TARA

Location: Massachusetts, USA

Mom woke us up. "Right now, we have to pick up your father from the hospital. We're going to meet Aunt Brooke and Uncle Jimmy at church before Matt's first RCIA class."

I decided to dress up for the first day of Matt's classes. I went through my closet and found a white dress with a purple flower petal design on it. I pulled out a huge purple gem necklace from my jewelry box. I placed them on my bed.

Mom checked up on me. "Do you want me to braid your hair?"

I nodded. "I feel like I'm a princess getting ready for the ball. I'm going to change into the dress after lunch."

She went to the bathroom drawer and got out a hair-tie. "Are you sure? You wash your hands so much changing clothes. Two changes in one day will wreak havoc on your hands."

My gaze fell to a fan on my jewelry box. "It'll be worth it to feel pretty."

Mom started braiding. "Aren't the tenth graders having CCD tonight? One of them might like you."

"And then he'll find out I have OCD and dump me."

She exhaled. "Tara, OCD is a common disorder. Maybe your Prince Charming has it, too."

I rolled my eyes. "Stop being fake. We all know I'll never get a fairy-tale ending. You said it yourself when I was in third grade at the gas station."

"What are you talking about? I'd never tell you that, especially because that's not true."

I divulged, "When Dad got out of the car to change the gas, you told me I had to get over the food fear because, if a guy asked me to dinner, I'd have to say 'I can't because I'm afraid to eat', and that'd scare him off. You're right, Mom."

"That? That was some advice in a parenting magazine."

I was appalled that mothers would recommend saying that. "What was the goal? To bring your child to an apathetic, lifeless reality at nine and crush the newfound hope in her blood?"

She huffed, "The goal was to get you to eat. The column said that, if I scared you, you'd eat. They were wrong."

I estimated, "More wrong than not telling me I had a twin brother for fourteen years?"

Mom admonished me, "Tara! Well . . . I finished your hair. Put on jeans and a shirt and eat breakfast."

After washing my hands after I took off my pajamas, after putting on underwear and jeans, and after putting on deodorant, I went down to see Matt.

Matt touched my hair. "Formality is nice on you."

I blushed. "You think so? I do get more social acceptance in a dress."

Matt smirked. "Because you look like the princess you are on the inside."

I'm not used to people being nice to me. It's unsettling after constant disrespect for fourteen years.

After I brushed my teeth and washed my hands, Mom brushed my hair, and I squeezed my feet into my shoes without touching them, we finally left for the hospital.

When we got inside, we were greeted by the same secretary as before. Matt shot him a withering look, and we made it to Dad's room.

Dad waved. "Hey! How are you?"

Matt waved back. "Great! My first RCIA class is today."

There are germs on the walls. There are germs on the floor, slapping against my shoes.

You're going to catch a deadly disease and die.

I was on the sidewalk, hacking up blood. Puddles of blood filled the streets, basking in bacteria.

I fell to the ground dead, with streams of blood staining my chin.

Mom fingered her purse. "What are we waiting for? Let's go home."

She drove back to our house, and Piper tore across our front lawn. "Hey Tara, did you decide to come to the Christian gathering at my house on Friday?"

I opened the door to the house. "Not yet. Today's a busy day; I won't have time to think about it."

Mom stepped inside. "They were fresh on Wednesday. I don't want any bad influences on my kids."

Piper coaxed, "I could see where they were out of line. But everyone coming to my house is really sweet."

I'd see for myself. "Who goes there?" She listed off the names. I relaxed. "I've heard of some of them. They have good reputations."

Matt started to get antsy. "Are we going to be late for Mass?"

Mom chuckled. "We didn't even have lunch yet; we still have time. Tara, you need to wear a long-sleeve shirt under your dress; it'll be frosty."

I forgot: the dress had short sleeves, so my birthmark would be exposed. Why no one could see it was another secret I didn't want to know. Surprise, surprise.

Piper jumped in, "Are you going to a birthday party or some other family event?"

I hope not. They think I'm a freak.

Matt bit on his thumb. "We're going to church, but I really think we're going to be late."

Mom waved it off. "We have plenty of time! Sorry, Piper, can you come back later? I have to fix lunch."

Piper waved at me and glided out the door.

Matt went to the window and watched her sprint away. "I'm glad pretending to be late managed to make her leave."

Mom cut up some carrots. "You can go to the group if you want. You said the kids there are well-behaved. As long as the kids are nice to you and respect Catholicism, you can go."

After lunch, I took off my jeans and shirt, washed my hands, put on tights, washed my hands, and slipped on my dress. After Dad helped me put on my necklace, Mom drove to church.

Once we got there, I headed toward the basement where Miss Ellen and the other choir members were.

Emma picked up my necklace. "Where'd you get it? You always have the best jewelry."

I told her the location, and she made a mental note to go there one day.

Emma's definitely a better person than the girls I sit with at lunch.

After Mass and two panic attacks about placing the whole Eucharist in my mouth all at once, choking to death on it, and going to Hell, I strolled over to where my family was.

The lights glowed like stars above us. Emma tapped me on the shoulder. "Want to introduce me to your family?"

I cleared my throat. "This is Emma. Emma, this is my brother Matt, my aunt Brooke, and my uncle Jimmy." They all shook hands.

Dad walked over. "Did you make a new friend?"

He loved it when I socialized. I hated socializing because most people were like my extended family, hateful, or allowing the cruel relatives to hurt me without a care in the world.

I said, "This is Emma."

After the introductions, Dad started conversing with Aunt Brooke and Uncle Jimmy.

Emma put locks of hair behind her ears. "It was cool to meet them! Later!" She ambled out the door.

Matt approved, "I like her more than Piper."

Once Matt's RCIA class ended and we got home, I had my hour-long shower, put on my pajamas, and went downstairs.

Matt traced my birthmark with his hands. "How'd you get that?"

This is the first time he's seen me in short sleeves.

I rubbed it self-consciously. "I got that mark from being born. Mom doesn't want people to see it. I don't know why."

Matt blinked. "That's weird. Hey . . . don't you have an algebra test tomorrow?"

CHAPTER 18: TARA

Location: Taunton, USA

It became the middle of March in no time, close to our birthday. As a treat, we were going to the La Salette Shrine in Attleboro, one of my favorite places, and Matt wanted to see it for the first time.

Matt was in shock. "Tara, I'm done with the course. I took the final test. If I pass, I'm going to school."

I high-fived him. "Awesome! You'll do great!"

Mom came in with groceries. "Meatball subs for dinner!"

Matt opened his notebook. "I want to check to see if I wrote down the right answers. Can you help?"

Matt and I went over various history topics until Dad came home from work. Mom placed the bowl full of meatballs on the table.

I munched on my meatball sub when, all of a sudden, I could tell blood was rushing faster in my body, and my brain became a battlefield.

Stress bombarded me with the force of a cannon.

You're can't eat that. You're too afraid to choke that you won't eat anything again. You're going to starve to death.

My skin erupted into goosebumps. I rocked back and forth, hoping that, once I finished the sub, the agony would stop.

Dad noticed. "Tara, are you okay? You're rocking really fast."

I feebly replied, "OCD's being a bear. Once I finish, I'll be fine." I kept measuring how much food was left.

This thing is endless!

Fear exploded in my temples repeatedly.

I can't do it anymore. It's too much.

I spotted my arms and legs shaking like they did in third grade before OCD was identified. "I can't eat it! I'm too scared!"

Mom took the meatballs out. "Do you want to eat just the bread?"

I solemnly agreed, and my chest squeezed. I managed to consume it after forty minutes, but significant damage was done. I was terrified.

I'm afraid to eat everything now, just like in third grade!

I'm going to starve to death!

I used all my effort to beat OCD then; I'm too drained to do it again! I'm going to die right after I got my brother back!

And then, after I starve to death and lose my brother, I'll go to Hell because God will reject me because I sold my soul.

I hate my life! I don't want to sell my soul!

I retreated to my room, where my whole body convulsed with terror.

Saint Dymphna, help me. I'm going to die! Don't leave me here all alone! I can't be alone in this dark world.

Someone put a hand on my shoulder. I cried, "Mom, I'm going to starve to death."

The hand rubbed my back. "I'm not your mother; I'm your brother."

"I know I will for a fact, and then I'm going to Hell because I sold my soul."

Matt put his arm around me. "What? Can you

even sell your soul?"

I threw my pillow at him. "I don't want to! When I want something, like a good grade on my algebra test, a thought pops up like, 'If I get an A, I'll sell my soul to the devil.' So, I usually say, 'No, I don't,' to make that clear, but then sometimes that thing happens immediately, and I can't take it back."

"This sounds like scrupulosity."

I flopped on my bed. "But what if I really did?"

He urged, "That really sounds like OCD."

He's like everyone else. What if this is real?

I would really be going to Hell. Doesn't everyone know that going to Heaven is the most important thing ever?

Matt inquired, "Did you tell Mom and Dad about that?"

I balled my hands into fists. "Yes! But they always say it's my OCD for everything. *Everything*! So, I don't tell them about it anymore. I just cry in my room. I want to ask Father Leon if it's possible for a soul to be sold, but no one will let me. Maybe, if I do, that'll make all the crying stop. Maybe that'll give me hope again."

Matt pointed out, "That plan has a flaw. If Father Leon reassures you, won't OCD pop up with questions like, 'Is he credible?', or 'Can I trust him?'? I want to assure you that you can trust Father Leon, but reassurance only makes OCD worse, right?"

He's right. That's exactly what would happen.

Matt moved on to something supposedly festive. "Our fifteenth birthday is Saturday!"

I covered my face with my hands. "Another disappointment. When I was a kid, I dreamed of turning fifteen because that's when I thought my Prince Charming would show up and sweep me off my feet, or I'd embark on a quest to save the world. That's not going to happen."

Matt bit his thumb. "Do you have any more taxing memories?"

A lot worse, kid. The tip of the iceberg.

I snorted. "Oh yeah. But I just want to go to bed and sleep right now."

I pushed him off my bed and covered myself with blankets like a caterpillar in its cocoon, the one that didn't get to be a butterfly.

He departed back to his room. "Night!"

I tossed and turned, and even my comfort novel, *Past Suspicion* by Therese Heckenkamp, couldn't get my endorphin levels up.

Ignore the dread moving around in your arteries; that's not going to stop your untimely death.

I shoved the book back in the bookcase and sobbed myself to sleep.

Matt tapped on the wall we shared in the morning. "How was your night?"

I tapped back, "I was being murdered by terror every second; how about you?"

Mom presented me with breakfast, a granola bar cut up into four dainty pieces. I took a bite, with the familiar cold clammy fear fueling my heartbeat instead of oxygen.

I took one miniscule bite at a time and consumed it all somehow and gulped down the juice. "I did it! I can eat granola bars."

How did I do that with fear washing over me like a tsunami?

But how am I going to do at lunch?

Mom went back into the kitchen. "Do you want me to cut the crust off your sandwich?"

A peanut butter sandwich without the crust. The first food I ever ate after OCD struck with choking fears for the first time.

I managed to give her a grim smile. "Let's do it."

Put on your battle face, kid. OCD is beyond games. If you lose, you forfeit your life and salvation.

The doorbell rang. I complained, "Piper this early? I'm not even dressed yet." When Mom moved back the curtains, it was Mr. Chives.

Mr. Chives exclaimed, "Matt aced the test! He can register for school today."

Matt and I got ready for school, of course, which included multiple hand washes on my part.

I have to deal with my brother who doesn't believe me about selling my soul.

Matt pumped his fists in the air. "It's going to be fun!"

No, Matt; it won't.

We scooted into the back of the car. Matt was silent, which was odd. Usually, he'd talk with me. He must have been nervous about his first day.

But I was anxious if I could really sell my soul, and I was getting weary.

Matt didn't understand me, so I'm going to give him a mild dose of what overwhelming anxiety is.

He only has to deal with it for six hours. I have to deal with it forever because, once I go to Hell, that'll be my punishment. I just know it.

Mom got out of the car with us. "I have to sign Matt up for school. I'm coming in with you."

I wanted to escape to my sanctuary. "I can go to the library, right? I don't have to be there with you guys signing up."

Mom acquiesced, "Go ahead."

I gave a fake wave and almost skipped inside.

I traveled to the library snuggled into a corner on the floor.

After a day of torture, Matt will realize how hard this is and experience firsthand what I go through.

Oh my gosh! I'm going to die because I won't be able to eat lunch! I'm going to die! I'm going to die! And then go to Hell. Life is so hard!

When it was time for me to put on my battle helmet for lunch, I sprinted to my usual place. A fluttery feeling in my stomach taunted me all day and was reaching its climax.

I took out my sandwich and my water bottle.

This is it. Your first timed meal. Can you do it?

Don't be nervous; you'll be a loser whether you eat it or not.

I just kept biting into the sandwich with small bites. Soon enough, I finished.

Whoa. Go me! Victory for the human, loss for the disorder. Not a loser after all.

Nope, you still have to eat a snack and supper. And that's just today. You'll have to do this every day until you die now.

I walked into Latin at the end of the day and saw a sight. Matt was in the class.

Ms. Greenwood handed him a piece of paper with all the things we did over the semester. "Everyone, this is Matt; he's a new student. Wait, you and Tara have the same last name. Are you related?"

"She's my fraternal twin sister."

Ms. Greenwood got excited. "No way! Matt, if you need any help at all, I'll be here after school."

He declined, "*Gratias tibi ago, sed scio omnia in chartīs.*" Everyone gaped at him.

Ms. Greenwood was pleased. "I've never met a student who uses conversational Latin."

He turned around to me. "It's complicated, and Portugal is involved."

I opened my notebook to avoid his eye.

She opened her teacher's book. "Let's review for Matt. We're on our mythology unit. Tara, our resident Myth Queen, can you tell Matt all the happenings our friends go on?"

I hid my displeasure. "Sure. Apollo fell in love with the beautiful Daphne. He chased her in order to forcibly kiss her, so she begged her father Jupiter to turn her into a tree so Apollo couldn't force himself on her. He granted her wish. However, when Apollo saw that she was a tree, he still admired her."

Ms. Greenwood lauded, "This is why Tara's the Myth Queen; she knew all about Roman mythology even before we went over the unit. Moving on to the Amazons . . . who wants to translate?"

When the bell rang, I went out as quickly as possible. Someone tapped my shoulder. I turned to see Matt. "We need to make up."

I coldly rebuked, "I'm teaching you a lesson. I did not help you for the entire school day just like no one helps me out about the soul thing. I've been doing the whole distracting method for years, and it's not working, but nobody believes me."

Matt frowned. "I'm sorry. But going to Father Leon won't help you."

"I just want to know if I can go to Heaven. That's all I want in life, salvation in the next."

He persisted, "Did you ever tell your therapist about this?"

My silence was his answer.

Matt suggested, "Uh-huh. You have to if it's hurting you this much. You need to respect yourself. Talk to her at the next session."

I hugged him. "I'm sorry I wouldn't comfort you when you were perplexed in the car."

He accepted the gesture. "Forget about it. How was lunch? Did you demolish that sandwich? It's okay if you didn't. Healing from OCD spikes takes

SARAH GRACIA

time. Years, even."

I showed him the empty paper bag. Matt teased, "Did you throw out the sandwich, or did you actually eat it?"

I moaned, "I did do it. You can see me in action when we have a snack, and then again at supper. I'm only halfway done eating today! The things an OCD victim has to go through!"

Matt sympathized, "You guys do a lot; you're role models of mental strength and resilience."

"I'll treasure that sentence forever. Or at least until I die and go to Hell."

He expected that. "OCD replays that a lot in your head, doesn't it?"

I descended the staircase. "Every second of every day."

We walked outside and saw Mom's car. We squished ourselves inside. Mom queried, "How was your first day, Matt?"

"Tara's in my Latin class. She's the Myth Queen in there."

When we get home, I'll have to eat a snack.
I won't be able to do it! I'm going to die!

When we got home, I threw down my bag on its usual spot and washed my hands before getting out the cookie package, ignoring my flesh becoming even more inflamed from washing too much.

Matt poured us some milk. "You can do it. I believe in you."

I started analyzing the situation.
I'll try to eat two cookies.

I felt like I was being stabbed in the chest with each bite, but I slowly kept chewing and swallowing. Before I knew it, four cookies were swimming in my stomach.

I ate four! Four!

He put the package back in the cabinet. "I am

now fully convinced you ate the sandwich."

I wasn't as exultant as he was. "Don't be too proud of me. I still have supper. And that's only today."

Mom put birthday napkins in the container. "What kind of birthday cake do you want?"

Matt licked his lips. "Chocolate!"

I don't even want to think about Saturday. I'll have to eat dozens of meals by then!

I pulled out my math homework. "I need to get algebra done and over with." I studied the problems and looked at my notes, but I was still clueless and jotted down random answers.

Mom reminded, "Tara, you're going to see Anne tomorrow!"

Matt paused. "Who is this Anne character?"

I never went to a session with Matt before. "Anne is my therapist."

He advised, "You should tell her about the eating thing, and the other thing we talked about earlier today . . ."

CHAPTER 19: TARA

Location: Massachusetts, USA

Anne sat in her chair after evicting my parents and Matt. "How are you, Tara?"

"I'm dying on the inside. I'm afraid to eat at every meal; I always eat it, but the torment never leaves. I don't know why."

She got out a pad of paper. "Make a hierarchy of all the foods you're afraid to eat; ten being the scariest food, and one being the easiest food."

I completed it, and this was the result:

Tara's Eating Hierarchy:
Grilled Cheese-1
Pudding-1
Peanut Butter Sandwich-1
Granola Bar-1
Cookies-1
Toast-3
Tuna-3
Pizza-3
Macaroni and Cheese-3
Ice Cream-5
Fish-5
Hot Dog-5
Ravioli-8
Tacos-8
Meatball Sub-10

She reviewed it. "I want you to go from the easiest food that's still a challenge and work your way up to the meatball sub. So, for dinner tonight, I want you to eat tuna, pizza, or macaroni and cheese. Keep going like that until you eat the meatball sub."

I was still frightened. "What if I eat the meatball sub and I'm still scared to eat?"

"It takes time to heal from a severe OCD spike like this, but you'll recover eventually."

"So, that's on the battlefield. What do I do when thoughts start coming, like that I'll starve to death? How do I make them go away?"

Anne pointed behind me to a shelf full of toys for her younger patients. "We've been over this dozens of times, Tara. Distract yourself."

"That doesn't work; I've tried that already."

She held out her hand. "Give me a toy." I gave her a stuffed animal turtle. "Pick out your favorite stuffed animal and pull out that chair so the animals can sit on it." I got out a cat and the chair.

She picked up the turtle. "Hello, Mr. Cat; I'm here for a library card. Can you please give me one?"

What does this have to do with OCD treatment?

I made the cat outstretch his hand to give her something. "Here you go. Have a nice day."

"Not so fast; I want to check out a book. Can you direct me to the section about chinchillas?"

I made the cat point in a random direction, and the turtle trotted off.

I don't feel any better.

Anne gave me the turtle. "Did you have any OCD thoughts while we were doing that? Didn't they go away for a bit?"

They were there the whole time.

I said, "No."

"This is what you have to do, Tara. I'm getting close to referring you for euthanasia. Your genes are proving to be a threat to society."

I was going to tell her about the soul thing, but I

don't want to be euthanized! I made enough progress for today, didn't I?

Matt's not going to like that I didn't tell. But I didn't inform him about euthanasia yet. One of those stupid eugenics laws . . .

I kept my head down in disappointment.

After my appointment was over, I returned to the waiting room.

Matt put a magazine back in place. "How did it go?"

I whispered, "I made a hierarchy. I have to eat the foods from the least scary to the scariest. Also, you'll hate me."

Matt concluded, "You hid the soul thing from her, didn't you? Next session, *I'm* going to have a talk with Anne. Anyway, the food treatment makes sense. It's like you have to defeat all the evil henchmen in a video game to get to the evil boss in the final battle."

If he tells her, Anne'll have me euthanized for sure! Change the subject!

I stuttered, "D-dad was showing you a video game magazine in here, wasn't he?"

Matt high-fived me. "Correct. What else did you do?"

The other part.

I scowled. "I was a cat today, and Anne was a turtle."

He surmised, "Did you play with those stuffed animals on the shelf?"

I covered my face with my hands. "Yep. The only time I don't like soft plushy creatures."

"Why was that so deplorable?"

It came out in a rush. "Anne says I have to distract myself to get OCD down, but it doesn't work. She keeps saying I have to keep practicing, but it never works. I'm a hopeless case."

"Do you know why it's not working for you?"

I sniffled. "Don't ask me; I'm the patient."

Matt turned to Mom and Dad. "What's up with this distraction method? Tara said it doesn't help her on more than one occasion."

Dad muttered, "We'll chat later."

After we got home, I scrambled out of my hour-long shower and into the kitchen. Mom took out ingredients from the refrigerator. "I have all three foods, pizza, macaroni and cheese, and tuna. Which would you like, kiddo?"

"Tuna." That was the most like grilled cheese.

Matt descended the stairs after his discussion with Dad and logged on the computer. He began to type rapidly.

I headed over to him and turned white at the screen. "OCD expert Helene Winter is saying that distraction doesn't work. Why is Anne making me do it? Is Anne a liar? Is the hierarchy legitimate, or is that wrong, too?"

He speed-typed. "The hierarchy is a real tool."

I fumed. "Why is Anne so caught up in distraction? Helene Winter's right; it only makes OCD go away for a short period of time, and then it always comes back. It always comes back. Always."

Matt turned on the printer. "I should show this to Anne at your next appointment. Dad told me she isn't an OCD specialist."

My heart dropped. "Then why am I seeing her?"

He did more typing. "Currently there are no credible OCD specialists near Taunton. There used to be, but they left after the government passed some obscure laws that I can't find."

I can tell you what laws.

I had nothing to say to the world except, "I hate people," and flew upstairs to my room to mourn.

Dad was just going down. "What are you doing up here? You never go upstairs before bed."

Freeze him out.

I yawned. "I'm wiped out after sessions with Anne. This is hard; having a new sibling and going through a spike . . . I need to recharge. All my days are filled with death and despair."

He passed me with no emotion and went down. I heard him say in a low voice, "Hildegarde, don't tell Tara about Bisavó . . . she's not healthy enough to handle it."

I went on my bed and grabbed the tissue box. A sharp pain pierced my leg, but that was the least of my concerns.

I'm bleeding on the inside.

I have no OCD specialist, Anne's considering me for euthanasia, and the distraction technique doesn't help.

I never thought it would come down to euthanasia. I never knew how much this world hated me.

I'm too afraid to admit I sold my soul. Especially that one time in seventh grade . . .

It was a tiring day. OCD was a bear, and I needed a break. Then I heard the start of a commercial that sounded like my favorite one airing.

I perked up immediately and the thought came. "I'll sell my soul if it's really the one I like," or "Satan, I'll sell my soul if it's the one I really like," or something like that.

Then my conscience or OCD (I couldn't tell the difference anymore) kicked in. "It really is the commercial! Was watching this commercial worth it?"

I thought of that day, my life of just OCD. Weariness settled over me. "I spent enough time in this fear. Yes, it is worth it; it'll make me feel better after today."

I can't believe I was that thick-headed! What if I

really did sell my soul that time?

Even if I meant it then, which I'm not sure I really did, I don't mean it now!

What is going on?

You sold your soul, worthless; that's what's going on. You're going to Hell!

That's so true.

No one will date me with all this stuff going on in my life!

I'm a loser! I'm the freak child in the family; I'm never going to have any real friends except for Matt and maybe, maybe Piper, and I'm doomed to be all alone burning in Hell!

Dymphna, forgive me. Forgive me . . .

CHAPTER 20: TARA

Location: Taunton, USA

Some time passed, but everything was the same.

I was still afraid to eat, and the whole distracting thing was a fiasco. I was still convinced I was destined for Hell because of stupid seventh-grade me.

Even the pain on my leg grew worse (Mom diagnosed it as a weird pimple).

I was still weary of Piper's friends, so I kept denying her invitations to attend the gathering. But she kept begging.

Before I knew it, it was Friday, the day before our birthday. The day before my dreams of meeting a handsome prince and saving the world were dashed.

Piper was over for a round of checkers before school. She wanted to accompany us that day, probably to throw in a last-minute plea.

Sure enough, she delicately laid it on the table. "Tara, did you decide whether you want to go to the Christian gathering at my house or not? It's today!"

If I go, will she stop pestering me?

I asked my parents, "Can I?"

Mom and Dad approved under one condition. "Matt has to go with you."

I tapped Matt. "Want to go with me?"

He slung his backpack over his shoulders. "Oh, Tara, that's a given."

Piper babbled, "It's going to be so much fun! We even listen to music about God. It helps us get into a prayerful state of mind."

I know some singers for this job.

I listed, "I like Audrey Assad, Marian Grace, Amanda Vernon, and Liz Cotrupi. Even though they were alive on the first Earth, they're still really good."

She passively dismissed it, "I've never heard of them."

I didn't expect you to. You only listen to modern music.

Matt chimed in, "I heard a couple of them. They have nice voices."

I invited, "Hey, Matt, do you want to hang out in the library with me before school?"

He accepted. "I'd love to. How about you, Piper?"

She brushed leaves off her jacket onto the floor. "No. I talk with my friends before school."

Matt put his hand over his heart as if he were mortally wounded. "I thought *we* were chums!"

She stammered, "We are, but I'm with my best friends before school."

He was still suspicious. "Earlier you said Tara was your best friend."

She was getting bored. "No, I said I was her best friend. I have others. I'm not anti-social."

That's mean. Thanks a lot!

I chided, "Piper, we should go. You don't want to be late for your best friends."

She took out a watch from her pocket and strapped it on her wrist. "You're right!" She bounded out of the house.

I confided, "Piper was so obnoxious today."

Matt remarked, "Indubitably. You should get another friend. How about that Emma from choir? She doesn't seem like the type to say those things. Or Cara?"

I liked where he was headed. "I have Cara's e-mail! I could ask her to text."

After a mundane day at school (Stupid algebra continued its quest to flunk me), Mom drove Matt and me to Piper's house.

Marcia noticed us. "You're new!"

Piper said these were new kids! They're the people-eaters!

Piper pointed at us. "This is Tara and Matt. You met them once."

Matt extended his hand. "*Salvētē! Mihi nomen est Matthaeus, et meae sorori nomen Tara est.*"

Ginny squinted. "Is that Latin?"

He was pleased with her correct assumption. "It is Latin. It's in our blood and inscribed on our DNA."

Molly was against it. "Latin's pointless. It's a dead language. Nobody but scholars speak it."

I had to take care of my precious language. "It's not pointless! It's beautiful!"

Matt was on my side. "Latin's the official language of science. Plus, a lot of languages are based off of Latin, and English has a lot of words with Latin roots."

Molly repeated, "It's a dead language. Let it go."

Piper put her hands over her own mouth. "I totally forgot! It's your birthday tomorrow! You guys are turning fifteen!"

Marcia commented, "It'll be the hardest year of your life. Hope you make it to sweet sixteen."

Yeah right.

I announced, "Nothing could top the events of year nine."

Marcia tauntingly retorted, "No. Year nine is

the longest of your life. This one will be the worst of your entire existence."

Matt grabbed my ear. "Were you nine when OCD was hounding you with food, and Mom and Dad didn't identify it?"

I fist-bumped him. "Yep."

He defended my statement. "Yeah, it's hard to beat that nightmare."

After reading a short Bible passage, Piper scanned the room. "Mom's upstairs, so it's safe for me to say this. Please pray for me. I got in trouble for bullying, and I lied to my mom about it. I told her it was because I had drama club."

You lied to me?! First the rude comments earlier today, and now this?! And you're a bully?!

Give her one more chance, Tara. Do it the American way. Three strikes and she's out.

Well, she already has three strikes, but two happened in the same day, so I'll give her one more chance.

Matt and I went out of the room to go outside, and I could hear the girls talk through the flimsy screen door. "I can't believe they like Latin. It's a dead language. Catholics worship Mary. The Catholic Church is a Satan-loving cult."

We honor Mary, not worship her! When will the world learn? That got old millions of years ago. This isn't the 1900s anymore!

Another sneered, "You actually like them, Piper?"

Piper's voice panicked. "Of course not! I only met Matt a few times, and Tara and I used to be friends before I came here. She's so weak; she always needs me to stand up for her. She acts like she has OCD and is really annoying.

"The only reason I didn't break up friends with her officially is because my mom is making me stick with her. On the bright side, she's great to make fun of with you guys, like Alicia at church!

"We put on a fake 'Christian gathering' here just to draw her in! It wasn't even that hard. We just read a Bible verse. That's all it takes! She has no idea what's really going on!"

Thanks for revealing your whole plot to me. And you made fun of Alicia, even at church? She's so nice! How dare you!

Matt bit his thumb. "Piper's a phony. You need to get rid of her."

I nodded. "First, there were the rude comments. Then she lied to me; she told Mom and me that she was in Drama Club to cover up her punishment for bullying. Lastly, you heard that. That makes it official. I'm no longer friends with Piper."

"What made you become friends anyway? You're better than her."

Long story short . . .

I elaborated, "She was the kindest girl at first, then she slowly started to become mean, but I overlooked it because she was always so sweet to me. But she hit rock bottom."

I noticed a girl whiz by chasing a runaway basketball. I mused, "Hey, she looks an awful lot like . . . Cara O'Sullivan! Hi! This is my brother, Matt. Oh my gosh, I was just telling him how I wanted to text you."

Cara jogged over to us. "Nice to meet you, Matt. I'm Cara. We're attracting attention to raise money for our team. We need money to fly to Czechoslovakia for the big tournament."

I high-fived her. "I didn't see any of your shots, but, since you made it to the tournament, you must be good."

She winked. "Thanks. Here's my number-" I took out my phone and added it into my contacts.

Cara continued, "Aren't you turning fifteen tomorrow? I remember your birthday is on March 22. You told me before . . ."

I was enthused that she knew. "Yeah! We're going to La Salette."

She was impressed. "Sounds cool. Can't wait to text you later, Tara. Have fun being fifteen!" She went back to her teammates.

I stood there, dazed. "Piper and I are done; our friendship is done. I can't believe they picked on Alicia. Those mean girls are the real Satan-loving cult. You have to eat thirteen people to join them."

Matt burst out laughing. "I'm sure Mom and Dad will make an exception to the 'don't walk down streets by yourself' rule for today in order to escape Piper. Let's go home."

CHAPTER 21: MATT

Location: Massachusetts, USA

I was as upbeat as I could be to try to make Tara's day special. "Saturday! Our birthday!"

She responded unenthusiastically, "We're both fifteen at 10:40 AM."

I could hear clothes being taken off hangers.

I went downstairs to eat breakfast. Dad put an unlit birthday candle in my toast.

That's a nice touch.

He glanced at Mom sideways. "Have a moment? There's an update on Bisavó, and it's not looking good." They went into the kitchen to converse in private.

Isn't Bisavó my great-grandmother? Is she sick? I really want to meet her while I still can.

I ate while Tara came down wearing jeans and a gray shirt that had a slogan about daydreaming on it. She patted her shirt. "I love this outfit. Daydreaming rocks."

Mom glimpsed out the window. "It's stormy out. Let's go to La Salette before it rains."

We rushed to the car and arrived at La Salette after half an hour.

I jumped out of the car in anticipation. There were other cars in the parking lot, but not one person was outside.

The gray sky must have convinced them to go in, but there were things outside to view.

Wouldn't there be at least one other person outside? We're completely alone out here! Something horrendous is about to happen!

This is ridiculous. Nothing bad is going to happen.

Tara voiced, "I want to go to inside. Something's wrong out here. Not with La Salette, but the atmosphere is . . . sinister . . ."

I pretended that I didn't feel it. "What do you mean? There's practically no one here."

We glided to the Rosary Pond. I gazed at the frozen ice with cracks splitting open.

I elbowed Tara. "Do you ever feel like a prisoner of war? Not in an actual war between countries, but a different one. Like your battle with OCD. Don't you feel like a hostage, OCD's prisoner?"

"OCD is actually described as a captor and the sufferer as a captive. It was in an article by Shala Nicely on the first Earth. So, yes. Adrian, Sophie, and Louis are prisoners to the kidnappers. They're fighting their own war. These are silent wars that no one knows about."

I admitted, "I had the same feeling as you did, the sinister one. La Salette is a great place; I can tell even though I just got here, but I feel like someone is here to get us."

She got in her thinking zone. "But La Salette is one of my favorite places. It's bizarre that the feeling would come at a safe place. What if the criminals stalked us and they're coming here to get us?"

My eyes averted to the ground. "What do you think, Mom and Dad? Mom?! Dad?! Where are you?" They were gone.

Tara pointed to a garden, but, since we were in the first days of spring, even from the Rosary Pond I could see that the garden was completely barren, without a single tiny bud in sight.

I could make out two shadowy silhouettes. "Oh. There they are. Come on; let's go over to them."

Right after I spoke, I heard a collision and something hitting the ground.

I whipped around to see if Tara was in trouble and saw her sprawled on the floor.

I instantly bent down to scoop her up in my arms. Blood trickled out of her head. I murmured, "What happened to you?"

"I came along." I looked up and saw a man wearing a mask.

He was holding a blood-splattered gun trained on me.

Smooth, Matt. You didn't even see the guy with the gun standing right in front *of you!*

The evil man continued, "Sorry to take you again on your birthday. As a matter of fact, it rained on the day you two were born like it will today.

"If you suspected something was amiss, it was foolish of you to get separated from your parents. Your sister won't escape me this time. That blasted Delaisan took her out of the cradle to take her thumbprint right before I came. Lucky for me, they already took yours, so you were there all alone and unprotected."

I blanched. "Mom! Dad! Help! Tara was shot!" He raised the gun and smacked my head with it. I crumpled to the ground, lightly aware of the scar opening up from the mysterious accident.

'Sorry to take you again on your birthday' . . . he must be Truman Shaw . . . I thought he was arrested.

He just murdered my twin sister! Tara's dead. Oh my gosh! Tara's dead!

And then everything went black.

CHAPTER 22: MATT

Location: Oristano, Italy

I opened my eyes to see a man standing in front of me. "If you play any games, I will rip you to shreds."

I crowed, "Where is my sister's body?"

He threw me against the wall. "You don't stand a chance against me."

"Where is my sister's body?"

Ignoring me, he started to beat me.

Why aren't I defending myself?

Too weak . . . they must've drugged me with something . . .

Oh. My hands and feet are tied. I can't believe I didn't notice that immediately. I must be really weak; my senses aren't as sharp.

"Where is my sister's body? A man had a gun and there was blood on it."

I don't think many kids go through this.

"You speak the truth. There was a man."

Pure fury made the weakness fade away. "She died!" I instantly started elbowing him viciously.

He tossed me on the ground and put his foot on my stomach. "She's not dead; she wasn't shot. Truman hit her on the head with the side of the gun like he did to you. Trust me, Tara is still alive."

"Truman Shaw was arrested. How did he get out?"

His foot dug deeper into my flesh. "No more questions. It's time for you to have a reunion."

The man who kidnapped me on the day I was

born strode into the back of the vehicle without the mask, but with the newly polished gun.

I jumped back in surprise; my brain flooded with all the memories it had lost.

There was a Sophie, and I knew all about World War I because two of her ancestors were Archduke Franz Ferdinand and Countess Sophie Chotek von Chotkowa und Wognin.

I knew about chastity rings because she always wore one.

There was a Louis; he was the voice of reason with hilarious commentary that always made me laugh.

There were more memories of Age.

Even though we were held in different parts of the world, sometimes they would bring us together to complete missions (while being spied on by captors posing as average citizens. They thought a child committing a crime would be in less trouble than an adult).

One time, Sophie and I almost kissed. Unfortunately, Truman Shaw was checking up on us and ruined the moment.

I also taught the gang religion, and they loved it. We thought highly of each other and tried to thwart the missions in order to help innocent people.

It worked a few times, but not a lot. The punishment for trying to get out of an assignment was Truman releasing bloodhounds on us and forcing us to run back to our bases for our lives.

I was wary of America when I first woke up because Louis used to be a hostage in Minnesota with the help of a corrupt politician.

I was practically caught up with the Golden Lake High curriculum at the start of Mr. Chives' lessons because Giovanni wanted me to have a good education despite being a hostage.

I could define OCD terms because Giovanni taught me everything about brain disorders, and he told me Saint Dymphna was the patron saint of them.

There was a captor named Clementine who wanted to date me, but I never liked her, and told her that (I might've sounded like a jerk, but she was a kidnapper holding me hostage, so . . .).

But there was more to my identity . . . there was one thing that my mind refused to register.

I snapped back to the present with Truman standing in front of me. "The guy said Tara's alive. I don't believe you! You took her life! I hate you!" I clawed him the best I could with my bindings.

He pushed me down to the floor like the other man did. "I merely hit her on the head with the gun itself like I did to you. After you were out, I checked her pulse. She's alive, and the wound wasn't life-threatening. She's in a lot better shape than you.

"As for you, you're going to see your old love Sophie again. That was quite a sight; you two almost kissed. I intervened, though. Love gets you nowhere in a life of crime."

I corrected, "We didn't want a life of crime; you kidnapped us!"

Truman tapped the back of my neck. "I installed a tracking device in you again, and I put one in your sister. We can't have another episode of losing you again. That was disastrous."

I snarled, "How did you get out of jail, Shaw?"

He cackled. "I know how to move around, but that doesn't matter."

Something else didn't add up. "How did you know Tara and I would be at La Salette if we didn't have tracking devices in us at that time?"

Truman smugly bragged, "We have informants everywhere. One of the henchmen found out a genius boy named Matthew registered at the public high school. I hacked into your records and found a photo of you. That confirmed your whereabouts. It also gave me your address, so I could stalk you whenever I wanted."

I rolled my eyes. "I never thought one of your people would be that smart. Anyway, why now? Why didn't you capture me once you found out where I lived?"

"I had to be cautious. Anyway, that was a cute chat, but I got to go. I'll be generous to you. I won't hit you on the head again; I'll just use knock-out spray. Henchmen, move the child into the stronghold!"

CHAPTER 23: MATT

Location: Oristano, Italy

I woke up to the sound of Sophie's voice. "Matt's here! I knew he'd come back! But he's bleeding. Let's see if we have anything to make it stop . . ."

The one thing my mind shielded was coming back to me.

"It's like you're a Delaisan."

There was one last memory.

"Matt! The authorities are coming to save you! But they're going to put you in hiding. Your family's also in hiding, for your twin sister Tara's safety. The creepy jerks wanted her, too, but someone took her out of the cradle for something.

"You're the Crown Prince of Delais, and Tara's the Princess. Your real last name is Garcia." Giovanni put his hand on my shoulder. "You're going to see your real family now."

Truman Shaw kicked the door open, grasping a heavy object in his hands. "The cops are taking over! They'll have the brat, but he won't be able to tell them anything! I bought something in case this happened, and I know one hit with this will knock the memory out of you."

He struck me with it right on my forehead, and I was out like a light.

"I'm the Crown Prince of Delais!"

Louis crossed his arms. "If you were, I would've found articles saying you were on the computer. How come I couldn't find any articles about you then?"

Sophie applied a wet grocery receipt on my wound and applied pressure on it.

I reasoned, "Giovanni said my family was in hiding. The secret must've been kept under wraps."

Sophie twisted her ring around her finger. "Louis, you need to tell him the news. The tragic news."

I wasn't in the mood for that. "What's going on? Is it about my sister?"

Louis' voice broke. "It's about Age. He's dead."

I breathed, "That can't be true. Do you know for sure? Did you see him die?"

Sophie butted in, "No. I couldn't bear to witness his final moments."

I got out of a wobbly bed. "There's a possibility he's alive. Where did they take him?"

Louis replied, "They just took him away! We don't know what's going on! Age is the Hereditary Prince of Liechtenstein, I'm the Prince of Belgium, and Sophie is a descendant of Archduke Franz Ferdinand!"

I blushed at the humiliation of forgetting a really cute girl. "Giovanni told me a long time ago about Sophie, but I forgot it. Truman smacked my head, and I got amnesia. I just got my memories back."

Sophie checked, "Giovanni Valisi? Why didn't you tell me I was a descendant of Archduke Franz Ferdinand before you got amnesia? That would've been the right thing to do!"

What's her problem?

I defended, "I didn't want to scare you! How was I supposed to say, 'Hey, Sophie, your ancestor Archduke Franz Ferdinand, the heir to the Austrian-Hungarian throne, got assassinated with his wife and that started World War I' to you? *How*?!"

She thundered, "Exactly how you just said it! Don't hide stuff from me. Don't. You got that?"

I relinquished the argument. "I'm sorry. On the bright side, I have a twin sister named Tara."

That's why, after I told Tara about World War I, I was so sad. Sophie was indirectly personally affected by it.

Louis wasn't shocked like I expected him to be. "Age told us. Did she by any chance go to a museum and meet us?"

I raised an eyebrow. "Not sure. Why?"

Sophie stepped in, "There was a Tara Garrings we saved from Truman's thugs. Age wrote a bunch of poetry about her. He had a crush on her."

I was deeply troubled. "One of my best friends might have had a crush on and wrote poetry about my twin sister? *That's* scarier than hearing that the assassination of your ancestors caused a world war."

Sophie punched me in the arm. "Hearing that the assassination of your ancestors caused a world war seems like a normal teenage thing to me."

The door opened, and Clementine entered, carrying crates. When she saw me, she dropped them. "Matt! You're here!"

I bit my thumb. "Here mourning for Age. He's dead."

Clementine's mouth turned into an 'o'. "He's not dead! Who told you that, Sophie? She's clueless. He's not dead; he's just unconscious until nobody needs him alive anymore."

Yes! He's not dead!

I grinned. "You're serious? Thank you."

Clementine gasped. "Does that you mean you're in love with me?"

I awkwardly set the record straight. "No! I'm

just thankful for your help!"

Sophie lashed out, "He doesn't love you! Everyone knows that!"

Clementine turned on her. "You're just jealous because you two almost kissed, and now he likes me."

Sophie held her head high. "Keep telling yourself that! There's no way he'd be in love with a kidnapper!"

Louis interfered, "What did you bring us? Food and water?"

Clementine patted the top of the crate. "And some medicine, but mostly water. Sophie needs a lot of it after the burn I gave her."

Sophie belted out a sardonic laugh. "I am not burned, but, if pretending that you hurt me helps you sleep at night, go right ahead."

I wanted to end their feud. "You were very helpful. Can I ask you something else?"

Clementine started to play with her hair. "Yes. What is it?"

"Do you know anything about what happened to my sister Tara?"

"Yeah, but I can't tell you; it would break protocol. It's not like we're dating or anything, so you won't find out! Unless you want to be my boyfriend . . ."

I sorted out, "Clementine, if I said 'yes', I'd just want to find out what happened to my sister, not because I liked you. I don't like you in that way. I keep telling you that. You and I will never be a thing."

Sophie muttered, "I told you so."

Defeat settled on Clementine's face for a few moments, but then she was thrilled again. "You're saying that now, because, once you do fall in love with me, you want it to be real! You're such a romantic!"

I was petrified at the thought of us together. "Clementine, you're one of my captors! Please go back to plotting against us!"

She exited.

I was extremely uncomfortable. "Can we go back to business? Louis, do you know how to use that small device?"

He turned it on and became quiet. "This has access to the Internet," he dared to utter, "which means we have access to the outside world. The device is small, so I can hide it easily."

Sophie's eyes widened. "We can use this to research your sister. Louis couldn't find her, but there might be a new lead. We might be able to find out what happened to her."

I didn't want to mess this up. "Thanks, guys. I appreciate you helping me find out what happened to Tara."

Louis brushed it off. "No problem, but it was by chance that it occurred to me that this would be useful."

I recited a prayer in my head for the fact that I wasn't dead yet. And a plea to Saint Dymphna to help Tara. That was important.

CHAPTER 24: TARA

Location: Westport, Massachusetts, USA

A cold breeze transported me back to the world. With a jolt, I noticed I couldn't move. I glanced down and found out why.

I'm tied to a tree on my fifteenth birthday. So, my first memory of being fifteen is being tied to a tree. That's just terrific.

I'm going to starve to death and go to Hell like I always feared!

I shut my eyes and leaned against the tree.

If I'm going to die and go to Hell, I have nothing to lose in remembering.

My mind locked that night away; the details are fuzzy and what really happened is distorted. Let's try to think . . .

The fateful day before the last day of second grade replayed.

Mom called, "Dinner!"

I perked up and ran to the table and bit off a giant piece of cheese sandwich.

It went down weird and scratched my throat. Dad checked, "Are you okay?"

I nodded. "It just really hurt going down. That happens to everyone once in a while." I took another bite, and it went down funny again.

I became unnerved. "It happened again!"

Mom took my plate away. "It must be the cheese."

I said to myself, "How can cheese do that? Mom must be lying to hide what's really going on."

The next day at breakfast, I ate half of a donut, and

I went to play outside on the swing set.

At lunch, I was terrified to eat the Chinese food Mom got. I went into the bathroom and told her I couldn't eat because of a stomachache.

At supper, I wanted to eat the chicken, but I couldn't swallow it. I was too afraid.

Mom was close to hysterics. "Why aren't you eating? Today you only ate half of a donut!"

"I need to go relax! I'm a wreck of nerves!"

She waved me to the couch. "Lie down until you're better."

I mumbled to myself, "I can't avoid eating forever; I'll starve to death. One time I ate a peanut butter sandwich watching a movie. I was totally fine then. Let's try that now."

I announced, "Mom, I don't want chicken; I want a peanut butter sandwich with the crust cut off, please!"

Mom made me a peanut butter sandwich with the crust cut off. I was still quivering. "Daddy, can you sit with me?" He complied, and I ate the sandwich in painfully small bites that took hours, full of fear that I didn't understand.

I knew I couldn't hide it forever, so I was going to be honest from the get-go. "I'm afraid to eat."

Mom was in denial. "What?! No! It can't be!"

In bed that night, I was shaken. Instead of the usual Our Father, Hail Mary, and Glory Be, I prayed, "God, please don't let me die. Please! I don't want to die before I enter third grade. I'm only nine."

An image of a teacher performing a tribute for me flashed in my head. "This is a picture of Tara Jane Garrings, a girl who was supposed to be in this class, but she died over the summer because she starved to death."

I wept silently until I fell asleep.

Another memory popped up.

Dad poked a seventh-grade me. "Before we found out the eating thing was OCD, Mom used to cry herself to sleep every single night because she thought she was losing her baby slowly before her eyes."

My soul felt like it was being strangled to death by grief.

The night when scrupulosity made its debut appearance raced in my mind.

In fourth grade, an ad for a movie came on. A girl stood in front of a mirror while the narrator claimed she sold her soul to Satan and now wanted it back.

I was scarred forever. "You can sell your soul? Evil is a lot worse than I imagined!"

A voice that sounded like my own whispered, "Maybe I should give mine to Satan for safekeeping . . ."

I fought, "No! He won't give it back! What have I done? I just gave my soul away! I want it back! I never wanted to give it away!"

Suddenly, in my mind, a dead, cold, black, frostbitten arm slung itself around my shoulder and pulled me close to the body attached to it, as if comforting me. *"That's why I keep your memories locked away, to protect you."*

Are you OCD? Is that what you are? A grotesque being only visible in the minds of your victims?

Too unsettled to stay in my own personal labyrinth, I opened my eyes.

Wait, this place is familiar!

I studied my surroundings. There was a beach and a tower. My childhood opened before me, before OCD got its death grip on me. I used to play there when I was little.

You can remember this place. You can do it.

I envisioned picking up seashells, getting a sunburn, and countless picnics in the car. Nobody lived there, a hurricane wiped out everyone. "Gooseberry Island! This is Gooseberry Island!"

Where's Matt?

In reliving my bruised past, I had forgotten

about him.

Idiot! You're the worst sister ever!

"Matt! Matt! Are you here?!"

A boy who looked strikingly similar to him approached and untied me. "Are you okay? I drove here to paint the Atlantic Ocean. Then I heard you shout and saw you tied to a tree. What happened?"

"I was at La Salette and now I'm here. Can you call the police and an ambulance?"

He took out a phone. "Yes. I'm Marcus, by the way. You are?"

"Tara. Thanks for saving my life. This is my first time getting tied to a tree."

He dialed the emergency number. "Hi. I'm in Gooseberry Island. I found a girl tied to a tree. She's not dead; she's standing next to me. Her name is Tara . . ."

The police arrived on the scene in about ten minutes. One examined me. "Are you hurt?"

I blanched. "I don't feel any pain! Do I look like I'm dying?!"

Another officer brought us to his car. "No, dear. Just a precaution. We should still take you to a hospital. Do you have amnesia?"

I beamed. "Negative. I'm Tara Garrings, and my family lives in East Taunton. We were in Attleboro, and then something hit me on the head."

The second officer relaxed. "That improves the situation. Do you remember your guardian's phone number?"

I nodded.

The first officer smiled. "Even better! After the hospital checks to make sure you're good to go, we can give him or her a call and you'll be all set to go home. Why were you tied to a tree?"

Marcus proposed, "Someone might have kidnapped and drugged her."

I frowned. "I don't remember being kidnapped and drugged!"

We got in the car. Marcus wasn't swayed. "Most people don't. We should send out an alert. I'll stay with you for as long as you need me."

The hospital workers determined I was free to leave. I gave them my parents' house number.

Not soon enough, my parents embraced me. Mom cried, "Tara! I was worried sick about you! We thought you and Matt were right behind us, but then we heard Matt scream. We ran over to you, but no one was there. You were both gone."

My heart plummeted. "Matt's missing *again*? I hate this! He just came into my life, and now he vanished!"

I slumped against the hospital wall and burst into tears.

Slimy bacteria coated my back and hair. They slithered on my skin, waiting patiently to penetrate my body and give me a deadly, contagious ailment that would cut my life short.

The staff figured I wasn't up for talking, so they turned to Mom and Dad. "Who's Matt? Is he your son?"

Mom and Dad retold the whole story. The police assured us they would update Interpol and now involve the FBI and the CIA.

Marcus was still there; he kept his word. "I'm sorry about your brother."

The irony of how similar they looked made me chortle. "You look like his twin and not me. I like that. It's like you're my brother until Matt gets back."

The authorities were documenting the situation. "Marcus, how did you find her tied to a tree?"

Marcus narrated, "I went to Gooseberry Island to paint, and then I heard her cry out for her brother."

Dad shook his hand. "Thank you for saving my daughter."

This is getting weird.

Marcus stuttered, "Your-your welcome, but I'm sorry I didn't save your son. Not that I could've, but . . ."

I hugged him. "You're a hero! You're going to be canonized!"

Mom thanked him. "We must repay you. What's your full name?"

Marcus blushed. "Marcus Niceren."

Dad faltered. "I think it's time we went back, back to the island."

Thinking he meant Gooseberry Island, I speculated, "To look for clues? That'd be helpful."

Dad gave me a what-are-you-talking-about look. "That's absurd! Oh, you mean Gooseberry Island. I meant Delais."

I didn't know where that was. "What? I've never heard of that place in my life! Where is it?"

Dad was getting impatient. "Delais is an island in the Indian Ocean. It's west of Australia, east of Mauritius, north of the French Antarctic Lands, and south of Sri Lanka."

Maybe we have family there that won't hate me for having OCD!

Hope blossomed in my chest. "Are there any relatives in Delais? Do you have any other secrets you're hiding from me?"

Mom took a step forward. "You bet we do. Your father is the King of Delais, I'm the Queen, you're the Princess, and Matt is the Crown Prince."

My jaw dropped.

Dad explained, "On the night you and Matt were born, Matt was kidnapped, and the kidnappers sent threats to people. They said they were after Adrian, Hereditary Prince of Liechtenstein, Count Rietberg, Princess Sophie of Hohenberg, Prince Louis, Duke of Brabant, and you.

"They told us they knew you had a red birthmark; we don't know how they found out. We had you hide it all these years so they wouldn't figure out you were the princess. We fled to America and changed our surname."

My whole life was a lie.

What else is new? They hid the fact that I had a twin brother for so long.

I blinked. "That makes no sense. We have family here. Didn't they know who we were?"

Dad answered, "My side knew, since they're the royal Delaisan family. Mom's side never found out. It's better to keep secrets that can kill."

I quizzed, "What are our real names?"

Mom returned, "Our last name is Garcia. Our real first and middle names are the same. We didn't want to deprive you of those names, too."

I tried it out. "Tara Jane Garcia. Matthew Joseph Garcia. Hildegarde Joy Barbara Garcia. James Brendan Garcia."

Mom frowned. "Since when was 'Barbara' part of my name?"

I illustrated, "Your Confirmation name. You picked Barbara, and Dad picked Brendan. He doesn't have a middle name."

Dad complained, "I told my mother that Confirmation names aren't middle names! She's convinced that my middle name is Brendan. It's not! That's my Confirmation name!"

We may have been undercover royalty for years, but Dad's personality has remained the same.

Mom suggested, "Let's call the Delaisans. We would have done it when Matt arrived, but he was found, not taken, so we didn't think there was a threat. Now we know there is. We have to go back. We'll be safer with guards protecting us."

Dad dialed a number. "It's James. It's time to make Delais a monarchy again. You don't understand! Matt was found, then captured again!"

Mom yanked the phone from Dad. "I know there's a lead in Sardinia, but that might not be where Matt is! I just lost a child again! Do you know how I feel right now? We live at the same address. You can pick us up from there. I still have Tara, barely. A boy named Marcus saved her from death."

I hugged Marcus again. "Thanks for rescuing me. You really are like Matt. You're like my protector until he gets back."

Marcus mumbled, "You shouldn't be thanking me."

Dad seemed to be serene for the first time since the ordeal. "Once we go back, we'll have Tara's fifteenth birthday ball. You're invited, Marcus. It would take our minds off of everything for a couple of hours."

I objected, "We planned a party, not a ball."

He countered, "That was before we were going back to Delais. It doesn't have to be a big ball. It'll be a normal party, but in a ballroom with fancy outfits and classical music."

I'm sold!

But there's one little matter to attend to.

I gulped. "We don't have to have a grand feast with a lot of people, do we? That'd be more of a birthday nightmare. They'd judge me."

Mom was starting to become composed. "The people there are compassionate. They'll understand your OCD and won't think any less of you."

That was amusing. "I find that hard to believe when my own family makes fun of me for it!"

She assured, "The Delaisans know that OCD sufferers have human emotions and are real people. We have to go back. The kidnappers know where we are; it'll be safer there."

I interrogated, "Do they have therapists in Delais?"

Dad high-fived me. "We even have trained OCD therapists. Let's go back home."

I clutched Marcus' arm. "Wait, what address do we send your invitation to?"

He told us, and Mom wrote it down. "Yeah, we forgot that. Knowing where to send the invitation would help. See you at the ball, Marcus. Thanks again for saving my daughter's life."

Dad drove home, and frighteningly massive uniformed soldiers in all white were at our house.

For some reason, I was convinced that they were the U.S. Marine Corps. "Are the Marines protecting us until the Delaisans get here?"

Dad was miffed at my ignorance. "No! That is *not* the current official uniform! I considered joining the Marines when we moved here! Have I taught you nothing about them? Nothing?"

The only thing you taught me about the U.S. Marines was the motto 'Improvise, Adapt, and Overcome'.

The uniformed people approached us. "We are not the U.S. Marines; we're the Delaisan Combat Team."

I was enamored by the tough, muscly agents. "That's so wicked! That's the equivalent to what branch of the U.S. military?"

One of them was offended. "What do you mean, 'wicked'? We're not evil! Anyway, we combine all the branches into one, which is why we're the Combat Team. We're too small to have branches. Yet we're still the mightiest military force on the planet."

One sentence and my subjects hate me already. Not good!

I apologized, "Sorry! 'Wicked' is Massachusetts slang for 'awesome'. How many people live in Delais?"

Another replied, "Ninety-six exactly, but counting your family, one-hundred."

Wow. We're tiny.

Will I go to school there?

I don't think I'll ever see Emma again. Or Alicia.

At least I have Cara's number.

Another asked, "Do you want to go to the helicopter now? It's parked . . ." I tuned them out, still digesting the day's events. They turned their attention to me. "Ready to go, Tara?"

I was caught off guard. "Huh? Oh, let me take some notebooks with me. They're in the house."

I'm not going anywhere without the chronicles of Lara.

Mom handed me her set of keys. "There you go."

The Combat Team and I ran up to my room. I held the notebooks to my chest. "Can I take a medal with me?"

Great. Now the notebooks are contaminated. Just my luck. With hospital germs, no less!

They didn't have a problem with me taking a medal. I snatched my Saint Dymphna medal. I ran over my list out loud. "Anything else? Story, medal, that's it. Are there pens or pencils in Delais?"

One snorted. "We have both. The top country in the world can afford pencils. What anxiety disorder do you have? In Delais, a lot of us have at least one. I suspect you do, too, because you have a Saint Dymphna medal."

"OCD."

They whooped, "She's one of us! All set now, Princess?"

I assured, "Yep! That's all I need in my room. Wait! Do I need to bring clothes?"

The one who picked up that I had OCD shook her head. "No. We'll get you a whole new wardrobe."

We hiked downstairs and into the kitchen. I went over to the kitchen counter. "I just need my cell phone."

They panicked, "No! The criminals could track you from it! Leave it."

I followed them outside, leaving my phone in the house. I took a deep breath. "I'm ready. Let's depart."

Tara Garrings was gone.

I was Princess Tara Garcia of Delais. The only difference was that, as a princess, I felt way more awkward and terrified.

CHAPTER 25:
TARA

Location: Amor, Delais

We landed in Amor, the capital of Delais, where a lot of citizens (with very big muscles) were waiting for us. There were no roads, only sand.

I asked, "Are there any other cities besides Amor?"

They pointed to the north. "Up there is Immortalis, but that's not the first thing you should see. It's nicknamed the City of the Dead."

That was spooky. "Why?"

A little girl's eyes were still trained up north. "That's where the dead are buried. There's nothing in Immortalis but the catacombs."

My face must've been petrified, because she coughed abruptly. "We should show you our cathedral! It's quite breathtaking."

For a five-year-old, she's very articulate.

I let her lead me inside, and my breath was indeed snatched from my lungs.

Crystal chandeliers lit the church, and frescoes worthy of Michelangelo were painted on the walls. Candles in the rightmost corner gave it a hushed, holy ambiance. Stained glass windows of Saint Dymphna, Saint Cecilia, and Saint Thérèse of Lisieux made it appear as though the cathedral were a medieval chapel in an isolated forest where the hero in books stopped at in the middle of a quest.

It was too angelic for words. A man interrupted the sacred silence. "We should show you your bedroom. You can decorate it any way you want."

We stepped outside, and I observed well-constructed houses and a castle. "Where's the school?"

The little girl jumped up and down with enthusiasm. "We have classes outside! It doesn't sound like a good learning place, but it's a calm area. The students excel; our classes are the best in the world. Plus, we have bottlenose dolphins! Do you get seasickness?"

That wasn't true for an East Taunton girl. "I've been on the Atlantic Ocean in December without getting ill."

The girl approved. "If you can handle that, you can handle the Delaisan waters. You don't need to learn how to drive in Delais since everything in Amor is within walking distance. I know getting a driver's license is a big deal for Americans, but here you don't need it."

I was puzzled. "What about Immortalis? What happens when someone dies?"

The girl stretched. "We sail there. Here's a random fact for you: Immortalis has heat sensors inside it that are watched at all times, so we'll know if someone is invading us by going through the City of the Dead."

I had nothing left to say except, "We're a bizarre country."

The girl considered that. "We currently have ninety-nine people on the island, we have a city of dead people, we're the smartest country in the world, and we're all the same religion. Most of us have an anxiety disorder, so people think we're weak. But all of us have advanced, intense physical training. We always come out on top with our iron will."

The girl stopped. "I'm ... I'm really sorry ... about your brother. That's why we're so peppy ...

we're trying to help you ... be happy."

They are so sweet!

Delais already became my sanctuary from the hardened world. "Thanks. I really appreciate it."

We went in the castle. The girl explained, "The castle is really spacious. It even has a grand ball-room. It's very striking. To your bedroom!"

The girl opened a door. "Ta-da! You can change whatever you want about it. It's babyish since it was styled for a newborn, but we made you this bed when your dad called and said you were coming back, so, at least you can sleep."

I defended my thoughtful countrymen. "It's not puerile! I have a regular closet, a normal bed, and a . . . jewelry box? You got me a jewelry box fifteen years ago?"

She explained, "We give every Delaisan princess and queen a jewelry box to store some of the crown jewels in. We buried them in Immortalis once you fled. We can dig them up now that you're back."

I wrapped my arms around the girl. "You missed us so much that you couldn't stand looking at the royal jewels? That deserves a hug!"

The girl beamed. "Aw! Well, it's true. The Delaisan crown jewels are based off of the Portuguese crown jewels. We experimented with the bracelets and necklaces."

My birthday ball drifted into my mind. I checked, "Hey, are you guys okay with me having a ball? Dad wants me to have one. Do we have to have a royal feast?"

A man in the group rejoiced, "We'd love to have a ball! They're so much fun! You don't like feasts? Why not? Don't feel pressured to have one; I just like to know what you're feeling."

They'll like you. They won't think you're a disgrace

to humanity like everyone else in the family.

I winced. "OCD with eating."

The girl threw her arms up in the air. "Yes! An anxiety princess! You're going to fit in here, Tara. You're one of us."

I was born to be the princess of that country. "Thanks! I love it here."

A woman in the posse shouted out, "When do you want to have the ball? It's up to you. You can invite your family or keep it simple with us."

If only I was in charge.

I sighed. "Mom will take over. She'll invite the whole family, and they'll make fun of me in front of you. They hate me so much! On a side note, we have to invite Marcus Niceren."

The little girl hugged my leg, since she was too short to hug anything else. "You think your family hates you? Why do you think that? Marcus Niceren . . . we'll talk to your dad about that."

The Delaisans seemed to genuinely care about me, so I wasn't bothered by disclosing personal details with them. "They like making fun of OCD and comparing me to other relatives."

The man roared, "They make fun of OCD? What? Some of your family members used to live in Delais! This is the home of anxiety disorders! I'm so ashamed of them! Comparing you to other relatives is a petty family thing; just ignore them. It's beneath your level to acknowledge such narrow-minded blows."

I vented, "I get that the comparing thing is common. It's just so aggravating when you tell them an achievement, and then they say, 'Your older cousin did that five years ago.' Can't they just be happy for me?"

The woman soothed, "Everyone in Delais feels that way. You want to be you; you don't want to be

compared to anyone else because you're not anyone else. Your talents should be acknowledged,
not dismissed because someone else did something similar."

I died and went to Heaven. "I'm not the only
human being who feels that way? Everyone convinced me I was losing my grip on reality because
I wanted to be my own person. They're all like,
'There's nothing wrong with what we're doing,'
and 'What's wrong with your older cousins? Why
don't you love them?' I want to be me, not them.
Me!"

The little girl still clung to my leg. "That's the
Delaisan mindset."

Mom said there was an OCD specialist, and
that was the prime moment to find out who it was.
I cleared my throat. "Who's the OCD therapist?"

The man replied, "Helene Winter. We have
a BDD specialist, a Trichotillomania specialist, a
Dermatillomania specialist, a PANDAS and PANS
specialist, and many more."

*The lady Matt found on the computer? This place is
spectacular!*

I squealed, "I love you all! My old therapist
had me distract myself and almost slated me for
euthanasia."

The woman grew angry. "Euthanasia? If we
knew about that, we would've literally declared
war on America. And distraction for OCD? Does
she even have a degree in Psychology? That's one
of the worst things she could have you do! You do
ERP."

The man piped up, "You have to sit with the
fear until it goes down. I know that, and I'm the
computer guy."

The girl facepalmed. "Sorry. You're already
devastated because Crown Prince Matthew is

gone, and now we're reminding you of your extended family. Happy things. Let's go back to the ball."

I immediately thought of the one pleasant guest. "Back to Marcus, my dad personally invited him."

The man noted, "So, this Marcus Niceren, us, and do you want to invite your family?"

I made a face. "Mom will. You guys will have to save me from humiliation."

The little girl squeezed her arms around my leg tightly. "You bet we will! Let's take you to the ballroom! We can pick out a couple songs for the orchestra to play. What music do you like? I think your dad wanted classical for this . . ."

Classical was definitely my style. "That just so happens to be my favorite. Shall we go?"

Everyone eagerly pulled my hand and whisked me to the ballroom. The little girl greeted the cluster of people talking next to a collection of instruments. "Hi! This is our Tara! She's sad because her brother is gone. Can you play "Fantasia on Greensleeves" to make her happy?"

I stopped short as the orchestra picked up their instruments.

There's something important about this song!

But my mind was a blank. I closed my eyes and let the music serenade me.

If my future husband likes this song, this'll be the one we'll dance to at our wedding reception.

My pimple started to sting again. I clamped a hand over it.

This thing won't quit.

It's like a symbol of the kidnappers that wouldn't stop searching for Matt.

Or a symbol of OCD; it's sore and won't heal.

The endless possibilities of torture . . .

CHAPTER 26:
MATT

Location: Eastern Hemisphere

Sophie threw the bloody paper on the ground. "Your wound stopped bleeding. That took long enough."

I impatiently bounced on my heels. "Can we find out if we can solve the conundrum of what happened to Tara?"

Louis yawned. "Sure. I'll always help out a lady." Before he could get the device out, the door banged against the wall, then snapped back with a start.

A sinister kid welcomed himself into the room. "Matt recaptured. I wanted to see that with my own eyes. You couldn't escape us forever. After all, even the police are in on this. I heard you're concerned about your sister. I saw her with my own eyes. She's still alive and in Delais. How do I know that? I met and saved her."

He brought my sister into this? He's going down.

I bit my thumb. "From Truman? If you rescued her, why do you work for the kidnappers? Wait, you're in love with her."

The kid had no emotion. "I am not in love with her. Capturing and saving her is part of the overall plan. I must have her marry me."

I decided to make him angry so he might slip out some details about the master plan. "Tara would never marry you; she's out of your league. You'd be lucky if she even *talked* to you."

He wore a ghastly little smile that I longed

to punch. "I already charmed her by 'saving' her from starvation by being tied to a tree; it's only a matter of time before she falls madly in love with me."

I caught on. As part of the plan, Truman kidnapped Tara so that freak could pretend to rescue her and make her like him.

I wanted to find out more, so I kept digging. "That's the biggest load of gibberish I ever heard. Once Tara figures out you're full of it, she'll never see you again."

The freak sat on the floor, taking his sweet time. "On the contrary, she invited me to her birthday ball, which will be held very soon."

Tara must be having the ball of her dreams and hoping a prince will sweep her off her feet.

Unfortunately, she was getting that guy. "The Delaisans will see right through you."

The jerk put on his stupid smirk again. "Don't worry about it. Everything will come to place."

I didn't like the sound of that. "Your big plan seems to be winning over my twin or stealing something from the castle. Do you want the royal curtains?"

He tossed me a journal. "I've told you enough. If you're so berserk about your sister's safety, this will make you feel better. I found it while snooping around your house. I invaded your home. How does that feel?"

The creep belted out an evil laugh that prickled my skin and left. I opened the journal and found the handwriting of a young child.

Dear Diary,

Today was so scary. The field trip to the museum went wrong. Kids were being mean to me, and a boy named Age got me away from them and brought me to where he and his new friends Louis and Sophie were.

They all just met, too.

Age can ballroom dance like on the shows Mommy and Daddy watch. I know because we danced togeth-er to some song called "Fantasia on Greensleeves," but without the music since we were in a museum.

Then some people came and took them away. They were after me, too, but Age told me to save myself. So, I blended in with my classmates and hid until they went away. I didn't tell Mommy and Daddy. They'd think it was my imagination.

I think the teacher called them. She had to call every set of parents. After he hung up, Daddy laughed and said now the people think we live in Boston and now they'll never find us.

I hope I can forget everything that happened. May-be I can trick myself into forgetting somehow.

Bye for now!

Love, Tara

My heart warmed. "She had good grammar for a kid."

Sophie's jaw dropped. "Your sister is the girl we saved! Poor thing, she was so traumatized. Do you know what this means?"

I guessed, "That you met her?"

She was restless. "Change of plans! Forget Lou-is' small thingy for now! If one of us can escape, go to the ball, and warn her about this guy, she'll trust us because we saved her! Matt, you should go. You're her brother; she'll believe you."

It was too predictable for my taste. "They know I'm worried about her; they'd expect me to go. She mentioned Louis and you once, but Age three times."

Sophie cracked her knuckles. "Age is uncon-scious, so this is a job for Louis or me."

Louis burst our bubble. "Not so fast! Tara also wrote that she was going to try to make herself forget the whole incident. She may have succeeded. She might not remember us. We need to trigger her memory somehow. It's a ball, so there will be dancing. She and Age danced to "Fantasia on Greensleeves." If that song is played, it might jar her memory, especially if Age danced to it with her."

He took out the small device, typed on it, and turned it off in despair. "I couldn't find out when the ball is."

I didn't care. "No problem! We'll just sneak into Delais and hide until the guests show up. On to the memory thing, when I got an e-mail that talked about you guys, she didn't remember any of you, so whatever she did must have worked. We need to unlock that part of her past. How do we know they'll play this song?"

Sophie added, "Age can request the song. Once they play it and he dances with her, it should do the trick."

Louis was skeptical. "This is ridiculous. If we escape, we should go the police. What about the tracking devices?"

I reminded him, "Remember, the boy said some police were in on it! We can't trust anyone yet! We'll just have to ignore the tracking devices for now."

Louis reddened. "Forgot that part of his evil monologue. We need to figure out where Age is, get there, wake him up, find out when the ball is, bring him to Delais in time, and have him warn Tara. Any ideas?"

Sophie put her ear against the door. "Do you sense silence? That's it! I don't hear the guards talking; I don't hear them breathing. What if they're so preoccupied with getting that kid to Tara's ball that they neglected to put guards at the door?"

I opened it. "Not even locked. Something's up."

Louis urged, "Let's go to the room with the snow globe and walk down the path Age was dragged on. Maybe we'll find him."

They led me to a vast room with a lot of light that hurt my eyes. Louis started, "This is where it happened. The man took Age that way! Let's go to wherever that way is!"

The emptiness was nerve-wracking. "Why isn't anyone here?"

Sophie spoke, "They must've assumed we'd try to save Tara before waking Age, so they must be expecting us to walk out one of the doors. There must be extra guards posted outside, but none in here. They must have gotten cocky, thinking they outsmarted us."

We arrived at a dead end with the exception of an elevator. We ventured inside. Louis fingered the buttons. "Here are all the floor levels. Which one would Age be in, the deepest one? It would take longest for the elevator to get there, so, if the authorities came, they would have more time to get him out."

It didn't matter at this point. "Go with the deepest one. We don't have much time."

He ordered the elevator to take us to the deepest floor, and, as we descended, a nasty image of the cable snapping crept into my mind.

After a few agonizing minutes, the doors finally opened. We sprinted out and came across an ominous room. At the center was our missing friend. Age was unconscious, his hands were covered in blood, and he was strapped to some contraption.

I shuddered and begged, "Sophie Science Girl, there are containers full of liquid on the shelves.

Do you know if a combination of these will wake him up?"

She snatched a couple of bottles. "These bad boys will do it. Louis, Matt, open his mouth." We obeyed, and she trickled the medicine in slowly, until both containers were empty. "He should wake up soon."

I marveled at her talent. "How did you know which ones to use?"

Sophie replied, "I've studied all kinds of science for a decade. I know what chemicals do what."

Good to know.

I wondered, "How did you get so good at science while trapped in a room and everything?"

She kept her eyes on Age. "There's not a science savvy person in the criminal ring, so they give me science books. I couldn't use the information I learned to bust out, but it comes in handy to rescue damsels and menfolk in distress."

Louis gave her a weirded-out expression. "Out of all the people in the criminal ring, not one of them can do science stuff? Well . . . you did have to do brain surgery to save them before . . ."

I suggested, "Truman only likes to hire dumb people. So, there's that."

Age's eyes flew open. "Am I dead? Are we all dead? Why are we in the room I died in? We're not in Hell, are we? What did I do that was so wrong?!"

I straightened him out. "Age! Nobody here is dead! You were unconscious, and Sophie revived you. Do you remember Tara, the girl you saved at the museum?"

Age grinned. "Of course I do! I wrote poetry about her. Isn't your twin sister named Tara? Isn't that funny?"

I was trying to control my this-guy-likes-my-sister-so-I-have-to-destroy-him reflex. "It was her. You wrote poetry about *my sister*. She's the Princess of Delais, and I'm the Crown Prince. There's this guy who's out to get her, and you need to sneak into her ball and warn her."

Age's face fell. "How am I supposed to get out of here? Even if I do and make it to Delais, what if Tara won't believe me? You should go; she'll trust you."

I grabbed a piece of paper and a pen off the table full of plans to make torture more painful and started writing. "They'd expect me to go, and they think you're unconscious, so you might take them by surprise. Take this letter and give it to Tara. I wrote down stuff only I know about her.

"You'll recognize Tara because she has a red birthmark on her arm that is very long. But she might not remember who you are, so you'll have to dance to "Fantasia on Greensleeves" with her." I hurriedly scribbled the letter, cautioning Tara about the stalker boy's true intentions. "Take it, Age. Don't lose it."

Age stuck it in his shoe. "It's where I keep all my important stuff. So, if I give Tara the letter, she'll believe it's me . . . but how do I escape the base?"

Sophie gasped. "Age needs a suit! We all should escape, at least to be sure he's wearing the right stuff. Age, I don't trust you to buy the correct garb. We also need to wipe the blood off of him." She took blank pieces of paper and applied them to his hands.

Louis disagreed, "It doesn't matter what he wears as long as he gives Tara the letter."

She argued, "If he wears that ratty outfit while everyone else is in suits and gowns, he'll stick out like a sore thumb. That boy will know it's him and might kidnap him again before he delivers the message! If he's in a suit, he will be a regular boy with blond hair and blue eyes with an eerie resemblance to Age, but it'll 'just be a freaky coincidence.'"

Sophie threw the paper-slash-Age's-bandages on the ground. "Done! Let's hope they don't start bleeding again."

I offered them a pleading countenance. "We need to get out of here. Our prediction is that they're expecting us outside the doors. Anyone have an idea?"

Louis let out a relieved laugh. "There are vents here! All of us can crawl through them to freedom! By the way, why can't all of us warn Tara if we're all escaping to make sure Age won't pick out an awful outfit?"

Sophie broke in, "If all of us were spotted, it wouldn't be a coincidence like it would be if only Age went. Only he can go. We'll hide somewhere."

Age cleared his throat. "Before we go, where do we buy the clothes?"

I'm getting a headache.

Sophie boomed, "We'll wander the streets aimlessly until we find a store! Wait, we need money." She fished out countless euros from her pocket and put them on the table. "Sometimes people drop money in the crates. I saved these up for something like this."

I recounted, "We'll climb through the vents to freedom. Then we'll find a clothing store and buy a suit using the euros Sophie collected from the crates. Does everyone get the plan so far?"

Age questioned, "Yes, but what do we do after we get the suit? Where are you going to hide once we get into Delais?"

I was exasperated. "You put the suit on. The rest of us have to hide somewhere on the island.

After you reveal to the Delaisans what's going on, go back and get us. To the vents!"

Age took off his shoe and yanked out a screwdriver. "To unscrew the bolts." Louis boosted him up, and he unscrewed the panel. Louis put Age back down, and Age put the panel on the floor.

I hoisted Sophie on my shoulders (after she put the euros back in her pockets) so she could crawl in the vents. Then I helped Age and Louis get up there. I halted. "Wait, after you pull me up, let's screw the panel back on. If it's off, they'll know how we got out."

I grabbed the panel and flung it to Age.

He had a solid grip on it. "Got it. Take my hand and I'll pull you up. Aah! I might fall out of the vent! Louis, grab me so I won't!"

He bent over, with Louis' hands firmly planted on him, and stuck out his hand. Louis panicked, "Age! You're practically falling out! Matt, come *on!*"

I grasped Age's hand, and Louis pulled Age up, and Age pulled me up. I took Age's screwdriver and screwed the panel back where it belonged.

I breathed a sigh of relief. "That was a challenge. Ugh, it's so dusty in here. Do they ever clean these?" We inched forward for a long time.

We crawled past an opening to a new room. Voices wafted in. "Marcus has to marry Tara. He has to be a prince of Delais for this to work. We need to know where *it* is. A connection to the royal family is the only way to get it."

What is this 'it'?

Another time, Matt, another time.

A second voice cursed, "Those meddling children better not ruin this for us."

The other pursued, "What are you getting at? The teens are locked in that room, and Adrian is out. We have a guy who's giving him a drug to make him stay that way until we don't need him alive anymore. Once he's dead, we'll take his body, sail to Menorca, and dump it on the side of a road."

I had heard enough, including the helpful tidbit that the idiot's name was Marcus. I gestured that we should move on, and we all went back to crawling.

We made it to the end of the ventilation pathway with one final opening. Sophie leaned forward to see if anyone was in the room below us. "The coast is clear! There's nothing in here but a window."

Age unscrewed the panel so we could hop out. One by one, we jumped out and hit the ground. I glanced back up. "We should put that panel back in place. Leave no clues behind!" Louis once again gave Age a boost while Age secured the vents.

Sophie opened the window. "We're still on the bottom floor after the elevator trip, so we can climb out the window. The ground is really close, so we don't need to worry about falling to our deaths."

I didn't like our chances. "The window is a narrow fit. One of us might not be able to get through. Age, you're the one supposed to go to the ball; try it now!" I handed him his screwdriver, and he put it back in his shoe. He slipped out without a problem.

Louis and Sophie made it, but I had some trouble. They all grabbed and pulled on my head until I popped out.

Now I know why newborns cry after they come out of the womb. That was painful . . .

I cringed. "Thanks! That was tight."

Louis whipped the small device out of his

pocket, "I can look up directions! I forgot until now; I was busy with the whole escape thing." He started typing. "Got it! Let's go to the nearest chic suit store!"

We followed the directions on the screen, and a random man jumped in front of us. "Greetings, American tourists! Welcome to the island of Sardinia! I have rare, very rare items for sale."

He knows English?

I kept walking. "We're not American tourists, but good luck selling your merchandise!"

More men confronted us. "It's perfectly acceptable that you're not American tourists because he's not really an Italian salesman. We're kidnappers. You're Truman Shaw's captives, right?"

More of Truman's convict pals. Perfect.

We all bolted away from them. Age caught sight of the clothing store after a few blocks. We all raced inside and locked the door. The cronies started pounding on it, trying to break in.

Sophie rattled off in Italian to the clerk. The employee took a deep breath, told her something, and dialed a number.

Sophie put euros on the counter and grabbed a suit. "Some officers are in on the plot! We need to escape now!"

We fled from the store. Age panted, "Where do I change into my suit?"

I blurted, "In a public restroom!" We went inside a random store, and Age went into the bathroom while we hid behind a rack of finely decorated hats.

He came out shortly. Age was definitely more suave in it.

Sophie punched his arm. "Now it's believable that you're the Hereditary Prince of Liechtenstein! I can't do anything about your hair, though.

It's impossible to fix. You're just going to have to accept that."

Age wondered, "How do I get to Delais? Is there an airport nearby?"

Louis went on the small device again. "Yes, my dear Age, there is! The airport is a fair distance from here. Let's get moving and buy ourselves tickets."

A few hours later, we got to the airport. I greeted a man behind the desk wearing a formal nametag written in a fancy font. "Hello! I'm speaking in English! I need to buy a ticket to Delais!"

The ticket agent gave us an odd expression. "I speak English, and Delais doesn't have an airport. The best I can get you is a flight to Rottnest Island. Let me see the cost for all of you to go."

Sophie gave him the money once he told us the price. "Boys, the flight is in fifteen minutes! We should use this time wisely and go to the bathroom."

After we took care of nature's calling, we boarded the plane. We handed the flight attendant our tickets and sat in the back where there were less people.

Age's voice was a whisper so he could barely be heard. "We're actually going to crash a ball to save a beautiful princess from a kidnapper! How many people get to do that?" His eyes glistened with adventure.

I closed my eyes. "Not many. We have some time to rest before we land. Try to get some sleep."

After a long while, the pilot thanked everyone on board for choosing their airline, waking me up. I nudged Age. "We're here! Whoa, your hair is trimmed and doesn't have dirt or blood in it. What happened to you while I was napping?"

Age ran his hand through it. "A hairstylist two

rows in front of us saw it and demanded to clean it. I'm different."

He got that right. "Yeah. It scares me."

Louis was chipper. "That was the best sleep I ever had in my whole life."

When we stepped off the plane, I tapped a person's shoulder. "Is there a ship for sale we could buy here? Are euros the currency?"

He turned around. "No, the euro isn't. I'm selling my boat, but I'm planning a trip to Europe soon, so I'll accept euros." He told us the amount he wanted.

Sophie wasn't taking any risks. "Show us your boat and prove that you own it. We don't need to use it only to find out it wasn't your boat in the first place and then go to jail for stealing."

He took us to a boatyard. "Rico!"

A worker came over. "Yes? How can I help you, Mr. Williams?"

Mr. Williams pointed to the boat. "These young children want to purchase my boat, but they want to make sure I am not cheating them. Can you prove to them that it is mine?"

Rico showed us Mr. Williams' paperwork. Sophie handed him the euros.

Rico exclaimed, "That's not the currency!"

Mr. Williams interjected, "I want to be paid in euros. It's going to make my wife pleased. We'll have less of a hassle going to Europe due to your interest in our boat. It's yours; feel free to use it whenever you please. Rico, transfer the boat to them."

After Mr. Williams and Rico left, Louis suggested, "Should we buy a meal before we sail to Delais? There's still a large chunk of the Indian Ocean we have to go through."

Sophie put a hand over where the money

was. "In your dreams! If we crash the ball and Age warns Tara, we can eat. That can be our motivator to get to Delais."

We climbed into the boat, ignoring our growling stomachs, and set sail.

CHAPTER 27:
TARA

Location: Amor, Delais

A lady held up a needle and thread. "What would you like to wear to your ball?"

My request was practically impossible, but I still voiced it anyway. "I adored the pattern on my curtains back in Taunton. Can you get that fabric and make a dress out of it?"

"What was the fabric like?"

I painstakingly went over a detail from the old life I left behind. "It had red, blue, and yellow flowers on it. Is there a computer I can go on to try to find it?"

She brought me to her office, and I went on the store's website. I clicked on the "curtains" menu and found it. "This. It was this."

She printed it out. "This'll make an elegant gown. You have exquisite taste. I'll order the fabric and get right on it."

I was impressed. "Wow. You're really good."

Someone else came in. "Tara, what kind of flowers do you want for the ball? The native flower is *Acanthocarpus preissii*, commonly known as the prickle lily. But we can order any flower you desire." He held up a bloom that looked sort of like a cross between a dandelion and a buttercup.

"I like the prickle lily. Can we use that?"

He gave me an affirmative and walked out, almost bumping into a young woman slightly older than me. The newcomer asked, "Tara, do you want to unearth the crown jewels we buried in

Immortalis? We can do that if you want to wear some to the ball."

Go to the City of the Dead, shuffle around the crypts, dig up the crown jewels, and wear them to my birthday ball?

Eh, OCD has me do worse things than that.

I hoped I didn't sound too demanding. "If it's not too much trouble, we can."

Another man came in. "Hi, kiddo. I'm Anton, your bodyguard. What are you doing here, picking out a dress?"

I added, "And flowers, and deciding whether or not to go dig up crown jewels out of our catacombs."

He sat in a chair. "What did you choose?"

"The prickle lily and my old curtain fabric for the dress. Getting the jewels would be no sweat."

Anton winked at the girl my age in an avuncular way. "Don't worry about the jewels, Colleen; I'll go with Tara to get them out." Colleen smiled and went off.

Anton chuckled as he viewed the fabric on the computer screen. "That's cute that there are blue flowers on it because the official Delaisan coat-of-arms has blue in it."

I eagerly inquired, "What is our coat-of-arms?"

He described the image. "There's a lot going on in it. A blue shield with three pomegranate fruits on a tree, suits of armor holding axes, and a knight's helmet with blue, green, and white ribbon flowing out of its side. Plus, the helmet has a tiny crown on top with blue and white feathers shooting out from it."

There was no way I could picture that in my head. "Never mind. I'll just look at a picture later."

Anton sighed. "That was a lot of information at once. Anyway, that was King Eduardo's coat-of-arms. He was the first ruler. When he died, his son Diego ascended the throne. King Diego abdicated later on and gave the country to his son James, your father."

"Then Matt will be the king?"

He darkened. "If he's alive when it's time for your father to pass over the kingdom. But, if he is still missing, the throne would go to you. You'd be the first ruling queen."

Since I loved the medieval era with Catholic princesses, I studied a lot about royalty, including rights of succession. "Do we have male-preference cognatic primogeniture?"

Male-preference cognatic primogeniture was when a female only inherited the throne if she had no living brothers with no surviving male descendants.

Anton rubbed his hands together. "We're either male-preference cognatic primogeniture or absolute primogeniture."

Absolute primogeniture was when the oldest child of the monarch, regardless of gender, was the heir to the throne.

I put my hands on my hips. "How do we not know our own succession system?"

"The monarch's firstborn was always a male. We never decided whether the oldest female should inherit; we never had to."

We continue being Earth's oddball country.

That made more sense. "I get it. What other laws about succession do we have?"

Anton furrowed his brow. "The monarch-to-be has to be of sound character. If the heir is a murderer or other type of serious criminal, we remove him or her from the line of succession."

Dad came in. "Hey Anton, what are you doing here?"

Anton shook his hand. "Tutoring Tara about the country. She now has a better understanding of the island."

Dad cleared his throat. "Tara, even though we're not having a feast, we're going to have a meal with the family. You'll be fine; you're a Garcia. You're a fighter; it's in your hot Portuguese blood. One of our ancestors killed a Nazi officer during World War II on the original Earth. Besides, you're a talented eater."

Then Dad left to go file taxes or some other awful math thing.

Tears slid down my cheeks. Anton whipped out a pocket of tissues. "Here you are."

I mumbled my thanks and wiped my tears away.

I'm going to eat in front of my family, who'll judge me based off of a mental illness I have.

I cried even harder.

Anton gave me more tissues. "Do you want me to introduce you to some of our dolphin friends? That'll take the sting out of your OCD being exposed in front of an audience.

"It's like a gladiator entering the Coliseum, except, in our case, it's our family that torments us, not the Roman emperor. Instead of lions tearing our guts out, our family tears out our self-respect.

"The martyrs had no thoughts that they were going to Hell. We believe we're going to Hell and all life beyond death is torture, and that our births were a burden. It hurts having OCD. If you want to go to the dolphins, let me get a bucket of fish. The dolphins are our equivalent of therapy dogs."

Therapy dolphins and bodyguards who go through the same wretched thoughts I have? This really is an island paradise!

After Anton got a bucket, we sauntered outside

to the edge of the beach. Anton plunked the bucket down and whistled. A dolphin popped its head up.

Anton took a device out of his pocket and started typing on it. The dolphin seemed to understand what he was doing and turned all around.

He elaborated, "We identify them by the shape of their dorsal fin, fluke shape, and other features. The results are coming up . . . Hey, it's Herbert! He's a peach.

"All our dolphins swim freely around the world; we don't put them in an aquarium. But there's always at least one dolphin swimming here on its travels. Do you want to see Herbert's tricks?"

I didn't want to abuse the poor dolphin. "Does he like doing tricks?"

Anton beamed. "He must because, like I said, we don't put our dolphins in captivity. Herbert doesn't have to perform tricks for food. He can swim away whenever he wants, and we just track him to see what part of the world he's in. He's free to leave, so, if I want him to do a trick he doesn't like, he can refuse or swim away."

"How could I say 'no' to that?"

Anton put his hand high up in the air. "Herbert, jump!" Herbert rose out of the water and then returned. Anton tossed him a fish. "Good dolphin! Very good dolphin. Herbert, speak!" Herbert chattered. Anton gave him another fish. "Good dolphin! Very good dolphin. Tara, want a turn? Tell him to shake your hand."

I held it out. "Herbert, please shake my head." Herbert slapped his pectoral fin on my hand. I cheered, "Go, Herbert!"

Anton patted Herbert's head. "Do you like him?"

How can I not?

I tossed Herbert a fish. "He's the best."

Another dolphin swam up, and Anton started typing. The dolphin didn't move around like Herbert did.

Anton concluded, "This must be a new friend. I'll add him or her to the database." Herbert bobbed his head from the new dolphin to Anton and chattered. The new dolphin moved all around.

Anton started typing again. "Now I can put the little fellow in since he or she's giving me a good look at the features . . . let's go get the tagging equipment." He held up one finger to Herbert, and we zoomed off.

We got back out, and Anton tagged the new dolphin and checked out the underside. "Ooh, a female. Is she your girlfriend, Herbert? You have the honor of naming her, Tara. What'll the lady dolphin's name be?"

I want to name her after someone. Someone who has always been there for me when I needed her.

I chose, "Dymphna."

Anton gave Dymphna a fish. "Darling dolphin Dymphna. Alliteration. I'm a poet; I keep the internal flame of literature lit."

Writing nerd joke.

I giggled. "Internal rhyme. Author respect. You have skills, Anton. This is fun. What else can we do in Delais?"

"Would you like to go to Immortalis and get your jewelry back? Your first visit to the City of the Dead. Exciting!"

It certainly beats a dinner with my family.

CHAPTER 28: TARA

Location: Amor, Delais

The day of the ball arrived, much to my trepidation since I would be without my brother while having to dine with relatives.

I'm going to the Coliseum with my family condemning me to death and crushing words to shred my self-confidence.

Just another day in an OCD victim's life.

I saw myself in the mirror. I was clothed in the dress and wore a tiara with emeralds in it (which Anton told me was based off the Grand Duchess Vladimir Tiara encrusted with emeralds) and a diamond necklace with gems shaped to look like stars (which was a replica of the Necklace of the Stars).

Anton was being extra amiable the whole day, acting like the calm before the storm. "Tara, you're dazzling."

"I'm glad one person has that opinion."

He hugged me. "Hey, you don't give yourself enough credit."

"I'm going to eat with my extended family. I'm the unofficial main course."

He paced. "You're not alone in that regard. My family back in Puerto Rico was furious at me for having a mental illness before they sent me away."

"If it's not too personal, can you tell me what happened?"

Anton pulled me into his backstory. "I was fifteen, and, all of a sudden, I had to check things over and over. I'd be late to every event. I started telling my mama I was going to Hell because I dropped my Bible on the floor.

"My parents took me to the doctor, and he said I had OCD. Soon it was juicy gossip, and everyone in my city knew.

"All my classmates threw rocks at me and told me I was unclean. At CCD, when the teacher left to ask the priest a question about the lesson, everyone dropped their Bibles on the ground to mock me.

"My abuela told me that God punished her by giving her a grandson with OCD, and she called me her curse. Everyone in the family found out, and my nickname became 'The Curse'.

"Eventually, all the other families laughed at mine and said, 'They are the cursed ones. Anton belongs to them.' So, my family sent me to Florida so I would die penniless on the streets without a soul finding out.

"What they didn't know was that, at my new high school, I told my guidance counselor I had OCD, so she sent me to a center for help. I got treatment there.

"After some time, I had a better quality of life. I aspired to become a bodyguard. I wanted to protect someone, to save an innocent person from something they had no control over. Someone like fifteen-year-old me.

"After my training was complete, the Delaisans hired me to protect the royal family. The Delaisans are my real family."

Poor Anton.

I cried, "You weren't a curse! When you break your arm, you aren't a curse to your family. When you have cystic fibrosis, you aren't a curse to your family. When you have cancer, you aren't a curse to your family. So, when you have OCD, you can't be a curse to your family."

He shrugged. "The stigma in society is powerful."

I fiddled with my necklace. "The word 'stigma' sounds like a needle stabbing you and blood trickling out in pinpricks."

That caught Anton off guard, and he couldn't control his guffaws. "Let's go, Princess. We're going to show everyone how sensational you are. Shall we, milady?"

We entered the dining room. I started fanning myself so I wouldn't pass out from anxiety. "I can have grilled cheese, right?"

He whispered, "You can have whatever you want. You can even have us cut Herbert's life short and eat him."

I was appalled. "I don't want to slaughter Herbert! He's my dolphin buddy."

Anton pulled my chair out for me. "But you could if you wanted to." I sat in it, and he pushed me in.

"Thanks for the chivalry! Much appreciated. When are they coming?"

He dove in the seat next to me, eyeing the entrance. "Now. You can handle whatever they say. You're Portuguese; you're a tough nationality. From Taunton, no less! You were the first city to stick it to King George III by raising the Liberty and Union flag on the Taunton Green on the first Earth!"

"My heritage and home are impressive, but I'm just a weakling."

Anton's face was full of compassion. "I understand how you feel, but you'll get through it. If I could, you can. Just put on your game face."

A few minutes later, relatives poured in. The

chorus waved. "Hello, Tara! How are you faring?"

I took my fork, spoon, and knife out of my napkin. "Well. You all?"

They started discussing Herbert and Dymphna. Since they knew about her, I assumed they played with them before they went into the dining room.

My cousin Dolores offered me a genuine smile. *She's the only one that does.*

I returned her smile and internally vowed that once Matt got back, he'd meet both Bisavó and Cousin Dolores.

Anton bragged, "Tara's a natural with dolphins. Even with poetry. She's going to be a heck of an opponent the world will have to face when she turns eighteen. But the world will have to go through me first."

A second cousin sniffed. "Yes, my daughter already did that. She's such an animal lover. She adopted a dolphin when she was in fifth grade. Did you adopt a dolphin in fifth grade, Tara? You didn't because you were too busy being afraid to eat and screaming about germs."

How dare she?! That was the most mournful time of my whole life, and she has the nerve to mock me! I thought families were supposed to love each other . . .

You know what? I'm sick of being treated like this! I'm going to let the whole world know how Portuguese Tauntonians take care of business!

My voice dripped with sarcasm. "Yes, it really was a tragic time. What really kept me going during those sullen days was your support.

"It still is so inspiring when you compare me to your daughter and reiterate over and over that she was never such a hassle as I was, and how embarrassing it must be for my parents to have their only daughter see a therapist. That is what helps me sleep at night to this day."

Nobody said anything.

Way to go, Tara. The first time you stood up for yourself. This is awesome.

Anton prevented the delicate conversation from becoming even more hazardous by commenting, "Tara is radiant tonight. She picked out the material for her dress. She could be a fashion designer if she wanted."

Another relative derided, "My son got the highest grade in his design class, and he competed with the top designers of our time."

Spending time with family must have been an ancient tradition. Families now don't love each other. Sure, they say they love you, but it's fake. They're not really there for you.

I started to get a headache. "I'm going to go see if the others are here. Care to come, Anton?"

He rose. "I'll go to Siberia with you if necessary."

Matt would like him.

Don't think about Matt; it's like being gashed with knives every time you think of him.

We exited into the entryway. Anton slowly inquired, "Are you okay? Things got intense back there."

I closed my eyes. "I need a break from them. It hurts too much right now."

Why can't Cousin Dolores defend me?

I asked out loud, "Hey Anton, what do you know about Cousin Dolores?"

His face tensed. "A lot. Why?"

"It just seems like she's the only family member that kind of likes me. I mean, I know she doesn't stick up for me, but she actually smiled. So, I think she cares about me more than the others."

Anton wasn't pleased. "Be careful. We both

know that the family unit has dissolved over the years."

That surprised me. I expected Anton to compliment her skill at something. "I mean, I know that families only hurt each other nowadays. Do you like Dolores?"

Before Anton could respond, the other family members arrived to join the ball. My cousin Charlie admired the scenery. "You're the princess of this place? I want to move here."

A traumatic memory of Charlie cropped up, and I shoved it away.

I'm not ready for these memories. I can't even trust Matt with them.

I had to convince him that Delais was not a good match for him. "You always lived in big cities. We have two little cities, and one is full of the dead. You'll have to live in Amor for the rest of your life if you want to stay here."

Charlie suddenly wasn't as pleased. "You have a city full of the dead?"

Anton, in a tourist voice, pointed north. "Yes! Immortalis, also known as the City of the Dead. We bury the bodies; it's not like you enter and there are rotten blood-thirsty corpses staring at you. All you see is their tombstone, like in a normal cemetery. Are you ladies and gentlemen thirsty like those corpses? Let's show you the dining room with the rest of the guests."

Good. That should scare Charlie away.

I went back to my seat. Everyone was settled in, and a waiter came and took our orders. When it was my turn, I went with the usual. "A grilled cheese sandwich and a bottle of ketchup, please."

Charlie snickered. "She really has to put grilled cheese in ketchup?"

Someone replied, "She has OCD; she's all sorts

of wacky. Did you notice how she never had any friends except Piper? I bet her mom paid Piper to come over."

Anton abruptly snapped his head in the direction of the entrance, and I could see it was because he was hiding his lip curling in disgust.

He took deep breaths, and his tensed state relaxed. "Tara, I've never seen such a popular member of the royal family here in my life. Everyone wants to be your best friend, and it's not because you're the princess. It's from your warm personality and charming sense of humor."

I beamed. "The Delaisans are the kindest people I've ever met."

The waiter came out with my grilled cheese and plopped a huge bottle of ketchup on the table. "To be sure the condiments don't run out. Enjoy, Princess. The other meals will be ready shortly."

I caught the chef, a middle-aged dark-haired woman, wink at me. I waved back.

She must have heard everything.

Anton muttered, "News travels fast in Delais, especially unkind words."

This really is my country.

The rest of the meals arrived, and everyone was too busy chewing to criticize everything I did.

Dad drank the last of his wine. "Anyone up for dancing?"

We entered the ballroom. Dad greeted the performers, "Hello. How was the early meal Ms. Pichler fixed for you?"

The music started. Everyone got a partner and spun around. No one asked me to dance.

I spotted a balcony. "I'm going to go see the stars."

Anton didn't follow me, so I guessed he was giving me space to cope with the fact that nobody liked me.

I grasped my star necklace and looked up at the twinkling stars illuminating the sky.

God's arts and crafts.

God, I know Jesus said that it is rarer for a camel to go in a needle than a rich person to go to Heaven or something, but do I have a shot?

I have a habit of hoarding my money, which started even before I became a princess. What if I donate so much I can't support myself?

Now that I'm a princess, I like having long digits in the bank. It makes me feel secure, like I can handle a catastrophe like if the boiler breaks or if the ceiling caves in.

Am I evil?

Do You hate me?

CHAPTER 29: AGE

Location: Delais, Australian Continent

We hit land after a few days. Fear took over my body. "We missed the ball; didn't we? We're too late! I hate sailing!"

I hardly noticed Matt tremble. "Look ahead! Are we in Delais, or is this a stairwell to Hell?"

I viewed where he pointed and squinted. There was a huge structure we had to go through to venture further, and inky blackness shrouded it in mystery. The only visible feature was a dramatic elegant yet jagged amber staircase jutting downward.

It wasn't hard to imagine demons pointing at us and laughing, daring us to venture down into their domain, and that the steps would really only stop at the gateway to Hell.

Louis typed on the device. "This says we're in Immortalis, Delais. In order for Age to go to the ball, he'll have to pass through the City of the Dead, which is the building Matt's afraid of."

I wiped sweat off my forehead. "No one alive? Everyone's dead in there?"

Louis responded, "All the Delaisan dead are buried there. You might see dead bodies. We can hide in the City of the Dead until you warn Tara."

I wasn't worried about the dead body part. "I saw someone get murdered in front of me when I was five. I saw someone tortured and killed in front of me when I was six. I can handle dead people. But how are we supposed to see anything inside?"

Sophie went to the boat. "We make a torch. I'll show you." She opened the oil drain plug, disconnected the gas line and mixed them together, tore a part of her sleeve off, doused it in the mixture, and finally dipped the branch in the mixture, effectively making a torch.

I glumly stated, "We need to navigate through the City of the Dead before this runs out."

Another day's work for the royal teens, no big deal.

We crept inside. The torch revealed a staircase leading downward. I descended, my feet as light as a ghost's.

Many coffins and grave markers filled the city.

Talk about anticlimactic.

We kept going further until there was an unlit lantern on the ground. Matt scooped it up. "Sophie, light the lantern with the stick!"

She pressed the torch into the lantern and took it back out. "I'm going outside to throw this in the water so I won't burn down the island." Sophie left.

The whole lantern scene struck me as odd. "I'm guessing the Delaisans bring lanterns with them while they bury the deceased. Why is this one here? It was positioned too carefully; it wasn't dropped."

Sophie popped back over. "The island is no longer at risk!" We trudged onward. She made a face. "There are so many twists and turns in here! This place needs a map."

Matt was morose. "I'm the crown prince of this place, and I'm going to die in here for not knowing how this maze in my own country ends!"

I wasn't in the mood for sadness. "Matt, you were taken at birth. It's not your fault. Even if it was, it's not a big deal. We can make it out of here, but we can't stop seeking the exit."

After an agonizing amount of time getting lost and retracing our steps, we stumbled on a staircase going up. I was overjoyed. "Since the downwards steps got us here, this upwards stairway must be bringing us out of here!"

Sophie peered at the beach once we made it to the top of the stairwell. "Do we need to hide in here until the ball begins? No, lights are on in a part of the castle! It must be going on right now! Age, go in there this very second! We'll wait here until you come back with the Delaisans."

I glided to the castle door. A buff man was standing in front of it. A group of people were hiking toward the door, as well. I blended in with them to escape questioning.

The guard stepped aside. "I hope you enjoyed your walk on the beach, Queen Hildegarde's relatives."

He gave me a suspicious once-over and a glare. I ignored him and followed the crowd into the ballroom.

Tara has a long red birthmark on her arm.

I examined all the girls, but none had a red birthmark.

She's somewhere in here.

Only then did I let myself look at the decorations. Crystal chandeliers sparkled above, portraits of royal family members lined the walls, and there was an orchestra playing classical music.

I kept sneaking about when I came across a balcony. There was a lone figure gazing at the stars. A girl wearing a flower-patterned sleeveless dress with long dark hair crowned with a tiara had her back to me. I couldn't skirt around to see if she had a birthmark, so I coughed. "Excuse me, can I talk to you?"

She turned around, and indeed had a red birthmark. An inner warmth flowed inside me, and the innate instinct to protect her all those years ago at the museum charged back with an electrical power.

She is the most stunning person I've ever seen in my life. Stunning can't even begin to describe it. My poetry wasn't exaggerating when it called her "the jewel of eternity miners longed to find but died before they could be soothed by her touch," or "the treasure more valuable than the gold of Ophir."

Other people are called stunning; nobody would understand how much awe-striking wonder Tara possesses.

I need a word that mankind can compare her to, but none suffice to her extent.

I need a new word for her: Tarian, the grace only comparable to Princess Tara of Delais.

I'm pretty sure Tarian means "dance" in one language and "shield" in another, but this is whole other definition.

She broke my thoughts. "Why are you staring at me? Do I look ugly?"

"No! You are ... Tarian."

She raised an eyebrow. "I've never heard that word. What does it mean?"

I flushed. "Once the dictionaries approve of my definition, you'll find out."

"It means 'ugly,' doesn't it? Who are you? I only invited the Delaisans and Marcus. Mom let the family crash the ball. Are you a Delaisan I haven't met yet?"

I tried to play it cool. "I'm not a Delaisan. Can we keep my identity a secret? If I were dangerous, they wouldn't let me come in here."

The security was terrible. And where's her bodyguard? If we get out of this alive, I'm telling her to up-

grade her security. This is just reckless.

Tara accepted that. "Fair enough. What did you want to tell me?"

I took the paper out of my shoe. "I have a letter from your brother."

She turned stone cold. "My brother is missing; he couldn't have given you a letter. Did my family put you up to this? You're disgusting."

Her words deeply cut into me, but I didn't show it. "I would never hurt you. I love you."

Don't tell her that, you idiot!

And you met her once ten years ago; that's not love! There's something wrong with you!

Her voice became flat. "That's a lie. I just met you."

I shook my head. "We met once before at the museum. I'm Age. I helped save you from kidnappers."

Tara was unconvinced. "Out of all the times I went to a museum, there were never kidnappers."

Matt's words came back to me, *"But there's a problem. She might not remember who you are, so you'll have to dance to 'Fantasia on Greensleeves' with her."*

Icy terror circulated in my veins. "I see. If you danced with me, maybe it would all come back to you."

My gut told me she was close to hitting me, so I distracted myself by putting the letter back in my shoe.

"You pretend to know my brother, and then ask to dance with me? You're absurd!"

I held out my hand, praying she'd take it. "Just give me a chance! Please."

Tara relented. "One dance, and, if I don't remember you, I'm calling security. You'll be arrested."

This wasn't as triumphant as I imagined our re-

union would be.

Or romantic.

I tried to slow my staggering heartbeat. "We need to dance to "Fantasia on Greensleeves." If you don't remember me after that, then you can call the guards if you want."

She was startled at the mention of the song.

Maybe I'm already getting to her!

Tara raced over to the musicians and said something, then walked back to me. "Ready to dance, mysterious stranger who I suspect is shady?"

The music started filling the room. "May I have this dance?" I bowed slightly and offered her my arm.

She tentatively took it with a look of pure fear. "You may."

Oh no! She's frightened! You're safe with me, Tara; I won't let anything hurt you!

I started to perform the steps with her, reminding her of the song, reminding her of what happened, and, most importantly, I dared to admit in the tiniest corner of my mind, *reminding her of me.*

Half-way through the song, she started to remember the steps on her own and studied my eyes. "You really are Age!"

I was fearful that, if I opened my mouth, I would say something like, "Please marry me and spend the rest of your life with me," so I bit my tongue and nodded.

Tara's cheeks colored like delicate pink rose petals. "I'm so sorry that I didn't believe you, for calling you 'disgusting,' 'absurd,' and 'shady,' and for accusing you of lying. It all just came back to me now."

Yes! She remembers me! Dreams can come true after

all!

I assured, "I would've forgotten as well if I were in your position."

I twirled her, and she asked, "What happened to you? You told me to go back with my classmates, then you went to distract the kidnappers. I never saw you again 'til now."

I delivered the news as gentle as I could. "They took me away."

Her eyes watered. "You got captured to save me? That's the sweetest thing anyone ever did for me."

She likes the fact that I saved her! This is amazing! She might like me!

I played it off. "Oh, it was easy to do, considering you were the one I had to save."

That was when I noticed every eye on us. All the dancers stopped to watch us, the people standing on the sidelines were watching us, even the musicians were playing while watching us (which I assumed was no small feat). "Why is everyone staring?"

"Who cares as long as I'm with you? Would you like to finish the dance with me?"

I felt as if we were walking on water. The rest of the dancers moved out of our way like the Parting of the Red Sea (which was unnecessary, since I would've went around them), but I followed Tara's advice and didn't care.

All that mattered was being there with her, just being there with her. With the most precious human being in the world. I held my breath when our hands touched.

The song ended, and I coolly complimented her form, "You're an adept dancer."

Thanks for not letting me propose to her, God.

"It was easy when I had the best person to remind me of the moves."

How is she so good at talking?

I hoped that I didn't have a stupid expression on my face. "Thank you. Now, would you like to go back on the balcony so you can see the letter in private?"

We walked over there, under the shimmering stars, and I handed her the letter.

Tara blanched. "Only Matt would know the stuff in the letter! So, Marcus Niceren did that to me? He pretended to save me! How could he?"

I pictured Matt, Sophie, and Louis in the City of the Dead, and knew I had to get them out as quickly as I could. "I'm sorry about his betrayal. We must alarm the Delaisans immediately. I would have told the guard outside already, but I thought you deserved to be aware of the situation first since you were the one tied to the tree and being played."

She held out her hand. "Can we go together?"

I took it, putting the letter back in my shoe. "Anything for you."

If only you knew how much I meant those words! I love you!

There's something wrong with you, Age!

We hastened out to the guard while I simultaneously avoided whacking into a pillar with my head in the clouds.

Once we made it to him, I caught him up to speed. "Matt, Sophie, and Louis are in the catacombs. There was one lantern that was positioned carefully. Why did you put that there?"

He grunted, "We didn't. Something very wrong is happening. We need to tell the other Delaisans and increase the royal family's security."

We ran to the other guards and told them what was happening. A woman ordered, "You stay with

Tara; we'll go get the others."

When they left, I comforted Tara. "Now, when Marcus gets here, you can have him arrested."

Her eyes widened in escalated inner turmoil. "Age, Marcus is already here. He came before you. He went on a walk on the beach with my family and didn't come back."

That was unexpected. "Why would he leave? You didn't promise to marry him, did you?"

I want you to marry me *when we're older!*

"No! He must have gotten cocky, convinced I was already in love with him, and exited to do something else. Was there anything else he would want to do?"

The Delaisans hurried back. "Your Highnesses, Crown Prince Matthew, Princess Sophie, and Prince Louis are missing!"

I felt the color drain from my face. "That must be what he wanted. Them. But how did he know where they were? How did he know when to nab them?"

The tracking devices!

Hmm. Louis must be infuriated.

The woman stayed on the bright side. "We can still tell Adrian's parents that he's here. That would be the best news they've heard in years." They sped away to do just that, with a few guards staying behind.

The pig himself walked up to us. "What did I miss, Tara? Who is this blond ignoramus?"

Hearing that little bug talk to Tara like he owned her enraged me to a level I never experienced before. "I exposed your dark intentions, masked villain!"

The guards sprang forward to arrest him, but he sprayed another formula at them. They fell onto the sand.

I complained, "How many of those do you have, enough to knock everyone on Earth unconscious?"

Marcus grasped Tara's arm forcefully. "You're coming with me." He proceeded to drag her away. She was petrified with terror and therefore didn't resist.

I rushed in front of Marcus. "Let her go. If I was trouble for you when I wanted to escape without hurting anyone, wait until you've seen me when I actually want to be trouble. Even I don't know my full capabilities. Let. Tara. Go. Now."

Marcus smarmily taunted, "Suits me. You can come with her." He tried to punch me in the nose with his free hand, but I blocked him, officially wrathful.

Tara screamed, somewhat out of her frozen stiff state, but not enough to fight Marcus with me.

I kicked him in the stomach and knocked him to the ground. He let go of Tara's arm, and she ran into the ballroom. I stalely spat out, "You shouldn't pick on innocent girls."

Marcus rose. "How about I take you? You're easier to abduct; no one likes you enough to rescue you."

Marcus lunged at me. I jumped out of the way and swung at him. "You're going to regret hurting Tara. It will be the end of you." I advanced, ready to deliver more blows.

People streamed outside where we were. A man rallied, "Get him dead or alive! Dead or alive! I want my son back! I want my son back now!" People either ran in the opposite direction of the man or charged at us.

Marcus seized me, purporting that I was the felon to take advantage of the confusion. "I have him. Let me take care of him."

Tara spoke, "No! The blond boy has nothing to do with it! It's Marcus who is the criminal!"

Marcus argued, "She's delusional with grief over her brother. I saved her from the tree, remember? I'm the good guy."

What can I possibly say? "I didn't do it"? "Tara's right"?

Wait . . . show them the letter and those papers Louis printed out!

I kicked off my shoe, and the screwdriver flew out, but not the letter or the papers, which stayed firmly inside.

Stupid gravity.

I begged, "Read the letter in the shoe! It proves Marcus should be the one you're after!"

Marcus blared over me, "Why would he be hiding a screwdriver in his shoe? He must be a criminal!"

Is he kidding? What captive wouldn't want a screwdriver?

The people were silent.

A lone Delaisan stepped forward. "I'll take this scoundrel to prison. Can I take Marcus and Tara with me? They should learn how to properly arrest someone."

Tara cried, "Marcus is the one you should be arresting!"

The man who rallied everyone put up his arms as if to say "everyone, stop." "What is *really* going on here?"

The Delaisan shook me. "Allow me to explain. This young man attacked our countrymen sprawled on the ground and tried to kidnap Tara. He must be imprisoned at once."

Tara defended, "Marcus is the deceiver! He pretended to rescue me but is with the people who took Matt! The evidence is in a letter in Age's shoe."

The Delaisan retrieved the shoe. "There is no letter, but there was this screwdriver hidden in it. Tara must be suffering from some side effect of OCD. You can't trust her opinion; she's mentally ill and cannot understand reality. Age, as Tara called him, must be arrested. Now, can I take Marcus and Tara with me to teach them how to imprison someone?"

While grabbing me, he went to Tara and started to drag both of us against our will, without permission from Queen Hildegarde or whoever the king was.

I fought back when we were out of sight so I wouldn't seem even more like a criminal in front of everyone. "I am not a kidnapper!"

The Delaisan called out, "I have them."

People emerged from the shadows, took us, and threw us in the back section of a food delivery truck.

Matt, Louis, and Sophie were bound on the floor. Louis was lecturing them about proper safety precautions.

Some things never change.

I updated them on the situation. "I warned Tara, but we're captured now. I also lost a shoe."

Marcus snorted. "Like all the damsels in distress do."

Tara hugged her brother. "You're not dead! And Marcus, when you said I shouldn't thank you after you untied me from that tree, you were right!"

Sophie was touched. "She's so adorable. I'm glad there's another girl in the group."

Louis simpered. "We're in a truck on an island. Marcus can't take us off Delais. Trucks don't operate on water."

The Delaisan couldn't keep a straight face. "It turns into a submarine."

A masculine voice hollered, "Pedro! You didn't have permission! Come back with Tara! This is what I get for giving her space! Teenagers can't have any privacy nowadays! And what did you say about OCD sufferers not understanding reality?!"

But before the voice could catch up, the submarine dove into the ocean. Marcus savored the moment. "There's nothing better than seeing hope wash off your faces! Tie up the couple, minions. Happily ever after doesn't exist in the real world."

The henchmen wrapped our wrists and ankles with rope. Even that didn't crush my heavenly mood. "Tonight was the best night of my life despite all of this."

Matt was agitated. "What do you mean by 'the couple,' and why is Age enjoying tonight so much? Adrian, Hereditary Prince of Liechtenstein, Count Rietberg, you'd better not be dating my sister!"

I answered, "I'm not; I just danced with her . . ."

Marcus slapped me. "Snap out of it! Underlings, I have plans to go to Algeria with the Liechtensteiner."

He gestured for his posse to go into a huddle, and they were discussing amongst themselves for a while.

Tara beamed. "Thanks for saving me at that museum all those years ago, you guys."

Sophie grinned. "Any time."

Matt was shaken. "What's going to happen to us? Is he going to kill us? Was catching Tara part of their plan? Was all of this about getting Tara?"

Tara sighed. "I only know that the bozo's name is Marcus Niceren. What's going on here?"

Sophie recapped everything for her.

The huddle abruptly broke. The minions became statues at their posts. Marcus leaned in close to my face. "We're going to spend a lot of time together from now on."

I made an annoyed noise. "That's worse than when the torture man cut up my hands."

Tara interrupted, "What did the torture man do to your hands?! Marcus, leave Age alone!"

Marcus towered over us malevolently. "Any questions? Most information can now be revealed."

Matt took him up on his offer. "What's the overall plan?"

He faltered. "One of the only things you can't know. Anything else?"

Matt answered, "You bet! Who is the top agent in this organization?"

Marcus stepped back in a dramatic flair. "My father, King Magnus of Sterietol. I'll inherit the throne unless my cousin Demetrius sways him . . . but he's nice like you people, so I'll be fine."

Sophie interjected, "What are you going to do with us?"

Marcus smiled like a sinister demon. "I'm going to marry Tara, murder Adrian and Matt, and keep the rest of you captive *for now*. You'll all get killed eventually, except perhaps Tara."

I predicted, "Because I danced with Tara and foiled the plan, you hate me and want to destroy me?"

Marcus rolled his eyes. "You didn't foil the plan, but you made it more complicated. You and Matt are being killed because we don't need you two alive anymore. My father figured out your pieces of the puzzle. He told me yours, but he will soon tell me Matt's."

Tara had a query of her own. "Why is a Delaisan with you?"

The traitor himself said, "I'm the rebel Delaisan, so I distorted what really happened in Marcus' favor, and made your precious Adrian seem like a cold-blooded barbarian. How else would the kidnappers know you have a red birthmark? I told them."

She shot daggers in his direction with her eyes. "You are the scum of the Earth."

Marcus sarcastically consoled, "Don't feel bad, Traitor Delaisan; after I murder her Adrian, she's going to hate me a lot more than you. Let's start the process, shall we?"

There was one thing that was still fishy. "Hold up. What was the whole lantern business about?"

Marcus cursed under his breath about my apparent stupidity. "That lantern in Immortalis? That was so all the henchmen could sneak in the country. Duh. Pedro put it there. You really couldn't connect those dots?"

I scrunched up my nose in detestation. "Why don't the Delaisans have security outside of Immortalis? That's an obvious way invaders could enter."

The Traitor Delaisan came forward. "Yes. That was where I came in. Immortalis does have security; there are heat sensors inside it so we know if someone is going through the City of the Dead.

"I made sure I covered the security for Immortalis today, so I let you all traipse through, so we knew where to grab you. Also, I could sneak the rest of the convicts on the island that way."

Marcus praised, "The traitor was very helpful. Certainly better than Truman Shaw. Any other things you want to go over before you die?" A few bottlenose dolphins chattered outside during the silence. "Grand. Now, Adrian, I'm going to take you on a short holiday to North Africa."

Tara seethed, "I heard that expression before in a video game! It means you're going to take him there against his will!"

Marcus teased, "It does mean that. Unfortunately for you, princess, Adrian isn't coming back."

CHAPTER 30:
AGE

Location: Algerian Desert, Algeria

Marcus and the Traitor Delaisan "escorted" me to a desert. I was astounded at how vacant it was. "How are citizens not finding us here?"

Marcus concentrated on going forward. "We know where to hide you all." He stalked into the desert without expounding why.

Marcus came back with seventeen scorpions scuttling all over his right hand. "Bury him in the sand. These critters will do a favor for me."

They dug a hole, pushed me in, and buried me up to my neck. Marcus licked his lips, hungry for revenge. "These are a newly discovered strain of the *Leiurus quinquestriatus*. Its common name is the Deathstalker. These are much deadlier than the other strains. Your father was stung by one when he was your age and almost died. I believe he is still afraid of these little guys." He placed them all over my head and neck.

I assumed, "You're going to kill me with their venom?" The scorpions bustled all over me.

Oh my gosh. Oh my gosh. This is really happening.

Marcus strolled toward my head and yanked two stingers down in my flesh.

Ow! Ow! Ow! Waves of pain! Waves of pain!

He kept pressing stingers into me over and over and over again, even digging my lower body up to get stingers to poison my arms and legs.

After some time, sweat started to trickle down my face and drip onto the sand, followed by muscle spasms. Once an indeterminate amount of time passed, I couldn't move at all.

The Delaisan studied me. "Without treatment, seventeen stings should end him. His father barely survived five."

Marcus gave me the most hateful expression possible. "I don't know, but I'm getting bored waiting for him to die. Let's go to Sterietol. Adrian should die on the way there. We'll throw his body somewhere and focus on the others."

They lugged me back into the truck. Tara cynically barked, "What did you do to him?"

Marcus kicked me in the thigh. "Adrian, can you tell them?"

I was motionless. Marcus was clearly enjoying himself. "The scorpion got your tongue? Or are you just quiet?"

The Traitor Delaisan stated, "Paralysis must have set in."

Tara growled, "It involved a scorpion. What did you do to him?"

Marcus glanced at Sophie. "I'd rather not say with the science whiz Hohenberg girl here. I'll tell you this; he'll die in front of you."

CHAPTER 31: AGE

Location: Sterietol, North American Continent

I was pulled out of the truck, and the sight awaiting me rendered me awe-struck. A large palace covered in ice overlooked everything for miles. It was literally incased in an ice layer.

The Traitor Delaisan fumed, "How is he still alive? The scorpion stings should have terminated him!"

Marcus smirked. "No matter. I have a back-up plan. Do you like the castle's icy exterior? Father had an ice layer added. He thought it would make it more intimating."

Everyone else was taken out of the truck. Tara shivered. "How does the ice not melt?"

Marcus explained, "It's extremely freezing here; ice won't melt. Citizens, bring me coats to cover the hostages so they won't freeze to death. I have harrowing plans for them. Other minions, watch the hostages. I must deal with Adrian first. Mwahahahaahaahahaha!"

Marcus and the Traitor Delaisan each took one of my arms and flung me onto a horse. Marcus saddled himself on. "Sterietol doesn't have cars; we get around by horseback. We're medieval that way. Delaisan, make sure he doesn't fall off. He's unable to support himself at the moment."

We rode off until we got to a massive lake with a thick layer of ice on black water. Marcus tapped the ice with his foot. "Delaisan, break the ice."

The Traitor Delaisan got off the horse, picked

up a boulder where a mallet was hidden under, and swung at the ice. It broke, and shards fell into the watery abyss.

Marcus pulled my chin close to his face. He fingered my hair and murmured, "All this for Tara, Adrian? You could have left her behind and saved yourself. You wouldn't have died if you escaped. But you chose Tara. All of this torture for her. You're not a knight in shining armor; you're a drowned boy in a lake. Tara is mine; you will never lay eyes on her again."

The Traitor Delaisan threw me in the lake, and I was helpless as I hurtled further down, holding my breath.

I could hear Marcus confide in the Traitor Delaisan. "The lake will freeze overnight, so, after today, he won't be able to get out. But he'll die from drowning in a few minutes. Let's go deal with the others."

How did I manage to survive the scorpions' stings?

But there's no oxygen down here. I'm going to die. It doesn't matter how I survived the scorpion venom.

Everything else drifted away as the current pulled me to a huge rock that went from the lake's floor to above the water.

What under Earth is that?

It doesn't matter, Age. Stop thinking about it.

How much longer can I hold my breath? Not forever.

So, I really will die. I wrote poetry about Tara for ten years, but I'm going to drown before we can get married?

Life is a rip-off.

CHAPTER 32: MATT

Location: Sterietol, North American Continent

Marcus and the Traitor Delaisan returned. Their culpable smiles matched that of a weasel.

Tara burst into tears for her new friend (not boyfriend-because that was not allowed). "What did you do to Age *this* time?"

Marcus replied, "I had him thrown in a lake to drown. He'll be dead in a few minutes. If you want, I'll have his body fished out so you can see it for yourself. I'm being generous to my future wife. We'll marry after I get rid of your brother."

Sophie criticized, "You're a horrible human being. And I've met a lot of horrible human beings."

Marcus turned to the henchmen. "Lead them all to separate rooms. Father is in the library studying the book. Send some of our people to break into the Liechtensteiner parents' home and steal the Bible in there. Shortly, Father will send people out for Matt's object. Speaking of Matt, it's time for his execution. We've been saving all the trash in the country for years for you."

I put on a falsely civil tone. "Whatever for?"

Marcus snickered. "You're going to be crushed to death by all the trash. Truman Shaw exercised his creativity for you."

I closed my eyes, trying not to get emotional. "Tara, can you promise me one thing? If you manage to get out of here and have all these criminals arrested, I want you to follow your dreams. Don't ever give up. Do it for me."

Tara smirked mischievously. "I planned on that happening anyway. Besides, everything's going to be okay as long as Bisavó is around. She's been in this world for so long that I just feel safe being around her, even though I only see her twice a year. I guess it's a weird calming thing for me."

Didn't Dad tell Mom that Bisavó was dangerously sick on our birthday right before we went to La Salette?

Marcus snarled, "Shut up! Tara isn't going to leave whether she likes it or not! I love myself; I'm so powerful."

I wrinkled my nose. "You love yourself way too much."

Marcus crossed his arms. "How could one possibly love me too much?"

Louis was antipathetic. "I am revolted."

Marcus and the Traitor Delaisan each took one of my arms, like they did to Age. They took me through a range of lushly carpeted rooms. A boy who looked identical to Marcus, except for the fact that his hair was styled as a buzz cut, caught sight of us and flinched. Marcus was displeased. "Demetrius, what are you doing?"

He must be Marcus' cousin. The one who was "nice."

Demetrius cleared his throat. "Your father told me to get him lunch, so I was telling the cooks to prepare the meal. That is Matthew Garcia, and you are going to crush him to death, correct?"

Marcus scrutinized him. "You must have overheard me! I can't stand you goody-goody people. I learn how to kill people with scorpions, and you practice healing them with antivenom."

The Traitor Delaisan opened a door. "All the trash is in the room above us. Once we leave, I'll press a button on my remote that will make the floor give way, and this room will be flooded with a decade's worth of trash. All the filth will flatten you into a two-dimensional object!"

Marcus turned to the traitor. "Let's go murder your crown prince. Truman especially will be pleased with his death. You know how he has a special hatred for Matt." They left.

God, please save my friends and sister from my fate. At least I have salvation to hope for. Please let there be chocolate in Heaven.

I saw the trash tumble in, and then the floor beneath me collapsed. I hit the ground, and someone started untying me.

Demetrius apologized, "I built a remote that would make *that* floor give way, like the one Marcus made. I cannot let you die.

"I am sorry my family is like this. If it is any consolation, Magnus is not my biological uncle. Marcus' mother, Queen Monica, was my biological aunt. She was so unlike them; she took me in after my parents died."

This guy is awesome.

I concurred, "Queen Monica definitely sounded different. Marcus didn't murder her or your parents, did he? He says you might claim the throne and not him."

He was still untying me from the more complex knots. "Aunt Monica died from disease, and my parents died in a horse-riding accident. King Magnus did not name his heir yet, so I have a chance of ruling. But it is going to be Marcus."

The rope fell to the floor, and I stood. "We need to save Age. He was thrown in a lake; he'll drown . . ."

The door opened and a girl with bleach blonde hair and turquoise eyes stepped in. "Tree, did you save Matt yet?"

Demetrius introduced us. "This is my cousin

and Marcus' younger sister, Angela."

I was baffled at the thought of Marcus having a sister that looked so innocent. "Marcus has a little sister?"

Angela closed the door cautiously. "Yes. My mother left the country during the nine months she was pregnant with me on vacation. She came back after I was born and gave me up for adoption to a peasant couple in Sterietol.

"Father knew that she had given birth and gave me up, but he knew I wasn't a threat to his plan, so he didn't press the issue. I have lived with my adoptive parents ever since.

"When Tree found out they were going to kill you, he wanted my help, so I snuck in here a few days ago with the help of secret passages. This palace is so large that no one found me, and I'm here to help! I already made sure there is a horse waiting outside for you. I'll help you get out using one of those secret passages."

"Demetrius," I started, not comfortable with using his apparent nickname "Tree," "Marcus mentioned he did something to Age that involved a scorpion. He also just said you're good with antivenoms. So is Sophie. If I save Age, even with his paralysis, your combined brainpower will surely save him."

He blurted, "I do not think I am as good as you think. Sophie would have to do the heavy lifting. Where shall we meet after the tasks have been accomplished? Is the laboratory acceptable? I have many antivenoms there."

Angela pulled me out of the room. "Meet you there!" We scurried through a hallway, and she moved a giant tapestry aside, revealing a secret passageway covered with cobwebs.

This castle sure is something.

We scrambled through it and came across a cramped room. Angela walked to an old window. "This window will get us outside to the horse."

Remembering the window I had to climb out of after I emerged from the vents, I was not elated at having to do it again. She opened the window and jumped out. I did the same, afraid that she would have to pull on my head.

Not again.

I fell on the ground. It wasn't that big of a drop, but I felt twitches of pain. Angela examined me. "Are you hurt?"

I picked myself up. "I'm a lot better than Age. This is the horse?" I pointed to a black stallion.

"She's the one." Angela mounted on her. I got on behind Angela, and we rode off.

Once we arrived, Angela pointed at the lake excitedly. "It didn't freeze over yet! Oh wow. The water is the color of death. Come back here when you save Age, and I'll lead you both to the laboratory."

Saying that the water is the color of death isn't helping, Angela!

At least it matches the sky.

But the sky has stars. This lake doesn't.

Good-bye, world of light, beauty, and love. I'm going into the desolate waters of darkness and bleakness.

I leapt inside the hole and entered the new dark world.

I scanned the murky depths for any sign of Age, tribulation skyrocketing. I kept swimming but kept finding nothing. I was starting to despair when the current pushed me to a slab of rock where Age was unconscious and floating around, like the lake was flaunting him at me.

I grabbed him and kept swimming upward to reach the top of the stone. I didn't stop until

I found myself above water at the entrance of a cave.

I pushed us up, sputtering. "Age? It's Matt! Age? You're still paralyzed, aren't you? I'll get you to Sophie so she can counteract whatever Marcus did to you. Since I'm not sure if I can lug you back while swimming, let's see where this cave will take us."

I placed him over my shoulder and made small talk to get rid of the we're-waltzing-down-a-cave-that-might-bring-us-to-doom aspect of the situation. "I was about to be crushed to death, but Marcus' cousin, Demetrius, saved me, and Marcus' sister Angela brought me here.

"I didn't know Marcus had a sister, and she's a pro at horseback riding. We should catch up with each other after we meet up with Sophie, Demetrius, and Angela."

As I carried Age through the cave, words written in French on one of the walls were visible. I wished I could understand what it meant. "I recognize that the language is French, but I can't read it. You can read and speak French, right?"

I speed-walked (not wanting to make Age vomit. I wasn't sure if paralyzed people could vomit, but I wasn't going to take the chance) and covered as much ground as I could.

Eventually, the writing gave way to paintings of Our Lady of Lourdes and Saint Bernadette Soubirous.

I kept going until we hit the end, and then stopped abruptly.

Clementine was standing in front of us. I put my hand over my mouth to stop myself from screaming.

I blandly assumed, "How did you find us? Are you here to finish the job?"

She waved flirtatiously. "Marcus sent me to make sure Age was dead. I'm not supposed to be doing this, but our love story is too romantic for me to kill you both. Here are two horses for you to ride back into the castle and stop Marcus."

I mounted on one. "Age will have to ride behind me. He's paralyzed. You'll have to make sure he won't fall off during the ride there." She secured him on behind me, and our horses shot forward like a bullet.

The wind whistled in my ears as I whizzed by on my steed, and we passed by a scarce amount of pine trees. My voice fought over the wind. "We need to meet up with Angela! After that, we can handle the situation without your help, so you can go back to whatever it is you do!"

Clementine replied, "Be careful! Magnus is a ruthless monarch with no mercy! He bullies the entire population of Oprimida!"

I was unfamiliar with Sterietolan geography and let her know. Clementine clarified, "Oprimida is the city closest to Tirano, the capital! There's also a town called Afortunado. Even though Sterietol is a large country, most of it is wilderness. The cave brought you to the south, so we need to ride through both places to get to Angela!"

We eventually got to Angela after riding through Afortunado, Oprimida, and the majority of Tirano. I awkwardly acknowledged her help, "Thank you for coming to our rescue in our hour of darkness, but you can go back to your plotting now."

With the sigh of an annoying knockoff romantic figure, Clementine disappeared from sight.

Angela was not pleased. "You were supposed to swim back here! Who was that girl?"

I updated her on everything. She softened

when she learned the reason we didn't swim back was because I couldn't carry Age and swim at the same time. Angela said, "Let's go to the laboratory where we'll meet up with Tree and Sophie."

We crawled inside the window (Age needed to be carried through). She throttled a suit of armor and ripped off the left foot, which uncovered a hole. "We need to take this exit. Hop on down."

I dove in first, and my body hit a cobblestone path. Charcoal blackness surrounded me.

Well, that's discouraging.

Angela commanded, "Matt, can you catch Age? Don't let him fall! He might hit his head!"

I assured her, "I'll take care of him." I saw a darker shape of black than the regular darkness falling. I moved under it, caught Age, and put him on my shoulder. "Ta-da! I'll catch you now."

Another dark shape hurtled down, and I caught Angela. A disturbing thought struck me. "Won't someone see the hole and know we're in here?" I couldn't see her face, even when she was inches away, which was mildly unsettling.

"I took care of it. Let's hold hands so we won't get separated. This is the only way to the laboratory, so we'll have to go this way."

We kept moving forward until Angela tapped me. "Matt, give me a boost. We have to get up."

I assessed, "You know an awful lot of these passageways for someone who doesn't live here."

"I examined the whole castle to help rescue you all. I take this very seriously. I still need that boost."

I didn't object. She stepped on my shoulder and pushed on the ceiling. Angela shrieked, "Hi, Tree! And you must be Sophie! Matt and Age are down in that hole; Age's paralysis is still an issue. Tree, can you pull them up?"

I gave Age over to Demetrius, who thrust him out of the tunnel of doom or whatever the proper term was. Demetrius instructed, "Matt, take my hand."

There was a dilemma. "I'm not tall enough to reach your hand."

Sophie broke in, "Let me get in. Hold on to me, Demetrius, and I'll hoist him up."

I felt her hand. "Got it!"

Sophie pulled me up to a room full of potions and medical equipment. Angela moved a fake tree over the hole.

Sophie twisted her ring around her finger. "Time to heal Age. What happened?"

I panicked. "I don't know! Marcus mentioned a scorpion. Age must have gotten stung by one, but I don't know which species!"

Sophie peered at all the vials. "I was there when Marcus mentioned the scorpion, you know. Anyway, Age was stung in Algeria. The first lethal scorpion I can think of is the *Leiurus quinquestriatus*. Does there happen to be Polyvalent Scorpion Antivenom here?"

Demetrius picked up a bottle with a hand-written label in French and a hypodermic needle. "As a matter of fact, yes. But please do not make me administer the elixir. I do not think I am as good as you are. There are no hospitals and no nursing instructors in Sterietol, but I soon hope to change that. It is unlikely in captivity, but I must keep hoping."

Sophie stared at the needle. "Is it clean? Do you have any disinfectant?"

Demetrius' face flushed. "I feel guilty that I live in the only building with access to basic sanitation." He then promptly handed Sophie disinfectant wipes.

Sophie cleaned and put the maximum dosage of Polyvalent Scorpion Antivenom inside the needle and injected it into one of Age's veins. Sophie twisted her ring. "Demetrius, how many vials do you have? Since we don't know how many times Age was stung, it might take more than just one."

Demetrius gave her four more bottles. "From my basic understanding, five vials of the antivenom is more than enough for the majority of cases."

Sophie exhaled. "Yes, but for all we know, Age was stung five hundred times. I can safely administer one hundred vials . . ."

This science stuff is really complicated. I'm glad Sophie really gets it.

Demetrius brightened. "These vials do happen to be extra potent. Our donor horses are given higher doses of venom, thanks to Marcus' experiments."

Sophie cleaned the needle again and continued to inject the remaining vials into Age's vein. She put her hands on her hips, clearly exhausted from the mental strain of Age's life in her hands. "Get comfortable. It can take four hours for recovery, just for a normal incident. It could be awhile."

Time passed slowly. We all huddled around Age silently for what could have been a few minutes up to several hours. After an eternity passed, Age regained control of his muscles and slowly rose. "Thanks for saving me, all of you."

I took charge, "We have to crash the wedding-"

Age sharply interrupted, "What wedding?"

I reminded him, "Marcus wants to marry Tara."

Age's face turned red with anger. "Seriously? That's happening now?! That Marcus troll is going down!"

Demetrius proposed, "Should we break into the chapel? Marcus does not have a religion---he probably worships himself like a Roman emperor---but that is the only room suitable for a wedding. Tara is Catholic, correct? The chapel is the place we must penetrate."

Sounds reasonable.

I asked, "Where's the chapel?"

Demetrius pointed to the ceiling. "The very top. Aunt Monica wanted it as close to God as possible. Angie, are there any secret passages we can take?"

Angela scratched her chin. "Yes, but it'll be easier to climb through the vents."

I was just grateful that there was no more mention of windows.

CHAPTER 33: TARA

Location: Tirano, Sterietol

After Age and Matt were assassinated and Sophie and Louis taken away, Marcus turned to me. "Your prince can't save you from marrying me now. He's dead, and so is your brother."

"Why would you think I'd want to marry you after you kidnapped us? We will *not* get married, you loathsome lowlife."

He belted out an evil laugh. "You would to save Sophie's life. I'll make a deal with you. If you marry me, after her piece of the puzzle is solved, Sophie will be freed."

I was not going to be outfoxed by a slug. "She has your name. Sophie is aware of the fact that you killed Matt and Age. You won't let any of us go."

He paced, a habit I had, and the fact that we had something in common irritated me. "You're wrong. If you marry me, I'll let Sophie live in Sterietol as a normal citizen. She can experience life that doesn't involve endless laceration. She just won't be allowed to leave Sterietol. Your move, princess."

I stammered, "M-matt wouldn't want me to do it."

He countered, "He didn't know I would save Sophie! Trust me, he would want you to take the deal. He was in love with her. Truman Shaw caught them about to kiss."

"You can't prove that."

Marcus rubbed his hands together. "I can. There are secret cameras in the castle that have footage on them. The captives were always watched, and all the cameras reported to the headquarters in the castle. Everything they were forced to do against their will is in here. I'm telling you that because you won't leave here."

I called him out on his bluff. "Oh really? Then take me there."

He blustered, "Truman! Escort the princess to the cameras! Our guest needs to see when Matt and Sophie almost locked lips! I have a wedding to set up. Citizens, get me a priest!"

Truman Shaw ushered me inside. "Here are the cameras. Whoops! We can't have this book in open sight."

He shoved a black book in a drawer and resumed the confident meandering of his speech, "You're supposed to see when I caught Matt and Sophie almost kissing? Here's the footage."

He played it. I watched with my own eyes as they almost kissed and Truman ripped them apart. "Should I marry Marcus to save Sophie?"

He stuffed a piece of gum in his mouth and chomped on it. "Since I like you, I'll give you advice. He'll force you to marry him somehow even if you refuse."

I shot back, "You can't force someone to marry you in the Catholic Church!"

"He'll force you to marry him in a civil ceremony."

I did not like my plight. "All I wanted was my brother back . . ."

Marcus burst into the room with a bang. "I couldn't find a priest who would marry us against Tara's will, so we're doing a civil ceremony. You'll marry us, Truman. Take the bride to the chapel.

I'll be waiting."

I was about to vomit. Age, the prince with sparkling, clear sapphire eyes and sunny blond hair who went to the ball to warn me, was dead, and I had to marry his murderer. It was too evil to be real.

Truman seriously asked, "Would you like me to sing a bridal song as we go down the aisle?"

"No! No! Just, no!"

He patted my shoulder. "I'll have mercy on you. I won't if you say so. You remind me of someone I care about. That's why I like you."

I'm a younger version of one of Truman Shaw's friends? That is so sad.

We proceeded to the chapel where I was *supposed to be married* while I tried to remain calm in a hostage crisis . . . and ignore the pimple. It was so sore I had to hobble.

Truman yanked me down the aisle and tied me to a pillar so I couldn't flee during the ceremony.

The wedding started, but I was filled with fear.

So, you sold your soul and are destined for Hell, you're going to starve to death with a contagious disease, your true love is dead, and Marcus is going to be your husband?

You're going to have to eat wedding cake that he's going to put in your mouth afterwards, aren't you? He might put too big a piece in your mouth, and you'll choke.

And you're afraid of choking. Have fun with your life, Tara! You deserve all of this, you monster.

CHAPTER 34: MATT

Location: Tirano, Sterietol

I forgot about the blasted window we had to climb through to get into the secret room. I helped Demetrius get inside. "Do you know what the overall plan is?"

He paused. "Somewhat. I know that, for the plan to work, Marcus has to marry your sister."

I bit my thumb. "He wants to marry Tara to be a prince of Delais; I heard two agents say that while I was in the vents. Why?"

Angela moved a table over and stood on top of it. "Speaking of vents, let's go in them. There are some up here. Age, do you have your screwdriver?"

Age winced. "It's in Delais. That stupid Traitor Delaisan confiscated it from me."

Angela moistened her lips. "We'll have to use the secret passage to get to the chapel then. Trickier, but doable." She pushed on a section of the wall, and it crumbled, revealing a secret staircase going up.

How many secret passages does this castle have?!

We carefully tiptoed up the steps since there was no railing to rescue us from a fall. I noted, "After we crash the wedding, we need to save Louis."

Demetrius' tone was etched in guilt. "Did any of you discover his whereabouts? I was busy making sure Matt survived the trash attack."

Sophie lost her footing, and I reached forward to catch her. "We don't want you to fall down."

Sophie's ring twirled around her finger. "Thanks for the save."

I kept looking down, and thoughts came about falling. "How much longer do we have to go? I'm getting paranoid about falling down and having to start from the bottom all over again."

Demetrius darkened. "We have a while."

Age wondered, "How was your childhood in Sterietol, Angela?"

Angela wiggled her fingers. "Numb. I haven't had circulation in my hands for years. They have the feeling of death in them. Tree and I made our Confirmation this year, which sounds random, but it's an accomplishment."

She and Tara would hit it off as amigos. "You'll get along with Tara. Are you obsessive-compulsive by nature?"

A friend with OCD would help Tara feel less isolated from everything in existence.

Angela cocked an eyebrow like she didn't understand me. I brushed it off. "Never mind. Demetrius, are we close to the chapel yet?"

Demetrius replied, "We are here now."

Angela kicked the wall open, and there were Marcus, Tara, and Truman, faced away from us.

Age tackled Marcus to the ground and started beating him. "You can kidnap and torture me for years, but I draw the line at marrying my soul-mate!"

Truman was too flabbergasted to wrench Age off of Marcus. I went to Tara and untied her from the pillar.

Marcus was shaken by the fact that we were there. "How are they *still* alive?"

Tara and I sidestepped Truman and got to the group. I caught Tara up to speed. "Demetrius saved me. Demetrius' cousin Angela helped me save Age. She's Marcus' sister, but nothing like him."

Demetrius kissed Tara's hand. "It is a pleasure, Princess Tara."

Forget having to deal with murderous relatives; being close to my sister is what he should be worried about.

I warned, "Watch it! I still need to have a talk with Age about dancing with my sister. Don't add your name to the list!"

At last Truman snapped himself out of his dazed state and went after us. Sophie kicked him against the wall, but unfortunately Truman didn't tumble down all the steps.

I questioned, "Where's Louis? What did you do to him?"

He was the last one to liberate . . . wounded all alone . . . with no one . . .

Age was clobbering the daylights out of Marcus. "Don't make my buddy Matt wait long! What did you do to Louis, and where is he? Where is he?!"

Marcus trembled. "On the top of the East turret! The East turret!"

Age got off of him, and Marcus' skin was black, blue, red, and pink.

I was desperate for constructive news. "Demetrius, can you bring us there?"

He did a quick calculation in his head. "Yes! It is this way! Follow me!"

Tara mused, "You guys rescued me? Even with all my weakness? Maybe I wasn't a mistake after all!"

I declared, "Who told you that you were a mistake? I'm going to punch his nose until he has to go to the hospital! And I don't care that Mom doesn't like fighting!"

"Get them!" Marcus and Truman were only

a faint echo. We zipped past countless corridors, and our footsteps pounded like crackling thunder.

A golden bejeweled door creaked open, revealing an overweight guy with whitish-blond hair wearing a nightgown at the entrance.

We must have woken him up.

The man addressed us, "The Garcia twins? Liechtensteiner? Hohenberg? Random blonde girl? Demetrius, I'm very disappointed in you for socializing with them!"

Age glared at the man. "You're King Magnus, aren't you? Your son tried to marry Tara. It was a vulgar ceremony. Vulgar! You should ground him. He's coming now."

I'm face to face with the man who coordinated all of our heartache.

I felt nothing.

Why don't I have any emotion? I should feel something.

We made our leave with Magnus, Marcus, and Truman tailing us.

Demetrius brought us to a section of the castle that overlooked the rest of Tirano, with Oprimida in the distance. Louis was there, tied to a single plank that was doomed to fall with a single poke. I called, "Louis, we're here! We'll get you down!"

He whimpered, "Matt, I'm scared. I'm going to fall!"

God, Louis was always so virtuous; please don't let him fall! Please! We need him!

I ambled to where he was and started to untie him. "Don't be! You'll be fine!"

Marcus boomed, "There they are!"

Magnus was unamused. "You couldn't keep them under control, Marcus? Who are you, Truman? He's so wimpy he can't even have one identity."

Truman flinched at his superior's reprimand.

'One identity'? What does that mean?

Forget it! Just save Louis!

After all the knots were undone, I pulled him away from the edge. I motioned for Demetrius to come closer. "Can you get us out of this?"

Uncertainty flickered over his face.

Magnus screamed, "Soldiers, arise at your king's disposal!" Armed men with bows and arrows entered.

We're on top of a turret! This is too close range for arrows!

Magnus barked, "Kill the blond boy and the boy with black hair that's not my nephew or son!"

Demetrius bowed. "You are right, Uncle. I am full of remorse that I assisted these behemoths." He went to Magnus' side.

He's going back there after we crashed a wedding together? I trusted him! What a turncoat!

The soldiers started firing at us. Louis shoved me to the floor. "Duck! Does anyone have a master plan to get out of this one?"

Marcus snatched a bow from a soldier and fired at Age. The arrow sliced his arm, and Age sedately ripped it out.

Tara had a concerned lovesick tone. "Are you okay?"

Age smiled. "Whenever you're here, I'm completely well."

Age and I are so having a talk if we get out of this alive!

Marcus was boiling, and Demetrius noticed his anger, as well. Demetrius stole a guard's sword. "Adrian! Catch!" He cast it up in the air.

Age caught and yielded it with expertise. Marcus shot a volley of arrows at him, but he (having a proficiency in weapons as a survival skill) deflected them away toward Marcus' direction.

In a matter of a split second, Marcus also deflected the arrows (He must have received training, as well), but onto his father.

Magnus howled and fell on the floor, his side gushing out blood. The soldiers stood open-mouthed at their leader gasping for breath.

Marcus was dancing. "Glad you're out of the way, Father! That accident was a lucky one! I'm the boss now!"

Angela sprang to Magnus' side. "Daddy!"

All of us traveled to the moribund king. Age whispered, "Is there anything we can do to save him?"

Magnus exhaled. "No, Your Serene Highness, I'm finished." He gazed at Angela. "Are you the child my Monica gave birth to before she died? You are very beautiful; you remind me of myself when I was your age."

Demetrius affirmed, "Yes, this is your daughter Angela."

Magnus was glassy-eyed. "You are all mourning for me, the man who sought out your destruction, while my son is celebrating. Why?"

Louis spoke, "We're Catholics. It's one of our obligations, even if all we see in you is a slimy leech for doing this to us."

Magnus observed Louis. "You tell it like it is. So, this is what Catholicism is about, literally loving your enemy? Monica was Catholic. Church teaching was decent and all, but I was too obsessed with becoming powerful. And look at me now . . . my own son is dancing on my grave."

Angela held his hand. "It'll be okay now, Daddy."

Magnus started tearing up. "I wasn't an adequate father. I coached Marcus to feed on the meek. I was a failure. Too bad it took my son re-joicing my death for me to see it."

Tara's voice was scratchy. "We're still here for you."

Magnus leaned his head back on the floor. "You're right; you are here comforting me on my deathbed. I guess Catholics weren't wrong after all. If it's not too much to request, no, ask, can you baptize me before I die?"

Demetrius stood with an air of authority. "Soldiers! Do any of you have water on you?"

One handed him a water canteen. Demetrius proclaimed, "I baptize you, Magnus Erik Niceren, in the name of the Father, and of the Son, and of the Holy Spirit," as he poured the water on his head three times.

Magnus' eyes gleamed. "You did it? I'm sorry for conspiring against you all, kidnapping you all, telling Marcus to marry Tara, and killing a number of innocent people whose names I don't know. I apologize to each and every one of you! I'm sorry for everything. Wait . . . Adrian! Matt! I have something important to tell you both!"

Age leaned in close to Magnus, and he said something in his ear. Age scrunched his eyebrows together. "Isn't that disrespectful? Why should I burn-"

Magnus interrupted, "You need to do that if you want to stop the overall plot. It's the only way; I'm sure God will understand. Matt."

I kneeled down and scooted myself over so I could hear him. Magnus breathed, "The piece of your puzzle is your crown. My son will attempt to take it. End this before the twisted plot I created unfolds even more."

My crown? Is he delirious from his wounds?

Magnus touched his bleeding side. "I'm sorry

for everything. Angela, I love you. Soldiers, you have witnessed this: I declare Demetrius Gaudium as my heir, not my son, and I recognize my daughter Angela as my daughter, so she's a princess whether she takes my surname or not!

"Demetrius, I'm so sorry for holding you captive after Monica died. I have done the worst deeds to you that I deeply regret, but I won't tell you for fear you won't love me.

"Angela, I'm sorry if you are hurt by me not naming you my heir, but I just met you. After years of observation, I know Demetrius is fully capable. He'll make a grand king.

"Children, forgive me . . . innocent dead people, forgive me . . . God forgive me . . . Monica . . ." He moaned and died.

Angela hugged her stomach. "Oh my gosh! Oh my gosh! He died! He died!"

Sophie consoled, "Don't be sad! Since he turned good in the end, he's in Purgatory now, and will go to Heaven to be with your mom really soon."

Marcus ceased dancing and bared his teeth. "Wait, now I'll never know Matt's piece! And did my father just name Demetrius his heir? This cannot be! I am the rightful king of Sterietol by birthright! I will hunt down every last one of you and exterminate you!"

Demetrius considered him for a full minute. "You mean all the hatred that rises in your voice? Every word that cascades off your tongue is deliberately true? Correct me if I am mistaken."

Marcus sneered, "Why wouldn't I mean it? You're just a bunch of fifteen-year-old urchins! I'm a seventeen-year-old man."

Demetrius snapped his fingers. "You have made your choice. Guards, arrest Prince Marcus and Truman Shaw. They are now nemeses to the Sterietolan throne and to the entire country."

The guards turned on Marcus and Truman. Marcus screeched, "No! You shall not contain me! I am invincible!" He whipped his sword centimeters from Age's throat.

CHAPTER 35: AGE

Location: Tirano, Sterietol

Marcus lowered his voice so only I could hear him. "Give me one reason why I shouldn't kill you this second."

Since the soldiers' attention was on Marcus, Truman started to slink away. I provided, "Truman is abandoning you."

The majority of the guards went after Truman, but Marcus was still trained on me. "If I'm captured, I intend on making sure everyone knows how dangerous I am." He nicked me.

Tara's harmonic voice went into casual hysteria. "Marcus, stop! If you care at all that I was your hostage fiancée, you'd let him go."

Marcus thundered, "He ruined our wedding! He should die!"

Tara enveloped me in her arms.

If Marcus does murder me, I'll die in the arms of the most spectacular girl in the world. Out of all of the almost-deaths I've been in, this is the best.

Demetrius held up a hand in an undeniably commanding manner. "Guards, I gave you an order as your king, and I expect you to follow it! Detain the criminal Marcus Niceren!"

They grabbed Marcus from behind and tied his hands together with rope. One awkwardly expounded to a bewildered Tara, "We don't have handcuffs." They escorted him away while we remained in shock.

Marcus' arrest was a miracle. I breathed, "Is it

over? Is this all over? Magnus turned honorable, his brat is in custody, and Truman is about to be behind bars, too."

Matt's face was as white as the pale, shallow moon above us. "What about Clementine? She did save our lives, but she was still one of them. What about the Traitor Delaisan? What about all those other people in on it?"

"I'll let you ponder that until your last breath. You bleed a very appealing shade of red. I might get a vial and fill it with your blood to keep as a sample to use forever."

There were many others in on it.

Demetrius stealthily crept down the exit Truman took. "Let us check up on the guards capturing Truman. The ones with Marcus no doubt led him to the dungeon."

Matt was uneasy. "There was a Delaisan traitor . . . there could be a Sterietolan one, too! We need to split up so we won't all be in the same place. If there's a traitor waiting for us, at least not all of us will be recaptured. Tara, Sophie, and I will check up on Truman-while the rest of you make sure Marcus is detained. Got it?"

Angela, Demetrius, Louis, and I were in hot pursuit of Marcus' jailers. Demetrius waved his arms up and down. "I order you to stop moving! That is an order!"

The guards halted with Marcus in their custody. Demetrius huffed, "We wish to accompany you in the transportation of the prisoner to his cell."

Men in Delaisan uniforms marched down the hall with guns pointed at all of us. One woman yelled, "After Princess Tara went missing, we did another investigation and arrived here. Someone tell us what's going on!"

Demetrius put his hands in a surrender pose. "I apologize for meeting you all under such circumstances. I am King Demetrius of Sterietol; my uncle, King Magnus, just passed away . . ."

The woman wasn't convinced. "Magnus died, and he picked you over his own son to succeed him?"

Louis chimed in, "Yes! Magnus converted to Catholicism before he died, and Demetrius baptized him. Then Magnus named Demetrius his heir. Magnus' body is still unburied in the castle."

A man questioned, "Marcus appears to be in custody. You had him arrested, King Demetrius?"

Demetrius affirmed, "Yes, I did. I also had Truman Shaw arrested, but he might have escaped."

The Delaisans nodded. "Prince Louis, Duke of Brabant, Adrian, Hereditary Prince of Liechtenstein, Count Rietberg, and an unidentified blonde girl are safely with you."

Angela waved. "I'm Princess Angela, Marcus' younger sister."

Other people in three different brands of uniform burst in. "We're Interpol, CIA, and FBI agents. We worked together with the Delaisan Combat Team. Care to explain where Princess Tara is?"

I blurted, "She, Matt, and Sophie went after Truman Shaw after he tried to flee. Demetrius is on our side; it might take a while to go over the story, but he and Angela are innocent. And, in captivity, we were forced to do illegal things. We never wanted to do them. Are we going to jail, too?"

The woman took charge. "This is highly complicated. You all were obviously in captivity, but we don't know what you were forced to do yet. Is there any way to know right now before we do anything else?"

Demetrius respired. "The footage! There is footage in a room that has all the evidence. But, since Matt was kidnapped at birth, there is fifteen years' worth of video evidence to watch. I can take you there. Please transport Marcus to a facility where he can no longer hurt anyone. I have had enough of his childish games."

We went to a room (with the Delaisans still pointing guns at Demetrius and Angela) that was full of technology. Demetrius hit the "play" button, and the footage started. Demetrius rocked back and forth on his feet. "You are welcome to view it all. Are we all going into custody?"

They did a quick overlook of the film. "That is one option. But there is another: we check in on you all to make sure that you haven't fled the authorities and gone into hiding. If you go into hiding, you're under arrest. King Demetrius and Princess Angela, how can you claim innocence in this matter? That is key information to grasp."

Angela reviewed, "My biological mother put me up for adoption soon after I was born. My parents have the adoption paperwork; you can check with them. The only thing I had to do with the plot was rescuing the hostages."

They inquired, "Who are your parents?"

Angela stated, "Pierre and Antoinette Bernard. They live in Afortunado."

A few Delaisans put their guns away. "We'll ask to see the papers and make a photocopy of them for the courts. They'd like to see it."

The CIA agents brought us back on track. "King Demetrius, you need to prove your innocence."

He elaborated, "When my parents died, Queen Monica took me in, and I lived with the Sterietolan royal family. When Queen Monica died, Magnus held me hostage in the castle. He was relentless in his quest to make me like Marcus and him, but I pray that did not work."

How could he say that about himself?

I defended him. "You're nothing like them! If you were on Marcus' side, Matt and I would be dead! Then, worst of all, none of us could've stopped Marcus from marrying Tara against her will! You're the very model of nobility!"

Demetrius grumbled, "You have not even known me for a full day."

I pointed out, "And yet you've already helped save two lives and crashed a wedding!"

The agents took us outside. "Where are Princess Tara, Crown Prince Matt, and Princess Sophie? They weren't recaptured, were they?"

I wracked my brain with all the possibilities. "Not likely."

Demetrius gave directions on where to find them to the Delaisan Combat Team, Interpol, FBI, and CIA. Some members headed off in that direction, while others stayed with us.

Angela was deep in thought. "To pass the time, would you like me to sing the national anthem of Sterietol? It's called 'The Melody of the Glaciers.'" Angela sang,
"People try
People do
All they can
To stop Death
Never to succeed
Life blooms
And withers all the same
No mortal can change that

But here we are
Despite the odds

In mighty Sterietol,
Survivor of blustering storms
Shining like a diamond
Glistening like a snow-capped dove

When the tempests merge with vengeance
And I am left for dead
Sterietol, bring me to your Savior
Carry me to the heavenly skies for eternity

People try
People do
All they can
To stop Death
Never to succeed
Life blooms
And withers all the same
No mortal can change that
No
No mortal can change that . . ."

It's true. We're powerless without the greater things around us. I wonder why all the fairytales never mention that the prince needs saving, too. As a prince, I know we do.

Our hope, like that of all humans, is the joy of salvation. I wonder what life would be like without the hope of Heaven.

What a cruel world that must be.

CHAPTER 36: MATT

Location: Tirano, Sterietol

With Tara and Sophie at my side, I had no fear of going after the man who took me from my family several years ago. I called after the guards, "Did you get Truman Shaw?"

The guard who gave Demetrius the water bottle to baptize Magnus spoke, "Truman Shaw has disappeared, and so has the traitor of your country."

I fumed, "They're here somewhere! We have to keep searching!"

Right then, the Traitor Delaisan and Truman jumped out of the shadows, the former pointing a gun at me. "Gentlemen, exit at once, or my dear crown prince will be injured."

I want to squish his face under my shoe so much right now . . .

The Sterietolan soldiers sprinted out like they had never handled a rescue operation before. The Traitor Delaisan snatched my arm. "Come with me."

Tara punched his arm. "Let him go, you oaf!"

He cruelly cracked a smile that showed rows of pure white teeth. "You all get to come with him! I can shoot any of you at any moment I choose."

Ew. Are his teeth made from human bones?

I narrowed my eyes. "Why did you commit treason against our country?"

The Traitor Delaisan's voice rose an octave. "That has nothing to do with the fact that you're being held at gunpoint. Go where I say, or you, your sister, or your girlfriend will be murdered."

Sophie is not my girlfriend! She is not! I almost kissed her once! We didn't even kiss!

I shut my mouth. He jammed the gun against my back. "Bravo. All of you go around the corner and then down that corridor."

We all obeyed, and I was personally stirred that neither girl was taking any chances since my life was in jeopardy.

The Traitor Delaisan took us to a bench with rope on it. Truman tied us all up. "That wasn't too troubling, was it?"

Tara licked her chapped lips. "The traitor had a gun against my brother's back. He was acting like Charlie! That was petrifying!"

Truman's voice dripped with sarcastic ridicule, "The girl with OCD was scared of something. Shocker. All you OCD sufferers do is cry. The world would be better off without any of you dragging the rest of humanity down."

If only Truman's opinion mattered to me...

Maybe the experience of the adventure had washed away her timid nature, or maybe that was the last straw, because she said something that everyone with OCD who had ever bullied should have said to the society that persecuted them long ago. Long, long ago.

Tara bared her teeth like a savage with a pure Portuguese flame that outshone the stars. "You should realize that there is so much more to OCD. You understand that the world thinks I'm a freak? Because it does. Even the childhood shows make fun of OCD in general.

"When a character sees a psychologist, he gets made fun of by the 'heroes'! It may seem like I'm being overly sensitive. But here's another fact to consider before you make a conclusion: the laughing track is on, like having OCD and seeing a psychologist are legitimate reasons to get made fun of.

"Do the networks know what we go through? But the fight isn't just with entertainment. It's society in general that hates us.

"Does society know I was once a little girl praying to God every single night to let me live?

"I guess, to the world, that's funny. I guess it's hilarious that, in elementary school, my supposed best friend betrayed me after I told her *everything*, and that everyone thought I was a pathetic excuse for a human being because I was the only little girl with an anxiety disorder.

"All my classmates left me for dead when I was afraid to eat; I could've starved for all they cared. But guess what? I wasn't hurt because I was used to it. I guess that's everyone's entertainment, making fun of people with mental health problems.

"Sometimes we can function-that's right, sometimes! Sometimes the disorder is so severe we can't get out of the house. But I guess that's hysterical to you. A disorder doesn't make us worthy of insults.

"Do you know what else we do? Some of us cry in the middle of the night every single night, over and over and over without stopping, because we're trying to shake off the feeling that we're deadweight. And, meanwhile, we get made fun of by everyone!

"This is comical to you all? Why aren't I surprised? Oh right, because I'm used to it!

"So, someone is fighting a mental disorder, and, in the very next second, people like them get made fun of! For a mental disorder! That's revolting, you shriveled-up zombie of a society! Do we deserve this?

"And, if you say yes, that I, with all my OCD panic attacks, afraid that I sold my soul, afraid to eat, or flat-out afraid of everything, am less of a monster than you, you slimy disgusting low-life who acts like a pompous Roman emperor, getting enjoyment out of making fun of people with an anxiety disorder in their brain . . .

"If you say yes, you are less of a human being than I will ever be."

I was so proud of her.

Tara is fierce. She's a lot tougher than people give her credit for.

Armed, uniformed agents entered. A CIA agent elaborated, "We heard Tara yelling, so we went in the direction of her voice."

One man in all white was close to tears. "That was the most outstanding speech I have heard in my life! That was breathtaking. If only I did that when I was your age."

Tara squealed, "Anton! You're here! Matt, this is my bodyguard Anton." The uniformed men untied us and handcuffed the Traitor Delaisan and Truman.

Tara smiled in a very sweet and captivating way. "May I please punch Truman in the face until he's barely alive?"

Anton was amused. "We could fudge the paperwork and say he fell, but I'm sure he feels very embarrassed that he was apprehended by an infuriated teen princess with OCD. Because that's what scum do."

Sophie murmured, "I knew your sister had it in her. You could tell from the innocent gleam in her eye . . ."

Anton turned on Traitor Delaisan. "Pedro, why would you do this to us? You treasonous snake!"

Pedro's eyes smoldered. "I wanted power. Once these nitwits croaked, King James and Queen Hildegarde would have renounced the throne that slaughtered their children. Then I could've overthrown the next in line; Dolores' too old to stand against me. Delais is the most powerful country in the world! Our raw intellect cannot be matched! We could blackmail the whole world into doing anything we wanted!"

Anton refuted, "We don't blackmail countries because that is *not* how model citizens behave! When you're in prison, will I have to send you the First Level Ethics curriculum? Don't think I won't!"

That was the perfect response. It really was.

Anton peered at Truman. "Have I seen you before? You look familiar."

Truman wrinkled his nose. "No. I would've remembered such a strange person like you."

The authorities took Pedro and Truman away (minus Anton since he was Tara's bodyguard). Anton pulled Tara into a hug. "I worked nonstop day and night until I found you, kiddo."

After the embrace, Anton brought us outside, where Age, Louis, Demetrius, and Angela waited. I informed them, "They got the rogue Delaisan and Truman. But Clementine and Giovanni are out there, plus countless other people."

A Delaisan clapped me on the back. "We'll keep an eye out for Clementine, Giovanni, and all the other people involved."

Louis raised his hand. "There's an American politician named Senator Goodwin Scarlett who was in on it. He's in Minnesota. I'm still not over it! I am outraged with Minnesota despite the state's innocence, and I will be until the End of Time!"

Poor Louis.

He's strong. He'll be okay.

Sophie smirked at me. "There are some people in Sardinia, with some police involved. At least that's more specific than Matt's 'countless other people.'"

I stuck my tongue out at her, and an FBI agent assured us, "We'll search Senator Scarlett's home and investigate the 'countless other people.'"

A man in very formal attire walked up. "Even before we get to the legal stuff, you need to go to the hospital."

Age volunteered, "Tara didn't commit any crimes."

The formal man's tone grew more serious. "Don't worry about the legal stuff right now. Your health is more important. We're aware that you were under duress."

Sophie informed him, "We have tracking devices in us and need surgery to get them out."

The formal man cringed. "There aren't hospitals in Sterietol. We'll fly you to Canada, where they can do surgery."

Louis tapped an Interpol agent. "Magnus' body is still in the castle. Can you put it in a morgue if Demetrius gives you permission?"

The Interpol agent high-fived us all. "Don't worry. We'll take care of it. We'll make sure Magnus gets a proper burial."

I bragged, "I prayed to Saint Leonard to get out of this alive, and we did!"

Catholicism works.

Age grinned. "You took down an evil prince by praying. Go, Matt!"

Louis had a mystified twinkle in his eyes as he watched Angela. "She has eyes like the sky and hair like the sun. She's stunning."

Age entered another world, but wasn't love-struck with whatever was on his mind, so it wasn't Tara.

Magnus told him to burn something and told me Marcus would be after my crown.

What's going on here? Not all the puzzles have been solved in this mystery.

CHAPTER 37: TARA

Location: Inuvik, Canada

After the check-ups to make sure we weren't going to die, our parents were allowed to visit us. Since we had no life-threatening injuries, the staff let us be in one room together.

Louis had his back to me. "I'm a little apprehensive. This is such a change."

Age slouched in his seat. "I am, too. Now we won't have to move place to place every year. It's going to be very different."

Sophie butted in, "Everyone knows who we are. I saw reports about us on the international news. They interviewed our parents. Age, yours were really beaten up. They were sobbing uncontrollably."

Age reasoned, "It must have been the recent torture session. A lot of blood spilled out."

Since when was he tortured?

I demanded, "Age, what happened to you?"

Age shrugged. "A man blindfolded me so I didn't see what was going on. Clementine popped in, too. Her croons about Matt were the real torture."

Matt cowered, "We saw his hands covered in blood. Age really looked dead. And I've seen many dead bodies."

A blonde lady with green eyes and a man with brown hair and blue eyes ran to Age and hugged him over and over. Age quietly shook with emotion. "Mother? Father? Is it really you?"

Age's mother cried, "We were so worried!"

Age said, "Mother, Father, I'd like you to meet Tara. She is a very significant person to me. She's a gem."

I was touched that he introduced me to his parents right after seeing them again for the first time in a decade. I shook their hands. "Hi, your son is the real gem. He's such a gentleman."

His mother declared, "I've heard all about you, Princess Tara."

Oh no! She must've found out about my OCD! She knows I sold my soul! Great. Now she thinks that I'm not good enough for her son.

Age's mom finished, "They were all splendid things. I hear you are an impeccable student."

That's a lot better than I feared.

Don't burp in their face or something!

My heartbeat quickened. "Why, thank you! It's a pleasure to meet you both."

His father dismissed my awkwardness. "The pleasure is all ours."

Age finally spoke again, "Dad, one of the kidnappers told me you were bitten by the *Leiurus quinquestriatus* scorpion."

Age's father froze. "I was. I hate them. They're tough buggers. In fact, after you were born, I made sure . . . never mind. I'll tell you later. We have company."

A group of adults stood in the doorway.

Louis sprang up. "All our folks are here! Well, Angela's parents cover Tree's deceased relatives. Hi, Mom! Hi, Dad!" The group crowded us after a split second.

Mom and Dad's eyes were red. Dad apologized to Age, "I'm so sorry I had you arrested."

Age laughed. "I don't blame you. Marcus made me look like a criminal. It takes one to know one."

All the other parents were hugging their child. One child. I addressed the group, "No siblings? None of you have siblings except for Matt and me?" Being part of the only sibling unit was a little eerie.

Age's mom explained, "After the threat was sent regarding our children, we concluded that, if we had more, they would be in danger, as well, so we didn't have any others."

I immediately felt guilty after the words came out of my mouth. "Logical. If I were you, I'd do the same."

Now they hate you. Way to go, Tara.

Although, it doesn't take much for people to hate you. You sold your soul; you're a despicable person.

Don't question anything from now on; you're too stupid to understand reality.

A nurse piped up, "I hate to interrupt, but the children should be more fully examined for medical reasons."

Sophie vouched, "She's right. We have tracking devices in us that should be taken out. We don't want the criminals to track us."

Our parents waved and left. "We'll visit you when we can."

The nurse grinned. "You'll see them soon enough. Let's make sure you don't have any minor ailments."

CHAPTER 38: TARA

Location: Inuvik, Canada

The cause of the pain in my leg turned out to be an abscess, not an unusual pimple. The medication the doctor gave me didn't make it go away, so I had a day-long surgery on it. The hospital staff found the tracking device in me, so I had surgery on that, too.

OCD was a tiger, but the Delaisans were doing ERP with me, especially with food. I actually completed Anne's hierarchy, but still had some jitters left over.

I was the only one still in a hospital room due to the tracking device surgery because, while I got the abscess removed, everyone else got their tracking device taken out.

The Delaisan Combat Team and other uniformed people came in. "Hello, Princess Tara! It has been affirmed that all illegal activity done by the hostages was against their will, so all charges have been dropped. They're free to go."

I beamed. "That's amazing! How is everyone else doing?"

A Delaisan updated me, "Princess Angela, King Demetrius, Princess Sophie, Hereditary Prince Adrian, and Prince Louis already checked out of the hospital with their parents, and are in the area . . ."

I wasn't following. "Why aren't they back home?"

An Interpol agent interpreted, "We had them

stay in an area where we could keep tabs on them until we were sure they were under duress while committing the crimes. It would also give them time to bond with their families before their parents had to go back to work."

The Delaisan went on as if I hadn't said anything. "Your brother's head is under observation for trauma because Truman hit the scar, and it was bleeding."

I was prepared to cover my ears in case of bad news. "Is he going to live?"

The Delaisan quickly said, "Yes. Your parents have also asked me to give you something . . ."

Sophie and her parents bounded into the room. Sophie sat in the chair next to my bed. "Hi, Tara! How are you? I wanted to visit you."

I divulged, "I just got out of surgery. OCD's high; I'm so nervous when I eat, but, when I do ERP, it gets under control eventually. The Delaisans are teaching me how to do it right. I feel safe with these people."

Sophie asked, "What's OCD?"

After I summed it up and told her my forms of it, she got it. I changed the subject. "Enough about my OCD. How are you?"

She was as excited as Matt was when he discovered chocolate. "Fantastic! I'm united with my family, and I'm leaving to go home to Austria in a bit. I'm going to attend a school with other teens! That sounds crazy."

I felt a twinge of sadness. "Will I ever see you again?"

Sophie's mother put a hand on my shoulder with maternal concern. "Demetrius bought her a cell phone. Your parents told us about how you broke off your friendship with a mean girl before the whole ordeal."

I bared my teeth. "Piper. She was extremely rude, lied to me, and trash-talked me behind my back about OCD. She judged me based off of a disorder I have."

Sophie raised her chin. "You don't need her then. Mom, do you have a piece of paper and a pencil I can write my number down on?" Her mother went through her purse and got both items out.

Sophie wrote her number down for me and placed it on the desk where the nurses put my food.

How did she memorize her number so fast? I haven't memorized my number in two years.

My face felt hot. "My phone is back in America, and I haven't memorized the number."

The Delaisan who was cut off by Sophie's arrival intervened, "I get to be the hero. Tara, the object your parents want you to have *is* your cell phone. After their talk with the Hohenbergs, they thought it would be a good idea for you to keep in touch with Princess Sophie of Hohenberg."

I thanked him and wrote my number on the piece of paper before ripping it in half. "This is so stellar! Do Age, Angela, Demetrius, or Louis have a number, too?"

Sophie responded, "Demetrius bought all of us a cell phone on behalf of Sterietol. He claims it's the least he can do after Marcus and Magnus' involvement in our kidnappings. Now, focus on getting better after surgery. Recover. Recover."

I giggled. "I will; I feel so much better now that you're here. You didn't even freak out when I told you I may have sold my soul! True friend, right here. Now I have friends who really care about me, and one of them is a handsome blond prince. It's a shame it took me fifteen years to find you all. But the past is the past. Let's focus on moving forward."

CHAPTER 39: TARA

Location: Amor, Delais

Helene rubbed her hands together in anticipation. "I'm glad your parents are letting us meet once a week. You'll improve faster. This is my overall goal for your scrupulosity based on your hierarchy you made for me last week."

Week 1: Sit with the uncertainty.

❖ *When the thought that you sold your soul comes, say, "Maybe I did sell my soul; maybe I didn't."*

❖ *Rate your anxiety on a scale of one to ten, one being "no stress" and ten being "OCD is murdering me" and sit with the feeling.*

Week 2: Look up if you can sell your soul on the Internet

❖ *Rate your anxiety and sit with it.*

Week 3: Imagine what Hell looks like because you sold your soul

❖ *Rate your anxiety in the same fashion as before.*

Week 4: Write a script about you selling your soul

❖ *Rate your anxiety in the same fashion as before.*

I wondered, "What's next after the four weeks?"

Helene answered, "Either it will take longer than a week to go over a step, or we'll move on to your eating. You're afraid of choking and starving, right? I'm only the OCD specialist; I make mistakes."

I adored her. "You're a miracle worker, Helene."

She simpered. "Appreciate it. Did you sell your soul?"

I grew worried. The memory from seventh grade filled every corner of my mind. "I hope not."

Helene pointed at my sheet. "That's not what you're supposed to say. Can you read it for me?"

I trembled. "Maybe I did sell my soul; maybe I didn't."

She clapped. "Did you sell your soul?"

I repeated, "Maybe I did sell my soul; maybe I didn't."

Helene was ecstatic. "If that thought comes up, you'll know what to do."

Anton commented, "Man, you're already admitting you might have sold your soul? It took me five months for that, and this is your week one."

Helene covered the sheet I was holding with her hands. "Turn your back to us, Anton! This is supposed to be confidential!"

He argued, "I'm her bodyguard. I'm her human version of a German Shepherd; I won't tell anyone."

She rolled her eyes. "All men are human versions of German Shepherds. Anyway, Tara, that's it for this week."

Matt came by. "How's ERP coming along?"

Anton grumbled, "She's doing better than I did at her age. She's already doing OCD homework."

I gave Matt my paper. "You have proper clearance. How are you?"

Matt bit his thumb. "All right. I just texted Age."

My favorite person to talk about!

I gushed, "Ooh! How is he?"

Matt looked at the sky. "Fine. He's taken up poetry again."

Poetry about me?

I blushed. "That's spectacular! What else is new with you?"

Matt brightened. "After Demetrius' coronation, I'm moving back to Taunton so Father Leon and I will have some one-on-one lessons to make up for the classes I missed. RCIA, here I come."

I was happy I didn't have that cross to bear. "I was so thrilled when I found out I hadn't missed any CCD classes."

Anton coughed. "Sorry to interrupt, but it's time for a Princess Lesson. Tara, I need to teach you how to throw a knife properly."

I put my hands over my heart. "I've always wanted to, but my parents weren't delighted with their only daughter touching weapons. That mystifies me, considering the event that happened in middle school. That Charlie, what a cousin."

Matt's temper was aroused. "This Charlie is related to us? What did he do to you? I'm going to beat the evil out of him! Does this have anything to do with Mom and Dad saying someone would take you away? You never told me about that."

I became uncomfortable. "No, it doesn't. I'll tell you when I'm ready! Patience. These matters are not for light conversation. When it is time, you will find out."

TWO WEEKS LATER

CHAPTER 40:
TARA

Location: Tirano, Sterietol

Dear Diary,

The OCD treatment in Delais is a dream. Helene is legendary. I bet my buddy Saint Dymphna put in a good word for me with God.

Senator Goodwin Scarlett's home is still being searched for clues. Still. It's difficult to find subtle clues in a humongous mansion.

We're still waiting for Easter to roll around for Matt to receive the sacraments.

Scientific researchers discovered why Age wasn't killed by the Deathstalker, but they aren't releasing the results, so I don't know why. My Prince Charming defies physics.

Not really, but I get to write what I want in my diary.

Demetrius invited us to his coronation. I'm currently in Sterietol now, as a guest in the castle.

There's going to be a ball afterwards, and Age asked if I wanted to be his date! He also said he has a gift for me.

But we're not dating. Mom and Dad have a "no-dating-until-sixteen" rule, and I'm fifteen, so it's just a one-time thing.

I'm sure Age and Matt had a long talk about it. A long, long talk. Matt said it was a four-hour seminar. Matt's going to watch us like a hawk. It's still going to be magical!

I picked up my pen, incredulous that all that happened during my freshman year of high school.

Matt poked his head in the door. "Tara, it's time to go to the church for Demetrius' coronation."

I closed my diary and put the pen away, following Matt outside to where the horses, Age, Sophie, Demetrius, Louis, and Angela (and my parents) were waiting for us.

I asked, "Angela, are you going to change your last name to Niceren, or are you keeping it Bernard?"

Angela bit her lip. "I haven't decided yet, but I'll let you all know when I make a decision."

Matt mounted on a horse, and I jumped up behind him and put my arms around his waist.

Sophie twisted her ring around her finger. "Are we all ready to go?"

The rest of the gang (and my parents) got on their horses, and we rode to the church.

When we arrived, we filed into the pews and waited for the ceremony to begin.

At the end of Mass, the bishop held the crown. Demetrius knelt on one knee in front of the congregation. The bishop queried, "Do you, Count Demetrius Alexius Linus Gaudium, solemnly swear to rule with justice and mercy to the best of your ability?"

Demetrius replied, "I, Count Demetrius Alexius Linus Gaudium, do solemnly swear to rule with justice and mercy to the best of my ability."

The bishop placed the crown on his head. "I present King Demetrius Alexius Linus Gaudium of Sterietol. Arise, Your Royal Highness."

Demetrius rose, with all of us applauding and Angela and the Sterietolans crying with happiness.

Louis predicted, "He's going to do marvelous

things."

Age offered his arm to me. "Time to go to the ballroom, my lady." I grasped it, and we mounted on a horse.

Matt pronounced, "Not so fast! I'm riding alongside you!"

I hugged Age. "Thanks again for warning me about Marcus even when I was mean to you. You really are a prince."

Matt objected, "No hugging, Tara! You're only allowed to hug him when we're all close to dying."

We galloped to the castle and walked into the ballroom, where an orchestra was warming up.

Demetrius came up to Age and me. "I did a favor for you. The first song the orchestra will play is 'Fantasia on Greensleeves.' My only apprehension in making this request was inadvertently vexing Tara's brother, but he will forgive me eventually."

Age shook his hand. "You're the best, Demetrius. Thanks so much. Congratulations on becoming the king! You'll be a good one."

I fist-bumped Demetrius. "Age took the words out of my mouth."

Demetrius smiled. "It *is* my responsibility as a Catholic monarch to rule with kindness. It is a contrast to the Roman emperors, is it not? They ruled by fear, but we are obligated to reign with love, and I will rise to the expectations."

I offered, "If you need any help, you can always go to your royal advisors. Don't think you're alone. It hurts to be alone."

Demetrius' eyes shined. "I am not, and I am grateful for that. Life is starting to be like my childhood again, when I would play treasure hunt in the wilderness. There was a strange, one-of-a-kind fountain-like . . . structure that made the perfect destination."

I was starting to think of him as a friend. "Points for creativity!"

The song started playing. Age bowed. "Tarian Princess, may I have this dance?"

I took his arm. "You're the only person with whom I would dance to 'Fantasia on Greensleeves.' But what does 'tarian' mean?"

We went to the center of the room like we did at my ball. "It means 'the beauty of Princess Tara of Delais.'"

I was flattered. "You made up a new word to describe me? I want to be an author when I grow up, so I really like that. What do you want to do when you're older?"

Age halted. "The only thing I've dreamed of was staying alive. But I suppose being king; since I'm an only child, I'm the only heir. I also figured out what 'Prince Over the Water' means. Marcus was talking about the House of Wittelsbach. That's one of the royal houses I'm descended from. So, tell me about yourself. You're my favorite topic to discuss."

He was so thoughtful. "Delais feels like home. I get along with everyone there."

"You're an exceptional princess. The Delaisans hold you in the highest regard."

I had affection for the Delaisans, the lovable oddballs who had a city full of dead people, anxiety disorders, and who enjoyed balls with an Ivy League education system. "I have a lot of things in common with them."

He twirled me. "What's your favorite color? Mine is blue."

I was enchanted by him. "If I had to pick, purple. But I love all the colors. What's your fatal flaw?"

"I spent so much time escaping that I'm not

sure."

I had no clue. "I don't know my flaws, but I have them. Everyone does."

I can't draw the line between OCD and my faults.

The dance ended, and I had a desire to kiss Age's cheek, but I restrained myself, envisaging Matt's reaction.

It doesn't matter. Age will never like you once he figures out you have OCD, sold your soul, and have eating problems.

I inquired, "Do you hate people with obsessive-compulsive disorder?"

Age was puzzled. "I don't know what that is but hating them for having it sounds dumb."

Like with Sophie, I detailed my issues, from germs to eating-to the fact that I sold my soul, especially that one time, but those weren't the only problems OCD could cause.

Naturally putting my guard up, I backed away from him and bumped into the bishop. "Excuse me, sorry."

Oh my gosh! The bishop was standing too close not to have heard all that OCD! Even the part about selling my soul in seventh grade!

The bishop winked. "Your face is very pale, so I'm going to assume you knew I could hear you. You don't need to be concerned about selling your soul. You can't, even if you wanted to, so that has to be your OCD; that's the only option."

But is he really qualified to tell me that?

The bishop saw the doubt on my countenance and continued, "I'm very credible. Before attending the people of Tirano, I traveled around the world. I know all about Catholic theology."

Helene would say he's enabling OCD by reassuring me. He was trying to do the right thing, but I'm not sure if that'll help me.

I thanked the bishop for his magnificent intentions, turned to Age, and sassily remarked, "So, do you think I'm a demon or not? I used to think I was."

Age pulled me in close. "You are not a demon. You are a princess and always will be. Nobody should like you any less because you have OCD. I do not like you any less than I did when I didn't know you had it.

"You will always be the girl for whom the word 'tarian' was invented. Tara, you're still special to me. Nothing could change that. Even if you did turn evil, I'd go to the ends of the Earth to turn you good again.

"This is the perfect time to give you your present; I bought you something."

Age reached into his dress shirt pocket and pulled out the type of velvet box that held jewelry.

I was caught off guard. "You aren't proposing marriage to me, are you?"

"No, this is something else."

I opened it, and saw a key necklace with Jesus, Saint Peter, and Our Lady of Grace on it.

Age elaborated, "This is a symbol for the Keys to Heaven that Jesus gave Saint Peter. You're afraid that you sold your soul and are going to Hell, but you're really going to Heaven. In case OCD says otherwise, you can wear this necklace and be reminded that God's love defeats OCD any second of any minute of any hour of any day."

Oh man. More reassuring OCD. But this is beautiful. Just beautiful.

I touched it lovingly. "How did you know beforehand that I was afraid of selling my soul?"

Age blushed. "I didn't. I was at a Catholic store back in Liechtenstein, and I saw this necklace and thought it would be a nice present for you. I didn't know how perfect it would be at the time."

Dad stood in between us. "Tara, I just got a call from Grandma. Bisavó died."

She never met Matt!

I said aloud, "She was ninety-eight years old when she died . . ."

Bisavó couldn't be dead. She refused to walk with a cane in her eighties. She was too resilient for anything to happen to her.

Whenever someone died, either a family member or a tragedy on the news, I knew I'd be fine if Bisavó were there-since she was so buoyant, even in her nineties, like a protective matriarch.

My inner peace was shaken. "You're lying! She can't be dead; she's healthy!"

Dad broke down crying. "No, she had health issues even before you and Matt were taken away at La Salette. She was frail ever since we got back from Anne's that day, but I didn't tell you because I was afraid the OCD spike would get even worse than it already was."

Matt, Sophie, Louis, Demetrius, and Angela came over. Sophie put her hand in mine. "When your dad broke the news to Matt, we heard, as well. Do you want to have a moment outside? We'll go with you."

They're true friends. They're my best friends.

We went out, and the brisk Sterietolan air struck through me. I wasn't sure how crying and weather worked in the Arctic. "If I start crying, will my tears freeze on my face?"

Demetrius swallowed. "Uh . . . that is not important right now."

Age stroked my hand. "I'm sorry about your bisavó."

Matt hissed, "You're not her boyfriend; don't touch her."

Angela pushed Matt away with feigned annoyance. "My dad died; I know what you're going through. You'll be okay again someday."

I shared, "But, now that Bisavó is gone, it feels like we're unprotected, like the evil can get us now. Now the despair is coming to get us."

Age pointed out, "That's true. Thorny times are coming toward us. After all, many of our former captors are still out there and could come after us at any given moment. But, if we stick together, we'll make it."

Even in my silent misery, I had to feel better at his words.

He warned me about an evil prince, saved me when Marcus was going to force me into marriage, invented a new word to describe me, comforted me after my grief, and likes me even with OCD?

He's a keeper.

Age's also right. We're going to get through all the challenges together. We have each other now.

I asked, "Do you ever feel like there are a bunch of wars in life, and we're all prisoners of a war at some point? Whether it's literally a prisoner of the battlefield, a prisoner of OCD, or a prisoner of anger, we're all at war. We were all prisoners of war at some point."

Age approved, "Like how we were prisoners of those people, and how you are a prisoner of OCD? That's a solid observation, Tara."

I corrected, "I *was* a prisoner. The Delaisans are helping me with OCD, and I don't consider myself a captive to it anymore. And you aren't hostages anymore. None of us are prisoners. We're free."

ACKNOWLEDGEMENTS

To God and Saint Dymphna, for never abandoning me even when I couldn't do it anymore and guiding my journey from beginning to end, and still steer my course in life.

To everyone with OCD, I want you to read this book when life is too much, even if it means every second of every day. To quote the video game *Radiant Historia*, "When it rains we soak together. When it is hot we burn together. We endure as clouds, peacefully".

Jansina Grossman, you deserve a gold medal for putting up with my annoying questions and being the super sweet Boss Lady.

To the fairest flower in the field, Rebecca Kuttner, your friendship was priceless. We connected in ways that would bond two people for life. We're special, beyond best friends. With that said, my darling, TEXT A WOMAN BACK! I MISS YOU! Everything about you.

My 9th grade English teacher, Mrs. Cathleen Charest, thank you for giving me hope that I could one day finish a novel I started. And thank you for teaching Honors English. I wouldn't have met my darling Rebecca Kuttner otherwise.

The family members that love me—you are true gems in a world of darkness. Shine on.

My Gina Marinello-Sweeney, for editing diligently to make her baby sister's dreams come true. I love you, Italian (or should I now say Delaisan?) Princess. You have a special place in my heart.

For Stacey Rice Dobrinsky, thank you for being my OCD therapist and real-life Helene Winter. I wouldn't be able to function without your help and dedication. I always nominate you for the IOCDF's Hero Award. They really ought to pick you one of these days. Until then, I hope you'll settle for being immortalized in literature and praised throughout time until it echoes into itself.

The entire staff at McLean SouthEast—without you and Stacey, I'd still be trapped by OCD. Thank you for setting me free and giving me a chance to live. You're the best of the best. I consider you to be my safe haven. Never change. By the way, my puppy Rosa's middle name is McLean. This is NOT a coincidence. You deserved it! I couldn't have gotten her without your treatment.

Leslea Wahl, for proofreading the first two chapters and bolstering my confidence to submit my work for publication.

Olivia Ploude, for listening to the first edition of Prisoners of War at lunchtime and commenting on it. Your friendship really helped me cope with that huge long panic attack I suffered that was mentioned in here!

For my special friend in the OCD support group, thank you for always asking about this novel and spurring me on with Leslea. It made my day when you remarked that seeing me well was your Christmas present.

Special thanks to Father John Murray, Deacon Joseph McKinley, and Father Jason Giombetti for answering my very specific theology questions!

Ms. Jessica Charlesworth—thank you for reviewing my Latin and making sure I wasn't making a fool of myself in front of the entire world. Even though I always somehow got a B, I'm very bad at Latin.

Nancy Cable, even though you weren't an OCD specialist, you took me in because there were none around me until Stacey. You did your best to help me and started me on my path. You lit my spark. Thank you. I love you.

Mr. Thomas Coute, for teaching me so many things about Taunton. Since a history textbook publishing company refused to include the fact that Taunton was the first city that "stuck it" to King George III, I squeezed it in here for you. Enjoy!

Margarida C. Silva and Alessandro Viaro, the photographers who made the cover happen. Keep at it! You two have talent!

Mr. Steve Kilpatrick, Mrs. Shira Marcure, Professor Alan Richmond, and the expert scorpion queens Lauren Esposito and Professor Leslie Boyer, I am eternally grateful for your scientific help related to the scorpion venom scene. All of you are geniuses.

Last but not least, I want to thank my late paternal grandfather, Gil Gracia. When I was four years old, you asked me what I wanted to be when I grew up.

I said, "A princess." You frustratingly replied, "No, really! What do you REALLY want to be?" I still said, "A princess! I'm GOING to be a princess!" With this book, I am indeed a real-life princess. Thank you for making me realize my destiny at such a young age. I inherited my talent from you, you know. You were an artist; I am a writer. Even though you had dyslexia and couldn't read, you mastered art. I wrote a novel. I conquered literature for you. I hope I make you proud.

AUTHOR BIO

Sarah Gracia always had OCD and ASD, but was diagnosed with the former when she was nine and the latter when she was eighteen. She daydreamed the events of *Prisoners of War* her high school freshman year while suffering the six-month panic attack Tara goes through in the book and finished writing the novel right before the start of her high school junior year. Sarah decided to publish the Prisoners of War trilogy under her real name to let people know that no one should be ashamed for having OCD.

Currently, she is attending college to (keyword: attempting to!!) earn a bachelor's degree in Psychology and plans to become an OCD researcher to cure it once and for all, despite everyone telling her it can't be done. When Sarah isn't writing books or studying, she can be found cuddling with her Cavalier King Charles Spaniel, Rosa McLean Gracia.

RIVERSHORE BOOKS

www.rivershorebooks.com
info@rivershorebooks.com
www.facebook.com/rivershore.books
www.twitter.com/rivershorebooks
blog.rivershorebooks.com
forum.rivershorebooks.com

www.ingramcontent.com/pod-product-compliance
Lightning Source LLC
Chambersburg PA
CBHW030532270626
47155CB00024B/2796

* 9 7 8 1 6 3 5 2 2 0 0 4 9 *